SAMMY TSUNAMI
AND THE
SHADOW ARROW

Luke Gatchalian

authorHOUSE®

AuthorHouse™
1663 Liberty Drive
Bloomington, IN 47403
www.authorhouse.com
Phone: 1-800-839-8640

Published by AuthorHouse 2/14/2012

ISBN: 978-1-4685-4584-5 (sc)
ISBN: 978-1-4685-4583-8 (hc)
ISBN: 978-1-4685-4582-1 (e)

Library of Congress Control Number: 2012901424

1

KNOCK! KNOCKITY-KNOCK! KNOCK! KNOCK!

The woman's clenched fist hammered the wooden door to no end—and hard enough that the hinges almost came undone. When she got no response, she tried again, but this time around she made sure it was much, much louder. Although she had a slender and waifish figure that barely filled out the silk rose red dress that she wore, she was anything but frail.

On the sixth knock the second time around, the bolt finally gave in and broke, leaving the door slightly ajar. Through the narrow opening, she saw her son still bundled up in his sleeping bag on the dingy kitchen floor fast asleep.

"Sammy Tsunami!" she yelled out loud at the top of her raspy voice. "Your school bus is about to leave! And you know what that means!"

Sammy Tsunami didn't like himself much that he wished that he was someone else. In the looks department, he was just plain weird-looking that he shuddered at the sight of his own reflection in the mirror.

His hair was sapphire blue and fiery shaped, which did

not blend well at all with his exotic features and subtle tan complexion. For some reason that defied explanation, his locks always stood up and stayed wildly disheveled, no matter how hard and how much he tried to comb it and tame it. As if being cursed with a neon-colored flaming mane was bad enough for his self-esteem, he only had one set of clothes to wear to school—and at home—each and every day.

For his top, he always had on a raggedy jet black sweater that was two sizes too large, with sleeves too long that they swallowed up his hands if he didn't have the good sense to roll them up. Printed on its front were six large yellow diamonds—three on top and three below—that glowed eerily in the dark. This baggy upper garment of his fitted himself quite nicely, although he didn't quite agree, fattening him up and throwing off any suspicions that he was really pitifully undernourished underneath all that Egyptian cotton.

His pants were likewise black, but not because they were dyed that way. They used to be some other lighter color but had, over the years, irreversibly darkened into the perfect shade of soot as a result of accumulating a lot of dirt and grime. There was a time when his worn out pair of jeans was too big for him. They used to sag all over his feet that he used to trip all over them every time he walked. Nowadays, they were too short for his long, endless legs and too tight that they literally choked his poor waist. And Sammy Tsunami, in all fairness, only had an itty, bitty waist because he was too scrawny and lean that his bones actually showed through his light auburn skin.

Lucky for him though, he had a pair of reliable navy blue running boots that were high enough to compensate for the lack of clothing covering his shins. Although they bore lots of wear and tear on them from their many years of reliable and dependable service, they were sturdy and had remained quite fashionable. They had several straps and buckles which made them complicated to wear. Notwithstanding this though, they were comfortable on his feet, which was a small blessing for him, especially given how stringently tight his pants were.

While Sammy hated the way he looked, he absolutely despised his two dark secrets which he kept to himself under heavy personal guard. The first one had something to do with the red scarf that was always wrapped around his neck. He has had it on for the longest time and never once took it off. He never ever dared to do so. His mother, India, who is his only surviving family, has made it her cross to bear to constantly remind him, day in and day out, to never even attempt to remove it—

Otherwise, his head would fall off!

As to how Sammy came to be cursed in this way, there is a story behind it which India herself has told the boy from time to time so that he could appreciate how fortunate he was that he was still alive to this day. The long and short end of the tale is that an evil alchemystic once tried chopping the boy's head off on a block when he was still a baby, but instead of lopping it clean off, the executioner's blade had shattered, leaving only a long, deep, gaping wound on the neck itself that could never heal.

To keep the gash from severing his head from his pencil thin torso, it has become his burden to wear, for the rest of his days, a red scarf made from a special fabric to keep the bleeding in check. As elegant as this solution was to his strange predicament, Sammy himself didn't enjoy wearing it all the time, most especially in the spring and summer time. More than the rest of his odd apparel, it was the red scarf that attracted the most attention because of its sheer crimson screaming bloodiness.

While he wasn't an ungrateful lout and did appreciate the fact that he was still breathing today and not a corpse, Sammy didn't like the awful, money-challenged life that he was living. If he was given the chance to magically transform himself into someone else—someone better off right here and right now—he would snap up the opportunity, just like that, without entertaining any second thoughts whatsoever. What really mattered to him more than anything else was escaping the crippling poverty that he and his mother were mired in. Unless a miracle happened and soon, there was no future, not even a glimmer of hope, to speak of in his case. He was just going to be another dead boy who starved to death.

The sad, awful truth was that the Tsunamis lived in a small, run-down cabin somewhere in the middle of what many believe to be a haunted forest. They had made their home here ever since they were evicted from their apartment by their landlord. India, the sole breadwinner of the family, had lost her job as a grocery clerk when the supermarket that she had worked in decided to use robots instead of people anymore. Unable to find work elsewhere and unable to pay the rent, the fortunes of the Tsunamis quickly worsened and worsened, until they ultimately ended up poorer than they had ever been. They became so dirt poor that they had to eventually move out of the city and into the wilderness, far beyond the outskirts of town.

This change was particularly difficult for Sammy, who still had to go to school in the city every day. He was eleven, and just about ready to start middle school this year in the sixth grade. His school was twenty-five miles away—a long ways from where he lived. The nearest pick up point for the school bus was a three mile walk across the darkest part of the forest, where the shadows were thickest and heaviest and gloomiest.

Not that going through them was a problem for him. All Sammy needed was time, and that meant rising up earlier than the rest so that he could catch his bus. The problem was, time was no friend of his—and whenever it pressed down on him, it pressed hard.

Unfortunately, today was one of those days when the clock demanded a lot from Sammy. It was the very first day of middle school, and he had been sleeping in late—really late. To get him to peel his eyes open and snap out of his extended slumber, his mother had to resort to something a little more drastic than just screaming her lungs out into his ear to spirit him back from his sojourn in dream country.

Grabbing a pail from a corner, filled to the rim with stagnant water and all sorts of leafy vegetation, she emptied its soggy contents on to Sammy, who quivered and bounced feverishly on his backside as he gasped for air like a fish freshly plucked out from the sea.

"Why did you do that, mom?" he angrily screeched, dripping wet and looking like a deep sea diver after a swim. His mother was standing over him as he groggily crawled out of his sleeping bag. She was grinning like a crazy lady, while holding up an empty bucket over her frizzy, emerald colored head. Sammy sneered at her as he begrudgingly rose to his feet.

"I found a water source—a spring!" she happily announced with her loony eyes lighting up. She lowered the bucket on to the rickety, wooden floor, and pranced around Sammy mockingly. "It isn't far from here. Now, you can finally bathe when you come home from school!"

Sammy ignored her as she turned away and hopped merrily toward the makeshift fire pit in the middle of the kitchen. This was where they cooked their meals and kept warm at night. It was nothing more than a hole really, filled with coal and all sorts of wooden debris, both burnt and un-burnt, which released smoke and the scent of boiled and grilled foods into a small crack in the ceiling that functioned as a chimney, if not for anything else.

The kitchen, modest and threadbare as it was, doubled as Sammy's bedroom considering that the only other one in the house was his mother's, which was much smaller and so much more cramped with clothes and wicker baskets scattered all over the place. Soaked to the bone and with no ready change of clothes, Sammy's initial reaction was to run inside there and wipe himself off with one of his mother's dresses. He was about to dart right in when his mother threw some celery at him, grazing his shoulder.

"No going in there!" she warned him strictly, as a raging blaze formed on the surface of the pit, filling the room with smoke and the curious scent of eucalyptus.

"I really wanted a bath, Mom, but not like this," grumbled Sammy as he stiffly rubbed the wet fabric of his sweater. "I'm going to get sick for sure, and you know that we can't pay for a doctor to treat me if that ever happens!"

"What are you talking about, darling?" she then asked him slyly, squinting her eyes as she beamed radiantly at him. "Are you still wet, you mean?"

To Sammy's surprise, his clothes were completely dry, thanks to the smoke that was blowing over him. It felt like sauna steam—hot, but not sweat inducing for some reason. There was an aridness that circulated in the air, which had the boy wondering how. He wanted to quiz his mother for an explanation, but he was too tongue tied to express himself, verbally or otherwise.

"I mixed something in the water that will get rid of your

body odor," authoritatively added India, crouching in front of the burning fire as she tossed pieces of wood into it to stoke it. Her stomach was complaining rabidly, but she was deliberately ignoring its indignant pleas for food that sounded off one after the other.

By sheer coincidence, Sammy's was tetchy as well. Secretly, the boy hoped that she would make them a satisfying meal to quell both their incessant cravings since it has been days since they have last eaten anything substantial and filling. Regrettably, she had nothing on her to burn in the fire, except for wood.

"It's guaranteed to last until you get home, so you don't have to worry about getting teased by your friends for smelling like a hobo, like they did in fifth grade last year."

Forgetting about his hunger pangs for a moment, Sammy returned his Mom's smile with an even bigger one—a grateful one. As soon as he started smelling the wonderful fresh scent of crisp linen on his clothes, his sour mood improved drastically for the better. But that would only last for a brief moment. Something more pressing had come up, as bright as a newly turned on light bulb inside his head.

"While we're on the topic of getting teased, Mom, don't you think it's high time that I get a new set of clothes. I've been wearing these old rags since I started kindergarten!"

"Ah! So you're at that age already where you're conscious about what you wear!" ruefully acknowledged India, crinkling her forehead as she picked up a brass spoon lying on the floor among the rest of the clutter scattered there. "What's style compared to function, hmm?"

Soon as she propounded this question to her son, she swiftly hurled the spoon in her hand straight at him, like a baseball pitcher's fastball special. It whisked through the air in a tick of a second before striking Sammy square on the chest. The force of the impact should have hurt the boy in some way, but it didn't. Instead, the spoon hit the stone floor, clanking and forcibly bent at an acute angle.

"Do I need to demonstrate how strong those clothes of yours are again?" she then waspishly added, producing a kitchen knife out of nowhere which she naughtily brandished in front of Sammy. At the sight of the blade, all the boy could do was purse his lips and hold his breath in terrified disbelief. "So do we understand each other loud and clear?"

"I'll keep wearing them if you promise not to throw that at me!" Sammy wheezed, his eyes bulging as they stayed transfixed on the glinting, sharp edges of the cutting instrument.

"Fair enough," agreed India, putting away the knife. "Just so you know, those things that you're wearing aren't made of cloth. They're alchemy steel, stronger than diamond but flexible and soft enough to provide you the soft comfort of cotton. Took me four years from the time you were born to construct 'em."

"I have no idea what you're talking about, Mom. All I want really is to get something else to wear for a change. But if that's not possible, I'll keep wearing these, no problem."

"You're afraid of what other people might think of you, is that it? Sammy, you're the most fearless boy I know. What happened?"

"Fearless, ha!" jeered Sammy, making a face when he said so. "You're saying that because you're my mom."

"When I gave birth to you, you never shed a single tear when you came out of my womb—not a tear! All babies come into this world crying. They cry because their souls, which are older than they are, fear. They fear the uncertain future ahead of their new lives—but not you! You didn't cry when you were born because you… are fearless!"

"Come on, Mom!" Sammy begged to differ, slightly embarrassed by the nonsense his mother was spouting. "You're just making that up to build my confidence. All newborns cry, of course. I couldn't have possibly been an exception!"

"Am I making this all up?" cheerlessly countered India, raising her eyebrows as she begrudgingly returned to her chore of throwing wood into the blaze dancing wildly in the middle of fire pit. "Then why are you still here when you have a school bus to catch? I'd pretty much say that's being fearless, won't you agree?"

As soon as his eyes fell on his weather beaten, rusty old wrist watch—which had stopped telling time at precisely 4:58—an overwhelming sense of dread and panic immediately seized Sammy. And he couldn't hide it even if he wanted to, for it was all over his newly minted pensive face.

"My watch is dead, Mom," Sammy declared with an obvious

air of disbelief and panic in his shaken voice. "The batteries must have gone out while I was asleep. That means I'm late for the bus, am I right?"

"Yep, yep, yippity-yep," replied his Mom who didn't seem to share the stress that was quickly percolating inside Sammy's churning insides. "I tried screaming that into your ear earlier. That's the other reason why I splashed with you with cold--!"

Before she could finish her sentence, Sammy was gone, off and running out the main door that he left wide open and flapping in the whistling breeze. When India saw the dust clouds trailing behind him, she felt an icy chill suddenly wash over her.

Unlike the cold shower that she gave her son earlier to wake him up, this one brought with it a lingering uneasiness that she had not known in a long time. It was a jarring experience vaguely familiar to her, and it forced her to try to remember a part of her past that she had long put behind her and tried to forget.

Something menacing circled the air, and noting its undeniable presence, she became deathly worried for her son. She was about to follow him when she noticed the shadows of the woods outside her humble home moving—as if they were alive.

"Where is the boy?" she heard them whisper. "Where is he? Where are you hiding him?"

Someone was out there, she thought to herself, as she stepped out the door of her cabin to closely observe and listen to the murmuring shadows creeping across the transmuting forest. Before she could manage to blink, the colors around her melted away and were replaced by a dull black and shadowy gray. It was like watching an old movie play out on the screen, only one that she herself was starring in.

"Who's there?" she hollered into the trees around her, whose leaves and branches responded by swaying back and forth as a passing wind noisily whooshed by. She then heard a faint growl in the distance, like that of a lion's. "Who's there?"

After she repeated herself, her eyes fell on her flattened shadow which was resting quietly on the moist, muddy earth. No sooner did she see it there, did it stand up by itself and confront her with its faceless visage. Had it any eyes, she would have certainly locked gazes with it. But there were no windows to its soul, for a soul was something it did not have.

As India pined for an answer, she was able to recall what it was exactly that she was trying to extract from her brute memory. And knowing what it was now, all her senses were overpowered by a great and terrible fear that left her completely numbed and paralyzed. She wanted to go after Sammy to warn him. But it was too late.

2

With only a desperate hope in his heart, Sammy Tsunami raced the wind that was blowing east in the general direction of the sun. Its rays struggled to pierce through clumps of leaves and intersecting tree branches that blocked their soft, warm glare from entering the woods. Sammy depended on the light they provided heavily—not only to illuminate his path—but to give him directions as to which way to go. There were no forest trails for him to follow, no visible path for him to go by, which brings us to Savvy's second and final dark secret: *his shadow.*

Unlike everyone else's shadow, Sammy's shadow had a unique shape. It was shaped like an arrow.

A shadow arrow.

Regardless of where the sun was, or where he faced, his shadow arrow always remained in front of him, flat on the ground, and moving only when Sammy himself moved. It always pointed him in the right direction, which was very useful since he never got lost with it. He just wasn't comfortable having it around whenever there were people—especially nosy, curious people that liked to ask a bunch of questions. It was bad enough that his hair was blue and sculpted like a burning flame, that his clothes were smelly threadbare rags, and that his head could lop itself off his scrawny neck at any second. If people found out that his shadow was out of the ordinary as well, he would be branded an even bigger freak than he already was. And that thought did not sit well with Sammy.

Still, that said, it wasn't all that bad, especially since all he really had to worry about were the outdoors. As it turned out, this shadow arrow of his was a very considerate embarrassment. It was kind enough to never appear indoors, always materializing outside, which suited Sammy just fine and dandy.

Not that it being exclusively outdoorsy was any great inconvenience either, since people hardly notice other people missing their shadows—especially outdoors. It was just like in the case of vampires and mirrors. Hardly anybody gets to spot a vampire not casting any reflection on a mirror. That's because most vampires aren't careless to be around mirrors whenever they're in the public eye. Just like them, Sammy has always made a conscious effort *not* to be around people in places where there was good enough light for shadows to be cast. That way, he didn't have to explain himself to anyone—especially to nosy and curious people that like to ask a bunch of questions.

It was an entirely different story altogether though, whenever it was just the two of them all alone. Not only was Sammy pleased that he had a natural compass at his ready disposal, he really enjoyed its quiet, helpful company. Although he would never openly admit this to any one, his faithful shadow arrow was more than just a handy tool. It was his reliable confidant and friend with whom he could talk to whenever he got lonely on a run. And Sammy did get lonely very often on a run, just like now was no exception.

"Do you think I'll have any real friends this year?" he asked his shadow arrow plainly, which sharply curved to the right as he passed a flowering undergrowth that was nestled between two young pines. "If it's a yes, make a U-turn to the left. If it's a no, make a U-turn to the right."

A cool summer breeze was blowing against his back, aerating his clothes and pushing him onwards. It almost felt like a hand—perhaps, the hand of fate, he thought. The day was young and there was much to look forward to.

"So is it a yes or a no?" Sammy then said impatiently, after waiting a while for a response from his shadow arrow that never came. "Can't you give me a straight answer anymore?"

The woods themselves were rich and deep and old. The dense emerald leaves that weighed heavily on the witchy branches that held them, cast far reaching shadows that threatened to drown whatever trace of light there was on the rough, stony earth. Scattered ubiquitously around the grounds were wild shrubbery that made hiking difficult around these parts, especially with thorns jutting out from them. They had roughed up Sammy's boots many times in the past, leaving hundreds of chalky white scratches.

Not that Sammy had ever noticed their damage to his

footwear before, callous as he was to care for this sort of things. He thought that he had stepped on something soft, like a rather large animal dropping, when he stole a quick glance at his boots to confirm. It was then that he finally caught the marks, chipping away at the striking blue color. He was considering taking a break from his run to pause for a few seconds to examine them more closely, when his shadow arrow suddenly wrung a hard left, sending his heart fluttering with a renewed sense of excitement and adventure.

"Good enough," he approvingly lauded as he followed it to the left, forgetting completely about the scars on his boots. "Not a U-turn like I asked, but good enough that I can't complain."

It didn't take Sammy long to finally reach the deathliest part of the forest, where there was very little sunlight for his shadow arrow to thrive on. The shades were greedy in this neck of the woods. They were ubiquitous and left mostly nothing for the eyes to see, except for a few scraps here and there that haven't been coated yet by their own wet brush of charcoal paint.

He had come by this way many times before, that it had become overly familiar to him. Nevertheless, he still made sure to take all the necessary precautions before embarking into the inky darkness. Foremost of these was making sure that he kept to the places where he could keep his shadow arrow away from getting tangled up with all the rest of its dark kin out there. It was a tricky sort of thing and did slow him down a bit, but not too much though that he had to relinquish running entirely.

"Now, be careful not to get mixed up with other shadows you don't know," he playfully told his shadow arrow as he tried to keep himself in the narrow illuminated middle of two wide banks of heavy laden blackness. He was sprinting on a tight rope of light that straightened and curved on a whim, while keeping his balance. It was no easy feat doing what he did on a dash. One slip, and his shadow arrow would be gone, swallowed up whole by the opaque darkness lying on either side. Not that it would be lost to him forever though. It was more of the inconvenience of him getting lost in the woods without it that bothered him most.

"I would appreciate an early heads up if you don't mind, thanks very much!" he told off his shadow arrow after nearly missing the last series of sharp turns that looked on hindsight like a heartbeat line on an EKG strip. Although he knew for a fact that it wasn't his shadow arrow's fault that the lighted path he was taking had gone all crazy, Sammy was deathly afraid to consider the other alternative explanation he was secretly entertaining inside his head.

Tried as he wanted not to believe it, the fact of the matter was: the shadows themselves were moving, and not naturally at that. It was as if they were trying to purposely close the fine gap he was moving through to lead him astray.

"We better blow out of here before we lose our light!" Sammy then said in a breath as swift as his quickened strides. As his brisk feet shredded the dirt, he heard the leaves suddenly rustle aloud like something heavier than the breeze was wafting through them. Whatever it was, it seemed to be getting closer.

"Who's there?" the boy asked coyly, hoping for no answer.

He was halfway through the dimly lit area when, from out of the dense shadows that lined the distant corners of the woods ahead, several distinctive forms emerged, startling Sammy enough that he almost stumbled to a fall. The creatures crept silently into the sliver of light that awaited the young lad, who was coming in hot from a few dozen paces away. He was on a collision course that was both inevitable and unavoidable. Even if he put on the brakes, it was too late for him to cut short his mad sprint —that is, unless he wanted to stop right in front of danger itself. The only option left was to speed up even more and hopefully pass the shadowy panther-like beasts, which seemed to be waiting for his arrival.

Panic-stricken and frightened as he was, Sammy maintained his composure. He manned up and injected more effort into his insane run. As he got close enough to steal a glance at their bestial forms, he was shocked to learn that the beasts themselves didn't have eyes—or heads for that matter! In their places above their necks were swirling dark clouds that had, floating in their centers, wide open mouths with serrated teeth that made great white sharks look like toothless old grannies. Not sure how to refer to them, he gave them a name—the "wild spooks"—after characters in a children's book his mother used to read to him when he was younger.

"I have no beef with you!" spewed Sammy, as he zoomed past the hideous creatures which collectively flashed their dripping fangs at him. He hadn't gotten far, when they began their relentless pursuit. The wild spooks were faster than Savvy gave them credit for, and more numerous that he thought them to be. Be that as it may, it didn't matter either way to him. He was leaving them in the dust, and doing it with a lot of style and flair.

The boy picked up his speed even more and ran like his life depended on it, chasing his shadow arrow around bends and turns despite obstructing thorny vines and brambles on the ground nicking his boots as he whooshed by. He didn't care to catch his breath anymore, nor did he care that his heart was hammering harder and harder at his rib cage and was about to burst right out. As if losing his heart wasn't already a bad enough possibility, a stabbing pain drilled deep into his legs and feet. The bus stop was only a short distance away now, and he could plainly see his big yellow ride pulling up any second soon. He was going to catch the bus one way or another. It didn't matter to him if he fell dead at its door step from complete exhaustion. He was going to catch it.

As Sammy was about to swoop down on his ride to school, he was taken aback by a sudden tug on his neck and immediately thought that his scarf must have gotten caught on one of the branches. When he spun his head around to see, he was shocked to see one of the wild spooks chewing on the end of his red scarf. It was tenaciously closing in on him with each greedy nibble. Worse than this, however, was the fact that the scarf itself was unfurling around his neck at a frenzied and alarming pace with every mad bullet-swift stride that he took. And with each inch of fabric unraveled, Sammy felt a piercing, rising pain on his neck, as if an old, unhealed wound was now making its presence felt in a big way.

"Stop biting that!" the boy scolded the beast, as he tried to yank his scarf out of its greedy mouth with a tug. In his ensuing panic, Sammy's lightning pace had doubled—as did the wild spook's. As if the shrinking gap between them couldn't make a bad situation any worse, Sammy had unintentionally jerked the beast closer to him in the course of his desperate struggle to escape its reach. In no time after doing so, the hot breath of the monster, like burning coals, was upon him, keeping his back warm and sweaty.

"I said, stop biting that!"

Channeling all of his remaining strength into his arm, he pulled as hard as he could for one last time. Although his determined efforts quickly paid off with great success, Savvy failed to realize that his actions only freed up the creature's jagged jaws, which now sought to chomp down on him any which way it could. What followed afterwards happened so quickly that it was a blur.

As soon as the scarf's fresh taste was gone from its mouth, it immediately made its play. With unearthly grace, the wild spook launched itself into the air, its mouth agape and salivating. In the fraction of a second that Sammy saw it dangling above his spiky head of hair, he felt its mouth bloom open around his head like a volcano erupted all over his face. Sammy took one breath of the heated air, and then braced himself quietly for the end, as knife-like teeth rained down on him from all directions. Just when he thought it was going to be all over, he struck something.

It was big… hard… and unmistakably yellow.

3

"Please tell me you're okay because I really don't want to go back to jail."

Sammy's eyes flickered, then wheeled opened. Although he was still in a daze and his head throbbed, he felt the blood slowly ebb back into his brain, which made it easier for him to come up with a snappy response at the top of his head.

"How come?" he replied in a feeble voice, as he got back on his legs and stood up. "Was prison really that bad the first time around?"

The first thing he laid eyes on was the round, crusty face of the bus driver, a balding short man in his advance years with a stocky built and a very distinctive handlebar moustache dangling under an overripe tomato of a nose. He was eyeballing Sammy, and looking every bit like he didn't appreciate the wisecracks. Seeing how it was with him, Sammy tried to apologize, but he was immediately cut off before he could put in a single word.

"What were you thinking, slamming into the side of my

bus like that, kiddo? Are you tired of growing up or something, that you want to cut your short enough life even shorter?"

The bus driver was piping mad when he scolded Sammy. He was so blinded with rage that he inadvertently threw an accusing finger straight at the boy's chest. It connected, even though he really didn't mean to. Still woozy from the impact earlier and weak, Sammy was defenseless, even against the softest of taps. One poke, and he was knocked over like a leaf.

"Oh, man!" ruefully lamented the bus driver, stomping his feet like an irate child as thunderous laughter erupted from behind him. The kids on the bus were so enthralled by the slapstick antics of the bickering duo that they literally went bananas. They were giggling and chortling, and hysterically pounding on the fiberglass windows in front of them, hoping to goad the funny pair into doing another spur of the moment comedy routine for their entertainment.

The bus driver was chatting up a storm that his lips moved so fast that Sammy couldn't quite catch what was glinting from the inside of his mouth. It seemed like there were mirrors in there or something equally reflective, like gilded metal. Whatever it was, it was shining brightly in the sun, blinding Sammy who could only avert his eyes to the safety of his left shoulder.

"That wasn't even a push, and here you are down for the count again!" the bus driver complained, as he gently snatched Sammy's arm to help the dazed boy back to his feet. Not meaning to get back at the old man, Sammy grabbed hold of the latter's khaki shorts, which he used to hoist himself up. The boy pulled at it so hard that it almost came completely undone. It was a good thing though that he was wearing some soiled trousers underneath. Otherwise, it would have been a bigger disaster than it already was.

"I really need this job, alright?" the old man added as he frantically worked to fix his partially shredded shorts. To Sammy's surprise, the old man didn't seem the slightest bit irritated at him for embarrassing him in front of an excited crowd of children.

"It took me two and a half years of my life to land this job, and you're going to get me fired! And on my very first day even! What a loser I am! What a loser! Tell me that you're not going to tell the principal about this. Pretty please, tell me you wouldn't!"

Sammy nodded and smiled. "Let me get on your bus, and I won't say a word, not a single word I promise," he assured the old man before proceeding to dust himself off. While doing so, he noted the name tag pinned to the bus driver's rumpled khaki shirt. It simply read: DOJO.

"That's Mister Dojo to you!" sternly warned the old man, who caught Sammy red handed staring at his name tag. "Today, that's just a name, kiddo! But tomorrow, it'll be a legend!"

Following that brief lesson on how to address touchy, sensitive, cranky elders, Sammy shambled on to the bus without so much as a protest or objection from the bus driver, who simply rolled his eyes away in resignation. As soon as the boy was inside, the most embarrassing thing—in the history of things—happened. It did so without warning whatsoever, catching Sammy completely off guard and reducing him to a metaphorical puddle of goo.

ROARRR!!!

His stomach growled, as if it was a lion announcing itself to the world. Everyone on the bus heard it, including the echo, which bounced around the confined space several times for a couple of seconds before disappearing entirely. Stunned and speechless, the students gawked at Sammy from their seats, their jaws dropped and their lips quivering. Sammy himself was blushing with shame, that he immediately retreated back towards the exit to escape their collective judgmental stares. He was about to cross the yellow line drawn on the metal floor, when the bus driver blocked his way with his enormous beer belly, which partially stuck out from right underneath his half-buttoned shirt.

"Is that a neglected tummy I just heard, kiddo?" he said in a theatrical booming voice. "Are you going to tell me that you skipped breakfast—which, by the way, is the most important meal of the day—because you were running late to catch your bus to school?"

"Umm… Yes, sir," the boy timidly answered with his head bowed in defeat. As soon as he spoke those words, everyone burst out laughing. Some even heckled Sammy, who stayed silent as a mouse throughout the harrowing ordeal. No one could tell he was deeply offended though, for he was able to keep a sheepish smile plastered across his flushed face.

If Sammy had a choice, he wouldn't have told the bus driver a partial truth because it was not in his nature to lie, even about the smallest of things. What Sammy tried to hide was, he not only missed breakfast that morning—but three square meals for two whole days on account of the fact that his family didn't have anything to eat at all. So by answering the bus driver's question in the affirmative, he figured that he had gotten away with not having to disclose everything about his family's dismal financial situation. Being made fun of for missing breakfast was a lesser evil anyway, when stacked up against being ridiculed for being poor, which was much more hurtful for him to bear.

"Please eat something when you get to school, okay?" The bus driver said this with as much fake sympathy as he could muster. He was still peeved at Sammy for making a fool out of him earlier, so he didn't bother to act concerned because he really wasn't. He took his seat behind the wheel and started the engine, which roared immediately to life.

Sticking out like a sore thumb was nothing new to Sammy. He was used to the judgmental stares and condescending smirks of complete strangers. They would steal glances at him, quick ones and long ones, making him feel like he was garbage polluting their clean air. Having endured this kind of abuse for years, the boy thought that he would be immune by now to their casual cruelties. But he wasn't. It still stung him, just like the first time.

Sammy marched in the opposite direction towards the back where the seats were completely empty. With feet that seemed to be chained to some heavy iron ball, he dragged himself painfully across the long narrow strip that separated the two great houses of the middle school world: the pre-teens and the new teens.

The pre-teens, the group to which Sammy belonged to, were a childish, unsophisticated lot of savages that behaved badly. They taunted and teased Sammy by sticking out their tongues and crossing their eyes. Some of them sniggered as Sammy inched pass them, while other jeered by calling him "mud sack" and "crazy top," names he was only all too familiar with after five years of hell in elementary school.

Although the new teens—the thirteen year olds and older faction—were not quite as vulgar as their younger school mates, they were certainly not as mature as they would want people to believe. Instead of acting like wild animals that just escaped from the zoo, these teenage wannabees got their kicks by giving Sammy dirty looks—condescending looks, in fact, meant to reduce him to a cheap non-entity.

To ensure the success of their cruel plan, they even made sure to put their made up faces out there for Sammy to see and remember, so that they, in turn, could remember him. Tried as they did to grab his attention though, the boy simply ignored them all, driving them crazy with a seething pent up rage. The stored anger that was building up inside of them got so bad for one girl that she tried to pull some of her hair off from her head.

4

When Sammy finally reached the end of the bus, a small boy with night black hair and a bowl haircut playfully seized the end of his red scarf and heaved at it. Suddenly and somberly remembering how the wild spook almost succeeded in decapitating him earlier, he was instantly overcome with terror and panic that he froze for a second on the exact spot where he stood.

"What's with the scarf and the sweater?" asked the small boy, as he planted both feet firmly on top of his chair. He stood on it to be able to talk to Savvy eye to eye.

The boy was shorter than Sammy thought. He was no taller than the average kindergartner, thin of body and thin of face, olive skinned with slits for eyes that were overshadowed by thick, bushy brows and a distinctive nose that was both flat and shrunken. Clad in a loose cobalt blue tee-shirt, a pair of short red shorts and some knee long tube socks that stretched all the way up from the edges of his basketball sneakers, he looked very, very young in Sammy's eyes—pre-school young in fact. Seeing him on the bus with all the middle school kids made Sammy wonder if this little boy was just hitching a ride to somewhere else.

"It's summer, not winter time, dude. Are you still using last year's calendar to tell today's date?"

Everybody was laughing their socks off again in the background. Sammy himself wasn't amused when he heard this, especially since he was worried about his head getting displaced from his neck anytime soon. Without saying anything in response, he quickly snatched away the dangling end of his scarf from the grip of the small boy, whose mischievous expression quickly soured.

"That was rude of you," pointed out the small boy, motioning to punch Sammy with a balled up fist. "Since you haven't had anything to eat, Sapphire Top, let me feed you a knuckle sandwich—on the house!"

"Leave him alone, Nark!" rang out a young girl's voice from out of the blue, stopping the small boy's fist cold, midway through its intended flight.

It came from the seat directly in front, from the pale faced schoolgirl with the rosy cheeks and the long curls who was peering suspiciously over the back rest. She was a brunette, no older than Sammy, with a strong, confident, charismatic face that was attractive enough not to be easily forgotten. She looked at Sammy first with tilted eyebrows that gave the impression that she was vicious to deal with. As it quickly turned out, however, it wasn't just a front.

No sooner did she train her hawkish sights on the scrappy

smaller boy, who answered to the name of Nark, did she grab him ferociously by the collar, yanking him to her with both hands to the point that their foreheads almost bumped into each other.

"I warned you and warned you and warned you!" she angrily reproached him, her saliva spraying his baffled face with all sorts of germs. "I'm going to have to arrest you for this, you bonehead jerk! Bullying is a felony not sanctioned by the Great Beagle Middle School Code of Conduct, Article 176, Section 9, paragraph A!"

This sudden twist in the unfolding drama had everyone in the audience either waiting with bated breath or biting their nails as they watched intently for what was going to happen next. They were anticipating that Nark would blow his top and engage in a down and dirty scuffle with the girl. They were preparing themselves for some punches to be thrown, even some scratching here and there, and maybe some hair pulling.

Surprisingly and completely unexpected, they didn't get any of that. Nark's reaction to being manhandled was either a brilliant one, or just plain dumb. Instead of mounting a protest over his shabby treatment, he simply turned docile, a move that startled even Annie, who was ready for some fisticuffs herself.

In her hands, Nark was just beet red and beaming like a drunken fool. He got so creepy too look at that she simply had to release him, letting go off his collar and sending him crashing down into his seat like a discarded rag doll.

"He seems happier," Sammy matter-of-factly commented, as he sneaked a peep at Nark who was flopped on his chair in a daze. Seeing him in that state, Sammy understood why, and knowing what he knew endowed him with a sense of empowerment. When he finally sat himself in the back, he was feeling really good about himself that he even stretched out his arms atop the back rest behind him in a relaxed position. He was grinning like a clown at everybody who met his gaze, including Annie who was looking at him suspiciously. They all thought that he was crazy or something to be acting that way.

"Don't mind her," chimed in another girl's voice, a sweeter and more pleasing one. It came from beside Annie, who was still kneeling on her seat with half of her body above the back rest facing Sammy. "That's the caffeine talking. She's been guzzling down cola drinks like water ever since she was five. That's why she's so hyper and high strung. My sister… Annie Pastrami."

The other girl emerged from behind the back rest with a friendly smile. She was chubbier, literally bursting out of the tight forest green athletic wear that she wore, with a roundish face framed nicely by a bob of red hair that had a natural ponytail extension attached to it. She answered to "Ruby," which was the name used by her sister in referring to her.

Unlike Annie though, there was a gentleness and comeliness about her.

"Chill out, Annie," she told her sister in a soft spoken voice that was almost too soft to catch. "Your blood pressure's gonna shoot up if you don't take it easy."

"It's chief!" Annie corrected her errant sibling with an ear-splitting shriek that shook the bus to its tires. "As in chief of police, my dear sister! Why can't you ever call me by my rank? I thought that we agreed to this over the summer."

"We did, Sis, but I didn't want this new guy thinking that you're irritating or something just because you always talk, like, at the top of your voice all the time."

Ruby's eyes were shifty, moving to and fro from Annie to Sammy, who was quietly watching the two siblings squabble, just like everybody else on the bus. She was trying to give the boy some kind of hint. Perhaps, she wanted him to intervene in their quarrel and side with her against Annie, Sammy thought. Then again, since he was not really sure what she wanted from him exactly, he just kept mum and shied away from getting himself involved.

"May I remind you that you're just a sergeant!" crossly asserted Annie, the veins on her neck inflating as she blew these words out of her mouth in a single, hasty breath. "You have the audacity and temerity to talk back to me like that? Why, I should demote you and put you back to latrine duty! How's that?"

"Whatevers."

Ruby's indifferent response silenced Annie, who was just too shocked at what she had heard. She wasn't the only one feeling that way on the bus though. Everyone watching her thought that she had a screw loose or something. As they began to gossip in muted murmurs behind her back, Ruby turned to Sammy and lost no time formally introducing herself to him. Appreciating the gesture, he reciprocated by giving her his name. The two then struck a conversation together—to Annie's astonishment and mild irritation.

"Pleasure to meet 'cha, Sammy Tsunami," she said with a hammock of a grin on her slightly pudgy face. "Are you a sixth grader too by any chance?"

Ruby asked this particular question with so much saccharine sweetness, that it immediately drew unwanted attention. An emo teenage boy with a goth fashion sense from the other side of the border was the first to launch a verbal attack. He booed and hissed at Ruby for trying to be cute, then hurled undeserved invectives at her one after another.

"Sixth graders suck!!!" he shouted out loud, empowering several nameless others to emulate him with their own potshots of insults. Soon, everybody jumped on the hate-on-the-chubby-girl bandwagon, and it got so toxic and loud that Ruby had to do something to quell the mutinous uprising.

"Laters, haters!" she snapped out loud at the rowdy mob. When her curt hostile reaction did not silence them, Annie joined the fray in defense of her sister and attempted to reason with the raucous rabble, diplomatic-like, but was hooted so relentlessly that she was rendered speechless.

"Shut up, or the Nanek Beast will take you all!" Nark screamed out loud, no longer able to tolerate the deafening ruckus. "I swear that it will go after each and every one of you, haters, if you don't zip it! You, losers, have been marked!"

Nobody ever mentioned another derogatory remark after that. In fact, nobody said anything anymore. They just went back to what they were doing before the commotion happened, pretending not to tremble or feel frightened over what their ears just heard.

Whatever it was Nark said, it worked, and Sammy couldn't help but feel great admiration for the small boy, whom he was fairly certain was some sort of genius for having made middle school at his tender age. Although Annie and Ruby were equally appreciative of and impressed by Nark's take charge attitude, they didn't say a word about it to him. They just proceeded with where they left off, like nothing ever happened.

"OMG!" exclaimed Ruby, who was chuckling uncontrollably when she learned that Sammy was in the same class as her, her sister and Nark. "I heard that Mrs. Galactrix, our homeroom teacher, is such a darling! She's just super, super nice! Just the sweetest gal there is!"

"Are you speaking from personal experience?" Annie waspishly jabbed with a sly smirk on her face. Whatever she was hinting at rubbed Ruby the wrong way that her chunky sister quickly turned to her with crooked eyebrows and fierce eyes. Annie could swear that she could see steam coming out of Ruby's large ears when she stared at her.

"You promised," Ruby snarled jiltedly. "You promised to keep it, cross your heart and hope to die!"

"And I broke no promise, my dear sister," Annie wryly insisted as she shrunk right back into her seat with a taunting grin. "I merely clued in the clueless. But they didn't get it. So no harm done, alright?"

Unrelenting, Ruby continued to glare at her sister with such intense intensity that it seemed as if sparks of electricity were actually flying from her eyes. As the two siblings preoccupied themselves with this activity, Nark stood up, slipped out of his aisle seat, and for reasons entirely his own, darted for the front end of the bus—with a horse whip in his hand!

What he was going to do and where he got his instrument of flagellation had everyone suddenly talking and buzzing. Even Sammy himself was stricken with the urge to yak about it that he called Ruby's attention to what was transpiring.

"Hurry up and drive us to school, Mister Dojo!" the boy cried out before cracking his whip in the air, frightening the huddled masses behind him and waking up the sleeping old man at the wheel, who had been dozing off all this time while his youthful passengers were having a row. "You may have started the engine, you old fool! But you haven't been putting the pedal to the medal! We are going to be late, so get driving!"

Acting entirely on instinct for he was still woozy from his

nap, Mister Dojo swiftly shifted gear, put down the hand brake, and buried his foot deep into the gas pedal—sending the school bus rocketing into the open road at a frenetic, frantic pace.

When their transport blasted off into the thralls of a nearby busy freeway, everyone was holding on to their seats for dear life, including Nark, who wisely leapt into the safety of the chair behind the bus driver and buckled up.

"You're going to get your comeuppance, Narky boy, for that little lion tamer impression of yours!" screamed Mister Dojo, bursting a blood vessel or two as his school bus blew through two police cars that promptly gave chase, their sirens wailing loudly as they sped up from behind.

"You think that was funny? I finally get to dream about swimming in money in my underpants, and you wake me up! How cruel you are! I'm going to get you for this!"

"Yeah?" Nark yawned apathetically before pretending to nap. "You and what army?"

5

Great Beagle Middle School was so much bigger than any of the elementary schools Sammy attended in the past. It looked like a gigantic mall with plenty of parking space outside.

"This is your stop, children. Now, get off my bus!"

When the bus doors folded opened, nobody bothered to thank the bus driver for the ride. Everybody just hurtled out of their seats and poured right out into the sidewalk in a bee swarm. They behaved like tourists visiting a new place in some foreign country, all giddy and all excited to take everything in. Some even took out their cell phones to snap pictures of the school's imposing façade, from the dazzling bright red letters of the signage that hung several feet up over their heads to the long train of golden school buses lining the drop-off zone.

While everyone else couldn't wait to tour the school premises, Sammy was taking his sweet time dragging himself away from the doors of the school bus. He preferred to stay incognito under the shade of the massive yellow transport, waiting patiently for everybody to disappear before he would follow. Not that he was being unsociable or anything, it was just that he didn't want anybody to see his embarrassment of riches—his shadow arrow. As long as he remained in a shaded area, no one would be able to see it because it would blend right in with the other shadows.

Besides, waiting was only a temporary hassle he didn't mind putting up with. Once inside the school itself, his shadow arrow would disappear altogether anyway. That was just how considerate it was, never one to burden him with an appearance indoors. Once gone inside, the only problem left to worry about was convincing people that he still had a shadow on him—a normal one. He figured that he would be able to best avoid these concerns if he either shied away from lighted areas entirely, or stuck close to the company of people with shadows and pass their own as his.

"We'll see you in class later, okay?" When Ruby told Sammy this, it seemed as if she didn't mean it. Not that she was being fake with her intentions, but rather, it was actually hard for her to part ways with the boy. She lingered for a while around him, holding on to an awkward smile as she waited for him to say something, anything, that might break the uncomfortable silence that was building up between them.

When Sammy finally got the hint after some ruminating, he coyly mentioned something about the weather. Dull as that was for a conversation starter, it somehow excited Ruby who suddenly became animated and talkative. She started babbling and rambling about things that Sammy hadn't the faintest idea about. And she could have gone on and on and on, had her sister not jerked her away.

"Come on, blabber mouth!" Annie belted out in her normal high pitched voice, as she impatiently seized Ruby's mildly plump arm and dragged it over to her corner. As she scolded Ruby harshly for dilly-dallying, Sammy noted the metal braces clamped on to Annie's teeth as she moved her lips. The wires were thin and nearly invisible. Staring at them glinting in the sun, he was surprised with himself that he didn't notice them before when they chatted on the bus. It was probably because he has a tendency to just maintain eye contact with the person he was talking to, he thought—and Annie's eyes, he recalled, were just so ridiculously striking that it was just so easy to lose himself in them.

"Are you looking at my mouth?" barked Annie, snapping Sammy out of his casual stupor. "Is there something in there? Oh Gosh! I'm pretty sure that I brushed really well this morning. I even flossed! I can't have food stuck in there somewhere! I have to make a good first impression this first day!"

"Relax, Sis," casually cooed Ruby, extending her arm out over her sister's hunched shoulders. "Sammy probably just noticed your braces." After uttering those words, she then turned to Sammy and enthusiastically beamed: "I can wear braces too, if you like!"

Livid and embarrassed by her older sibling making a fool of herself in front of a couple of passing-by random onlookers, some of whom didn't bother anymore to hide away their chuckles, Annie vehemently escorted Ruby away, leaving Sammy all alone in the middle of a flowing sea of humanity that was just growing and growing as more and more school buses arrived.

****

The entrance to the main lobby was a pair of sliding doors made entirely of transparent glass, which opened and closed as students came and went. Beyond their welcoming facade lay a grand lobby with all the trimmings of a first class, swanky hotel—elevators, escalators, grand staircases, the works. The floor was marble tiled and sparklingly polished with an ornate water fountain right in the center. Hanging from an elevated ceiling crafted entirely out of elaborate mirrors was a magnificent chandelier that radiated a soft, relaxing light.

Walking into the foyer for the first time filled Sammy with both a sense of hope and a sense of dread. A new school symbolized a new beginning for him, and closure to a past that needed forgetting. At the same time, he was frightened silly by the daunting prospects of having to face a new set of unknowns. Just the notion of having to deal with these made his stomach churn.

"Why's that kid dressed like that?" Sammy overheard one student say. "A scarf and a sweater in summer time? How tacky!" decried another. "And his clothes look all worn out."

Awestruck by the gorgeous spectacle that was the lobby and the snappily dressed and obviously well-to-do young students that populated the sprawling premises, Sammy felt small and out of place. He couldn't help but think out loud: *What is a poor slob like me doing in a high-end joint like this?*

"Not used to so much class are we? I can't really blame you. I, myself, can't help but marvel at how amazing this place looks. It can be overwhelming, especially for a country bumpkin like yourself. Am I right, or am I right?"

It was Nark. He snuck up behind Sammy and latched a heavy hand on his weary shoulder. The weight he placed only made the weight in Sammy's heart even more difficult to bear. Sammy wanted to just up and leave. And he would have certainly done so if his feet weren't nailed to the ground, no thanks to his strong sense of responsibility, which held him back from running away. He had never played hooky before, and he wasn't about to start now.

"You c-can… s-say that," Sammy stammered, breathing uneasily as he exchanged fake smiles with Nark, who seemed to relish having the insecure boy wrapped around his finger. It was evident from the way he grinned, the confident swagger he displayed, and the smoothness in his talk. He circled around Sammy like a vulture waiting for its prey to fall and die. He could see Sammy trembling with uncertainty in front of him, his knees shaking, and this delighted him to no end.

"I have to admit that this is way out of my league," Sammy volunteered, as he tried to keep his nerves in check. "When the school district zoned me here, I was expecting something nice, you know. Not something so… decadent, gosh. The public schools I used to go to were so, how should I put it, painfully modest."

"Of course, they were," Nark said, with a more obvious condescending tone this time. "This place may look terrific, but it's really ugly at the core," he added with a wink and a smile.

"Sharks swim here, the man-eating kind. Unless you're a shark too, you're just fish that'll get eaten. Most kids here are fishes, but I'm a shark. In fact, my name rhymes with shark. Easy to remember, right? Nark, the Shark. If you're going to survive middle school here at Great Beagle, you need friends who are sharks to protect you. And there are only a few of us around here, barely a handful, and I've got them beat by miles. So, do you want to be friends or not?"

From the time he started school, nobody has ever wanted to be friends with Sammy. He was just way too weird to be someone's pal, and everybody wanted someone "safe" to be their friend. It was probably because nobody wanted to be associated with a freak, unless they wanted to be branded a freak as well, and Sammy was just too out there freaky. So hearing Nark propose that they be friends felt really strange to Sammy. *Was it a trick of some kind? Or just part of his silver tongued charm?*

He thought that Nark's arrogance and conceit were major turn offs, even though he admired the small boy's guts and nobility to stand up for others, like he did for Ruby on the bus. The last thing he wanted was to be Nark's lackey, his stooge to order around. Although he didn't know Nark that well, it was apparent from his abrasive albeit charismatic personality that he had this tendency, and that worried Savvy who was hesitant to accept his very generous and tempting offer to be good buddies.

"So what do you say?" followed up Nark, extending an open hand in friendship. "Be my Buddy Dude?"

Whatever that meant, Sammy had no idea. But it sounded so right for some reason that he suddenly forgot his reservations toward the small boy. Without harboring anymore second thoughts, Sammy grabbed Nark's diminutive hand and sealed the pact. They were friends, and that was that.

It was difficult to contain the elation that was fermenting inside of him. For the longest time, sadness and frustration have been his constant companions, always around him and never leaving his side. Now, his status quo was changing, evolving into something he did not fully understand but could easily embrace. This new friend that just he made was the sign that he has been waiting for all his life—the sign that it would be better days for him from now on. As weird as it was to let go of the loneliness that has haunted him, it was even weirder for him to just be happy for once. The emotion was alien to his being. It took getting used to.

"Cool!" Nark excitedly exclaimed, shaking hands with Sammy, who was all smiles that he finally made a friend. "We're gonna be late for class. What say you we take the escalator over there?"

Sammy nodded, and dogged his new pal as they both took off. It was during the course of this playful pursuit of theirs that Sammy noted an oddity, catching his attention from out of the corner of his eye.

Although it made every effort to stay inconspicuous and secret, it lacked the finesse to do so, sticking out like a sore thumb—at least, as far as Sammy was concerned. Everybody else that trafficked the lobby was unaware of its presence, except for the boy. And why? Because most people hardly notice other people's shadows. It's just something that's taken for granted, which suited Savvy just fine—especially since his own was now missing.

At first, the oddity tried to blend right in, matching every movement, every foible, every nuance of every single shade it hitched a ride with. And then, it got careless, impatient and bold, leaping from shadow to shadow, changing rides whenever it could. It moved in a blur, probably thinking that no one would notice. But Sammy did. The boy couldn't have missed its distinctive sylphlike form for he knew it only too well. Initially, he thought that it was his mother's, clandestinely following him to school for some reason. Every inch, every contour, every line and shapely curve of the silhouette was hers—statuesque and willowy, and poured into a tight fitting dress that extended from the shoulders to the knees. Even the tousled hair, with all the split ends, was a perfect match despite the fact that it wasn't dyed in emerald green.

When he noted, however, the graceful gazelle-like

movements with which it conducted itself in its stealth work, he immediately dismissed this idea. His mother was a rough around the edges, frontier-type of gal, who would rather barrel in with all guns blazing instead of sneaking around like a thief. This one, however, wore the hat of a thief rather well, and was at all nothing like his Mom. And it was following him closely. Very, very closely.

6

The escalator they took was not only steep; it stretched so high that it missed two floors entirely. To ride it, one needed to hold on tight for dear life to the moving balustrade and keep one's feet steady on the flat surface below. Otherwise, it was a long, rough tumble down an endless flight of never-ending ascending steps.

Strangely, it was empty, except for the boys and one and two others trailing them from afar. Clean, sterile and thoroughly modern as it was, the desolate and discomfiting atmosphere that it radiated simply did not do for Savvy who kept fidgeting and squirming as he tried to stay still in his place. *"Where was everybody, and why aren't they rushing to their classes?"* he wondered, combing the area with eyes that couldn't likewise relax. The large circular clock hanging on the wall at the far end clearly gave them only a good eight minutes left to go before the tardy bell rang. His heart was outracing his muddled thoughts when he pondered the possibility of arriving late in class on the first day.

Something was afoot, he was certain of it. He looked around

his surroundings, craning his neck to try to get a better angle. It was then that he caught a large cylindrical glass elevator shooting upwards on the side of a towering marble pillar. It was sardine packed with students that didn't even have the elbow room to scratch an itch. A couple of seconds later, they were there, on top, with time to spare to casually shuffle their feet. Seeing them scamper out and head on to their classrooms made Sammy's heart sink. Nark and he still had a ways to go, and the clock up there seemed to suddenly be ticking a lot faster for some reason.

"This Nanek Beast that you mentioned earlier on the bus… is it, like, a cartoon character on a T.V. show or something?" quipped Savvy, who never ever in his life watched a single television program to dare make such a guess. He was trying to inject humor into their dried up conversation in order to revive it, if only to distract himself from the stress of what felt like having to deal with an impending deadline that he was this close to missing. Instinctively, he started walking uphill, prompting Nark to emulate him and follow closely behind. The escalator just had too many narrow and precipitous steps to climb that they eventually ran out of breath and had to speak to one another to keep each other going.

"Dude, that's Great Beagle's boogeyman," panted Nark, exhausted a bit and somewhat amused at how naïve Sammy sounded. "Last year alone, five students quit the school because that urban legend allegedly roughed them up. Three ended up in the hospital on account of multiple bone fractures, while one almost died. They all described the monster as this towering humanoid dressed entirely in black with boa constrictors extending from out under its shoulders instead of arms."

Fascinating story, Sammy thought, speculating right away whether it was true. In his short life, Sammy had seen many things of this sort along the way that he was no stranger to the unexplained and supernatural. Much as he liked to tell Nark about his past experiences, however, he decided to keep them all to himself for now, mostly because he didn't want Nark to get the wrong idea about him this early on in their budding relationship. The last thing he wanted was creeping out his new friend with his sordid tales of the macabre.

"Do you think it is real then?" Sammy asked instead, even though he was already convinced that it was, based on nothing more than a gut feel.

"Can't say myself, but everybody in the school believes it is," replied Nark with a serious expression waxing over his face. "You saw that kid on the bus, right? Soon as I mentioned it out loud, he was suddenly quiet and scared. Everyone was too. I guess that it's taboo to throw that name around. Works for me every time."

"You seem to really know how to navigate your way around these waters," Sammy complimented his dwarfish companion, who acknowledged his well meaning gesture with an approving nod.

"Sharks like me know the deep, that's all I can say," Nark pitched back, buttering up his own ego quite nicely as he strode upwards and overtook Sammy by a few steps. "That's why you and I should hang out together. You'll learn a lot from this little David who has taken down more than his fair share of Goliaths in this esteemed academic institution, if you catch my drift."

"Gee, you sound like an old hand here who has been around this school for a long time," Sammy shallow mindedly blurted out, realizing only afterwards that he had made a boo-boo when Nark's face suddenly soured.

"What are you saying then? That I'm not a first time sixth grader like yourself, just because I sound experienced?" the small boy angrily protested, frightening Sammy to the point that he had to retreat two steps back for his own safety. "Do you think I'm a repeater? One of those poor saps who couldn't quite cut it that they had to get left behind? Is that what you think of me?"

"No!" hastily answered Sammy, on the ropes and on the defensive, and breaking a nervous sweat while at it. He wanted to backtrack and clarify his previous statement. The problem was, he couldn't get what Nark just said out of his head: *More than his fair share of Goliaths in this esteemed academic institution.* What did he mean by that exactly? Did he have older siblings attending this school whose bullies he used to fend off for them every time he accompanied them here? Is that his case?

"Actually, my impression of you is that you've been accelerated or something," Sammy belted, finally regaining his wits and composure after getting flustered for a second there. "You probably skipped a grade or two or three because you look… so young to be in middle school actually."

"So you have a problem with my height then? I'm short, and short people don't deserve to be here. That's what you mean, eh?"

"No, no, no! It's just that…"

Nark boisterously burst out in hearty laughter. He was so beside himself that he almost slipped and fell down the moving steps, if not for a tight grip on the balustrade he was holding on to. "Just messing with you, buddy dude," he explained himself as he rubbed the tears off his eyes. "Chill already."

When Nark flashed his signature smile again with the deep dimples, Sammy knew that the danger had been averted. He was perspiring all over like a pig and was flushed. Although he was certainly glad that his friendship with Nark didn't suffer any irreparable damage, he was worried about the future, especially now that he was aware that his new pal had an explosive temper. Knowing this, he would be diligently taking mental notes from now on, filing them away in the file cabinet inside his head for future reference. That was how he was going to deal with him henceforth. He couldn't afford to let his guard down ever again.

"Look, we're here," said Nark, stepping off the escalator on to what appeared to be a metallic train station platform. Across from it was a caterpillar shaped roller coaster with several students already seated in it. Luckily, the conclusion of their little incident had coincided with their arrival, which suited Sammy just fine, as he not only ran out of things to talk about—he didn't want to get into another exhausting altercation with Nark anytime soon.

"Welcome to the Caterspeego!" Nark said aloud as he did his best used car salesman impression. "It may look slow, but it's fast as lightning! Or so I've heard."

Nark made this lively pronouncement within earshot of everybody already strapped in. Roused by the noise that he made, the students sitting in front lost no time twisting their heads in his direction to see what all the brouhaha was about. The second they caught his wolfish glare, however, they quickly and timidly withdrew in awkward silence.

When Sammy discerned their sheepish reaction, he couldn't help but be amazed by how ably his impish cohort handled himself in that situation. He wasn't just all talk as he originally thought him to be. He had teeth, and sharp ones too. As soon as both boys slipped into the last car in the back and sat right down next to each other, they buckled up as tight as their stomachs would allow them. By the time that they had finished, the traffic light beside the tunnel ahead turned green.

"Better get used to this, buddy dude," Nark whispered mischievously to Sammy as the roller coaster began to crawl and pick up pace. "Because you'll be doing this for the rest of the year!"

Right after Nark said those words, the ride was underway, rocketing on the rails like an unstoppable bullet. It twisted and turned, circling loops and dipping down hard, forcing Sammy's heart to skip a beat every time it did. Everyone screamed, thrilled and terrified at the same time to no end. Some even raised their hands to catch the wind that was whooshing right at them like a baby hurricane.

"I can't hold it!" squealed Sammy as he tried to keep his teeth from chattering. He was squirming in his seat as he held on tight to the rail in front of him.

"My ears are not hearing you!" replied Nark, happy as a clam as he enjoyed the wild ride.

When their coaster finally came to a screeching stop a few minutes later, Sammy couldn't wait to get off that he literally vaulted right out of his seat, leaving Nark stupefied and all alone in their car. Sammy then threw up a bit on his boots before dragging himself to the nearby water fountain to wash his mouth.

"Ewww! That's disgusting!" spritely chided Nark, patting Sammy on his bent back twice before walking off into the crowd that was amassing down a sloping marble corridor.

"I do disgusting pretty well," swiftly came back Sammy, lifting his chin up from the drink before wiping it off with the back of his fist. "You should see me do horrifying!"

Nark stopped in his tracks, right in the middle of an active current of people sweeping by him. He chuckled, zoomed in on Sammy approaching him, and nodded. If he had a hat on, he would have probably taken that off too.

"Funny," he dryly commented before shifting gears to a

more somber tone. "About earlier, before I forget, I wanted to apologize to you for pulling your scarf. I was being a jerk and all for criticizing your fashion sense, odd as it is."

Sammy listened to the apology, like his ears heard nothing else, and felt a change stir in him. Not only did he appreciate the unexpected gesture from Nark, it made him see him in a different light, something he thought a while ago could never ever happen. Suddenly, all the mental notes that he filed away on him were shredded, minced and thrashed. All the negative conceptions he had, erased.

Knowing now that Nark was really good person deep down, in spite of all his numerous shortcomings, made Sammy adore their blossoming friendship even more. Sammy was so relieved by this pleasant turn of events that he ventured to cast aside his earlier inhibitions, test the waters further, and delve into uncharted territory without fear or regret. And that started with how far a joke could go.

"My fashion sense is indeed very odd, I must admit," Sammy began, going in the opposite direction with a lighter tone. "But you're an oddity yourself, Nark. Shouldn't you be in kindergarten or something? I think I saw an elementary school right across the street where you can enroll in."

Initially, Sammy thought his plan had backfired when Nark's expression suddenly went blank. But that all changed when the small boy exploded into a mushroom cloud of uncontrollable laughter, prompting Sammy to join him himself in the ha-has, the guffaws and the chortles.

They were having a blast, tickling each other's funny bones with joke after joke after joke, when the next roller coaster arrived and stopped right behind them. Just as it was emptying itself of its cargo of passengers, the tardy bell rang, sending everyone still loitering around the corridor running for their lives to get to their respective classes.

As they all scuttled off into different directions, the two boys trailed them, content to just walk at a much slower and more relaxed pace, smiling and not taking themselves too seriously. Lost in each other's warmhearted company, neither one noticed the last commuter to alight from the last roller coaster train. This particular one sounded off no footsteps when it sauntered nimbly across the floor. It was quiet as a mouse.

Only that it was no mouse. It was the shadow that had been tracking down Sammy, the one with the profile of a woman—like his mother's, but not quite. And it was right behind the two boys, close enough to snatch them if it wished to.

7

Room fifty-two wasn't that far a walk from the platform they came in from. It was sandwiched between the rest rooms and the fire exit, and just right across the lockers. The entrance itself was hard to miss. It was a pair of sliding doors, but unlike all the rest commonly found around the school premises, these were the only ones that had sunflower stickers of different sizes on the glass.

"Welcome to the Sunflower Room," Nark said nonchalantly to Sammy as they stood side by side observing the floral motif. "The warden of this particular prison is Mrs. Galactrix, whom we will be meeting in a very short while. Once we walk through these doors, there will be no turning back. We will be her prisoners for one whole year. We will be nothing but seven digit student numbers. You and I will lose our names and identities as human beings, buddy dude. Are you prepared to surrender your freedom?"

"No offense, but you're being melodramatic," ribbed Sammy, walking through the doors that whizzed open, left and right, to welcome him. "If we're tardy, then we're--!"

The shoebox shaped classroom inside was just the right size, neither large nor small. It spaciously fit twenty-four computer mounted desks and their chairs, all facing front where an oversized touch screen board was suspended on the wall. It was also empty, except for two seats at the back.

"I thought we were late," remarked Sammy, surprised at the unexpected find. "I'm pretty sure we were."

"Lucky break for us, then," chimed in Nark, slipping through the entry way happy as a clam. "But we're not the early birds though."

He fingered out the last row. One of the filled seats there was occupied by a petite young blonde girl with tawny eyes, pouty lips, and a deadpan expression on her fair face. She had a black leather jacket on over an orange blouse and a bandana wrapped around her head that had the most striking image of a hundred Eyes of Horus printed on it. Between her indigo blue miniskirt and high heeled brown leather boots was a pair of long legs tightly wrapped in fishnet stockings.

The moment the boys walked in through the automatic glass doors, she spotted them immediately, training her piercing stare in particular on Sammy, probably because he was the more attractive one of the two. They exchanged silent glances for a while, before she ultimately decided to snob him completely and return to her day dreaming.

"That's Oleta Teytata," pointed out Nark, obviously referring Sammy to the snooty blonde ogling the wall beside her. "She's real friendly, that one. That is, if you can buy her stuff. Otherwise, she'll just ignore you. The only language she speaks really is money, money and more money."

"Sounds like my kind of lady," quipped Sammy.

The other student in the room was big, burly and hairy—so much so that he sported an untrimmed beard and unkempt shaggy locks, both black as night. From all conceivable angles, there was no doubt that he was an adult. That much was obvious from his six foot four heavy frame, and the bulging biceps that hung out of a dingy white undershirt that he wore over a pair of camouflaged military pants.

"And that bruiser over there is Timmy Tunabelly," continued Nark, singling out the much older student seated four seats across from them, who had a blank expression stamped on his hardened face. "He's the school's big bad bully. He doesn't look it right now because he looks brain dead, but trust me when I tell you that he's bad news. Don't ever make eye contact with him or he'll tear your limbs off from their sockets as soon as he looks at you."

Although Sammy was pretty sure that Timmy had overheard Nark talking about him behind his back, the bearded fellow didn't budge from his chair, nor did he make any slight movement of any kind to show his displeasure. He was like a statue, carved into his chair, unmoving and completely apathetic to the world around him.

"Just so you know, buddy dude," added Nark, the exact moment a torrent of students came flooding in from behind them, noisy and chatty as they scurried and searched for their individual desks. "Timmy's fortyish."

"Fortyish" snapped Sammy, genuinely surprised with the disclosure. "Then, why is he still in sixth grade?"

"That man holds the Guinness Book World Record for longest stay in sixth grade. He couldn't move on for some reason. Some say that he couldn't cut it, make the grade, you know? Others say that he enjoys flunking, but look at him— just look at that poor chump! Does he look like someone who enjoys repeating the sixth grade year after year after year?"

One long look at Timmy, whose vacant expression remained unchanged, and Sammy himself was convinced. His heart was awash with pity for the poor fellow that he was emboldened to approach him to say hello, talk to him, and try being friends with him. He was on a hot streak anyway as far as building friendships were concerned, so he was confident to his bones that he would be able to catch lightning in a bottle twice.

He casually walked over to him, leaving Nark alone for a second, with a ready hand extended. He was an earshot away of the bearded giant when he was suddenly derailed by another young boy, tall and thin like Sammy himself but not as quite. This one had earphones hanging out of his ears when he bumped into Sammy, and a large pair of circular glasses over his eyes that were partially covered by overreaching bangs.

"Sorry, dude," slickly apologized the boy using a California surfer's accent. He had long bushy hair, an acne-ridden face, and strutted in the loudest summer wear Sammy has ever laid eyes on. The vibrant and vivid colors of the Hawaiian shirt and the knee long shorts that he wore, including the sandals on his feet, just screamed out at Sammy.

"What's with the winter get-up?" he asked innocently. "Summer won't be winding up until, maybe, a month from now. Too early to be wearing a scarf and a sweater, man. It's scorching hot outside and you're going to sweat in that!"

"Keep walking, Mick!" rudely cut in Nark, who had his arms folded across his chest to show his displeasure with how the surfer boy was treating his new best pal. "Move along or the Nanek Beast is going to pay you a visit too!"

"What's a Nanek Beast?" Mick replied, dropping his eyes to address the dwarf who was staring at him reprehensibly. "Is that like a cartoon character or something? Because I don't watch T.V. at all."

"Keep walking!" repeated Nark angrily, clenching his teeth this time. "This is my buddy dude you're dissing here! Diss him, and you diss me too! Feel me?"

Gratified was how Sammy felt when these words reached his ears, like a sweet melody he's long wanted to hear all his life. Nark may be small, but he was large now in his eyes—someone he could genuinely look up to. His heart just swelled with so much joy that his eyes teared up a bit.

"Laters, people. Mick out!"

As soon as Mick departed for his desk, somewhat begrudgingly, it was Annie and Ruby's turn to pester the boys. Standing shoulder to shoulder, the sisters flashed their cutest, most adorable smiles at them, baffling the boys who couldn't figure out for the life of them what their strange motive was.

"Hello there, boys," Annie started, her metal braces sparkling under the light. "We were watching you get chummy and stuff. Do I detect a developing bromance here?"

"None of your beeswax, darling," teased Nark, who immediately lightened up and chuckles the second Annie met his icky gaze. "So you've been following us spy-like, huh? I really thought we had a moment there on the bus when you grabbed me by the collar and pulled me close… to your lips."

Nark was acting too sleazy for comfort that Annie had to recoil back when he strutted over to her corner. Sammy thought he was only being sly though, trying to give the girls a taste of their own medicine. Still, he couldn't shake the feeling that it wasn't just an act. The way he talked and his body language were all red flags going up.

"You don't have to keep interrupting me and my boy, Sammy, over here every time you have the urge to come and talk to me, darling," Nark teased, running his fingers through his greasy hair to keep his bangs from dropping over his eyes. "Now that I know that you can't get enough of me, I'll make sure you have me all to yourself anytime you want!"

Watching the girls wince as Nark got smooth with them got Sammy all riled up with his new best friend, who was going overboard with every passing second at being inappropriate. He felt obligated to step in and put an end to it himself, but he resisted because he didn't want to antagonize his pal—his only pal in the whole wide world.

"If you want to date me, sure, I'm available, babe," he said with a lot of sass and moxie. "The Nark is into you, like you are into the Nark! How's that sound? Exciting, right? I know. So what do you say we go out and catch a bite after school, eh?"

"No," sternly replied Annie, her tone resolute and decisive. "You are not God's gift to women, little man. And just to make sure that you get it, I am not into you, dig?"

Annie stormed off after dishing out those harsh words, leaving Nark shaking his head in disbelief. She managed to whisk Ruby away with her too, instinctively grabbing the wrist of her dazed sister as she hurriedly strode towards their desks, which were located beside each other in the third row from the front. When she turned and left, she never looked back, and Sammy couldn't admire her more for just how cool she had just handled herself.

"I can wait," Nark then said calmly, composed and poised as he quietly folded his arms over his chest again. No one was more shocked than Sammy when he noted how mature his friend was in handling the rejection, as well as the humiliation that went hand in hand with it. "These types of girls, I get them all in the end. It's just a matter of time, really. It's not a matter of 'if', it's a matter of 'when' and you can take that all the way to the bank, buddy dude… all the way to the bank."

In a show of solidarity, Sammy reached out to Nark and patted him on the back. Acknowledging his friend's kind gesture, he nodded at his tall friend, and then they both parted ways to be at their desks—Nark in front, and Sammy at the back, somewhere between Oleta and Timmy who remained as expressionless as ever.

They were the last ones to take their seats. As soon as they did so, the sliding doors zipped open and a sudden silence blanketed the room from corner to corner. All eyes faced front as the large glass screen on the wall came alive with a colorful fireworks sequence and letters that danced to a popular upbeat pop tune before settling down to form the word—

APPLAUSE!!!

"Hello, my new room fifty-two! I'm the one and only Gailforce Galactrix! That's Mrs. Galactrix to you, boys and girls! And I'm your homeroom teacher for this year! Aren't you all soooo lucky!"

On the outside, Mrs. Galactrix was a stately, elegant exotic beauty—tall, trim, almond complexioned with straight shoulder length black hair, and a killer smile to die for. She dressed herself in a short sleeved yellow blouse, sunny like her favorite sunflowers, over a black skirt that dropped below the knee. Her high heel shoes boosted her already impressive height, making her appear towering, like a catwalk model. Anyone seeing her would think she was too. She not only looked the part, she also moved with the grace and poise of one.

Personality-wise, however, she was a completely different animal, not the prim and proper lady everyone would expect from the way she sharply groomed herself. She was bubbly, effervescent, vivacious and so full of life that it wasn't hard for anyone to like her. Well, at least, almost everyone.

"I see a lot of new faces and some old faces here," she gleefully said as she scanned her class from the center of the stage. "Hello again, Nark. Nice to run into you again."

Nark reciprocated with an uneasy smile that was far from just plain coy. His lips quivered as he bit on them. Nobody noticed it though, because he was sitting in the middle of the front row. The only one who did was the teacher, who expected as much.

8

Lunch on the first day started on the wrong foot. The hot lunch line itself was nightmarishly long, stretching and snaking for miles out of the lunch room down flights of stairs to the lobby and even spilling out into the parking lot.

When Sammy joined the queue at five past noon, he found himself stuck at where else but the tail's end—the absolute farthest point—which was basically just the principal's empty reserved parking space, some twenty paces from the entrance of the school. There, the prospects of landing a hot meal before the one o' clock bell rang was slimmer than winning the lottery.

Being his usual pessimistic self, Sammy quickly resigned himself to the fact that, by the time it would finally be his turn, school itself would be over. That meant that he had to contend with a very hungry, very angry stomach again that has not been fed a single thing for two straight days.

ROARRR!!!

All Sammy could do was smile when his tummy was overheard growling again. Fortunately, there were only a few people outside and the wide open space of the parking lot wasn't conducive to acoustics. Although he got some laughs and a couple of heckles from the people in his line, he was good. There was no name calling or threats. Sammy worried though that his luck was running out fast, as his stomach began to churn and gas up on the inside again. It was only a matter of time before the big one hit, which was soon.

"Here's something to tide you over."

The chocolate bar in the yellow wrapper dangled in front of him like bait. Overwhelmed with an overpowering hunger, Sammy snatched it greedily from the hand that held it out to him, tore it open, then wolfishly scarfed it down. It was only after consuming all of the candy that he noticed his benefactor, Annie, looking terribly concerned at him. She had seen Sammy's bony hands trembling when he voraciously ate up her gift and the dark spots around his famished eyes. She felt so sorry for him that she threw her arms around him without thinking, and hugged him as tight as she could, surprising Sammy who was speechless.

"You, poor thing!" she exclaimed, before releasing her suffocating stranglehold of the boy. "You're more bone than meat!" she then added, a conclusion she had drawn from feeling his body up close.

Sammy wanted to put in a word in his defense, but Annie had shoved a whole bag of sandwiches into his chest before he could say anything. Then, without any explanation whatsoever, she rocketed out of there.

"What was that all about?" Sammy mumbled to himself.

In a twinkle of an eye, Annie was gone and a light drizzle began to fall. The pitter-patter of the rain on the ground was not enough to drown out the gossip that was spreading around the line. The topic was Sammy and Annie, and the brief hug that they shared.

"Dude, that scrawny kid over there with the spiky hair has a girlfriend!" one random student said to the other.

"Lucky."

"Yeah, and she's totally smoking!" seconded another anonymous one.

"And on the very first day even!"

"Must be a summer carryover."

"These school romances are sure starting early this year."

The chatter carried on until the line began to inch forward again. Worried that his presence might only further incite idle talk about him, Sammy didn't follow and stayed behind in the parking lot. Although the showers were beginning to pick up some gusty winds, he didn't mind the inconvenience, especially since he had a bag of sandwiches all too himself. Before long, he stopped being shy and started gobbling them up ferociously.

He was attacking the sandwiches one after the other, shoving them right into his mouth before he could even catch his breath. It was while he was making an animal of himself that he spotted Nark from a distance, who was staring straight at him with unkind, slighted eyes.

Wondering why Nark seemed so mad at him for no reason, Sammy motioned him to come over, but the small boy had other plans. Without a word, Nark stole away to the school, leaving Sammy soaked and with many questions that needed answers.

****

"Where did you put my sandwiches, Sis?" belted out Ruby as she rummaged through her tin lunch box, which was empty except for a single banana.

"I… lost it," replied Annie sullenly, as she noticed Sammy enter the lunch room and back in the lunch line again. "You can have mine, if you like, Ruby."

When Sammy overheard the sisters conversing, he was eighteenth from the front. He wasn't supposed to rejoin the line anymore, having walked away earlier, but his poor stomach just couldn't make do with the tasty sandwiches Annie had given him. It needed more nourishment, and seeing that the queue's back end had shrunk considerably from the parking lot down to the lunch room, he just had to jump back on the bandwagon. The lure of free food was just too tempting for him to ignore.

The lunch room itself was bustling with students, most of whom were already seated and enjoying their meals. Some brought theirs from home, while others got theirs either from the lunch lady at the end of the counter or the vending machines that lined the wall by the entrance.

The noise that reverberated around the place was ear-splitting, so much so that Sammy could hardly hear himself talk when he tried to ask the person in front of him for the time. He barely heard her say that they had a good thirty minutes left to go before classes started, which was good enough for him to finish a second serving.

As he waited patiently for his turn, which was any minute now, Sammy got bored and eavesdropped on a couple of seventh and eight graders—upper classmen in the school—who were spiritedly discussing last year's casualties.

Did you hear about what happened to so and so last year?

Their recap of the previous year's losses zeroed in on the mysterious disappearances of three sixth grade teachers, who allegedly just up and faded away into thin air right in the middle of their class lectures. Their sudden, unexpected departures brought the total up to seven in a span of three years.

The school's better off without them! Moving up's now a breeze!

As it turned out, according to the footnotes of the group, all these missing teachers were not exactly saints. They were notoriously known throughout the school during their heyday for deliberately holding students back in the sixth grade. Collectively known as the "terrors" because it was easier to draw blood from a stone than to get a passing grade from them, these teachers made it their personal mission to "protect the academic integrity of the school by weeding out all undesirables."

It didn't take a rocket scientist therefore to figure out that their "flunkies" probably held a grudge against them, and were probably responsible for their inexplicable exits. Be that as it may, terrible as it is to think that they're all gone, the sixth grade students at Great Beagle this year couldn't be happier. Without the "terrors" to flunk them out, advancing to the next grade level didn't pose a challenge, as much as it did in the previous years.

In similar fashion—since it was also brought up in passing during the discussion—the eight students, who unceremoniously dropped out last year because they were allegedly terrorized by Great Beagle's legendary Nanek Beast—were all bullies in their own right. With them gone, along with the seventeen others that left in the last two years when creature sightings started, the school has never been more peaceful, all thanks to an imaginary monster.

"Do you want grub… or grub?"

The lunch lady's accent was thick, just like the hair on her arms which showed below her rolled up sleeves. She was extremely efficient with them too, especially with a ladel. With a single graceful motion, she would swing it two handed like a golf club, scooping off grub out of a large, stainless steel pot, then depositing it nicely on to a plastic plate before the hapless student holding it could ask: *"What's for lunch?"*

Of course, her skill at serving food was much, much better compared to her skill of cooking it. Every student, who sat down to quietly eat the only thing on the menu, either: vomited, passed out, screamed in agony or… liked it immensely. Sammy wondered which of those four categories he would fall into come his time to taste the mysterious culinary creation.

When it finally came Sammy's turn with the plate, he held it up nervously and snuck a quick glance at the lunch lady herself. To his astonishment—lo and behold!—he recognized her immediately—or rather "him" immediately.

"You!" he huffed aloud, his jaw dropping hard. "You're the lunch lady too!"

Mister Dojo was standing across from him behind a granite counter that had baskets of various treats on it. He was wearing a shower cap, an apron and some industry grade gloves. He had a toothpick sticking out of his gritted full set of gold teeth, something Sammy never noticed about him before. That, and the fact that he was hairy all over.

"Grub… or grub?

Although the snub hurt Sammy's pride a bit, he simply pretended to just go along with the charade to get his grub… and go. As soon as Mister Dojo made his hole-in-one on Sammy's plate, he told the boy "to beat it" as he had another customer waiting in the wings. Sammy obliged and walked over to an empty seat in the corner.

He was right about ready to sit himself down when Oleta Teytata suddenly appeared out of nowhere. Although she didn't get an invite from him to join him at his table, she impudently sat herself down in front of Sammy, dropping her plate on his table without so much as a "May I?"

"This is turning out to be a really nice date, darling," she purred softly, connecting with his eyes like a predator.

Sammy found it strange that Oleta was being friendly towards him in an odd and uncomfortable way. Gone was the famous deadpan expression of hers, as well as her signature rudeness and sarcasm. For some reason, her natural abrasive personality has been completely replaced by a seductive temptress, and this made Sammy suspicious.

"So, what's up?" Sammy asked, trying to hide his anxiety and discomfort. "What do I owe the pleasure of your company?"

"I've had my eyes on you, Sammy Tsunami" Oleta began. And as those words smoothly rolled out of her tongue, the eyes of Horus on her bandana seemed to wink one after another to Sammy's shock and bewilderment.

"What do you say, we go steady?" added Oleta, reaching her hand out to Sammy and touching him gently on the wrist. "You don't have a girlfriend, do you?"

She gave him a sticky look, the kind that melted boys where they sat. Lucky for Sammy though, he was made of sterner stuff and did not turn to putty in her hands. Although he couldn't help blushing in front of her, he kept his head and thought things true. The last thing he wanted was letting himself get neatly wrapped around her finger.

"So what'll it be, handsome?" Oleta pressed on, batting her eyelashes at him. "Make me a happy girl and say you're mine."

"No," Sammy retorted, jumping out of his chair to confront

Oleta head on. "I've met girls like you before that only want to play around with the heart strings of boys. Once you have their heart and soul, you cut their strings and go, laughing as they cry. My heart isn't a play thing, Oleta. If you think that I'm some stupid country bumpkin, then think again. I'm on to you."

With those words left on the table, Sammy marched towards the exit, leaving Oleta completely stunned in her seat—but not before grabbing his grub and his plate. Nobody saw him make a scene as everybody was busy either chatting with friends or eating.

For a while, Oleta just sat there, wondering what to make of the pickle that was Sammy Tsunami. Then her cell phone rang, and she picked it up.

"Yeah, he left already," she spoke into the receiver, switching back to her usual dry, couldn't-care-less voice. "You owe me twenty bucks, okay?"

9

On his way back to class, Sammy stopped by the computer room. It was on the second floor—the same floor his classroom was on—but closer to the platforms and along the way. The sign on the door read: *OPEN FROM NOON*, which was a lucky break for him considering that he still had some time to kill. In his clock, seven minutes was more than long enough to Google something.

Peering through the glass door, and seeing all the eighteen inch monitors just standing around on their tables without anyone using them just made Sammy's heart soar. Finally, he thought, a crack in the wall that he can hang out in.

Without entertaining second thoughts, he walked right in through the door and darted for the nearest keyboard. After grabbing a swivel chair and seating himself down, he turned on the CPU and waited for the screen to light up.

His fingers were ready to go and type, when he heard a loud thud behind him. Startled at the noise, he turned to see. It was Mick, the boy he met earlier in class, the one with the glasses and the Hawaiian shirt with the crazy, insane colors. He had dropped a stack of books he picked out from the shelf in the corner—on the floor.

"Sorry about that, dude," he meekly apologized in his distinctive surfer accent, as he bent down to pick up his mess. "Clumsy hands."

"Hey!" said Sammy, who was actually glad to see his unexpected company, having missed the opportunity earlier to introduce himself to him. "It's Mick, right? Sammy."

"Oh, yeah, that's right," Mick interposed, gazing straight into Sammy's sapphire eyes through his large round, Harry Potter-like lenses. "Nice to meet 'cha, man. That's a rocking hairdo!"

"Thanks!" Sammy retorted appreciatively, amazed at the fact that this was the first time anybody heaped praise on his blue flaming tresses. "What are you doing here?"

"I'm embarrassed to say, research, man," Mick replied, just as he was done placing the books on a desk. "I wanna get a head start over everybody. I'm a grades rat, nothing but A's and a few B's all my life. Not that I'm bragging and turning you off, dude. I don't mean you to get the wrong impression about me, just setting the record straight."

"It's alright," chimed Sammy, who was genuinely surprised to hear that Mick wasn't a slacker as he originally thought he was, which was refreshing to know. "I'm a grades rat myself. Although, where I come from, they call people like me 'nerds' if you can believe that."

"A pleasure to make your acquaintance then, my fellow

nerd," good-humoredly rejoined Mick, who immediately flew to Sammy's side the second his screen got its graphics on. "I wanna show you something if you have a sec," he then told Sammy, intrusively leaning over the boy's shoulder and running his fingers over the keyboard until a strange website with a barking cat came up.

"This is my site!" proudly announced Mick in an excited tone before retracting his typing hand back to his side.

"I made it myself last year in fifth grade. I write and post news articles here about things that happen in school. You know, juicy and interesting stuff that people follow. Not gossip, mind you, because I don't do trash. I'm actually an investigative reporter when I'm not being a student, dude. This year I plan to investigate and uncover the mystery behind the Nanek Beast, Great Beagle's greatest and most dangerous urban legend. It's going to be an insane expose, man!"

"I thought you haven't heard about the Nanek Beast?" quizzed Sammy, whirling around in his swivel chair to confront his bespectacled acquaintance face to face. "I was there when you specifically told Nark earlier that you don't have any idea what it is!"

"Dude, I was throwing him off!" was Mick's snappy and sincere answer. "That kid's the main suspect, man! In the last two years when all these mysterious disappearances and dropping outs started, he's been right in the middle of the maelstrom—the one thing in common that links all these unsolved cases together!"

Mick was going in a direction Sammy didn't feel comfortable with. He was ragging on and dissing his new best friend—and yet, he was making such a compelling case about it that Sammy couldn't stop listening to his story. He had lent out his ears to Mick, and couldn't get it back.

"The teachers who vanished—they were known as the 'terrors' in this school because they made it a point to flunk as many students to keep a sizeable number held back in the sixth grade. They were all power trippers and jerks, but they didn't deserve what happened to them. These teachers have families too, who miss them, you know? Anyway, Nark's one of those who got held back—several times—by these teachers! So what does that tell you? Connect the dots."

Conflicted was how Sammy exactly felt about this whole Nark situation. On the one hand, there was his blooming friendship with him. Although they haven't been pals for long, they had something special going on between them—an honest to goodness camaraderie—that he didn't want taken away. On the other end, Mick's evidence against his dwarfish friend was strong and convincing, although not conclusive enough to pin the guilt on him entirely. It was adequate though to get the wheels in Sammy's head spinning. And boy, were they spinning!

"Do you think these teachers are… dead?" Sammy butt in, changing the topic for a second to have a burning concern of his addressed.

"Probably, dude," solemnly responded Mick. "Legend has

it that their bodies were spirited away to the otherworldly dimension of the Nanek Beast, where their souls would be devoured by the monster. I heard he pulled their souls out right through their eyes!"

"Why, their eyes?"

"Because the eyes are the windows to the soul, dude."

Hard as it was to swallow what Mick had told him, Sammy gave his story the benefit of the doubt and left it at that. Still, he was in a quandary.

On the one hand, there was Nark, his only friend in the world so far. The fact that Nark lied about not getting held back was something Sammy was willing to overlook, considering that anybody in a situation like that would probably be too embarrassed to disclose something like that anyway.

Granting even that it turns out that Nark is a pathological liar because that is his nature, Sammy didn't think that his friend should be zeroed out for simply being at the wrong place at the wrong time. It was all just coincidence, and in the absence of proof that he had something to do with the disappearances, people should not be associating him with them.

Then again, Sammy considered, what if the allegations against him are true? What if he is indeed the culprit in this crime? Could Sammy overlook something as serious as that just because they were friends and friends have to watch out for each other. Sammy was so confused and couldn't make up his mind on what to do.

"And there are the dropouts also," continued Mick, "those students who were terrorized allegedly by the Nanek Beast itself!"

Sammy had heard about these traumatized kids in the lunch room, along with the missing teachers, when he stumbled upon a couple of upper classmen raving about their tragic fates. He thought that Mick's spin to the story, about how the teacher's souls were devoured, was a nice touch—even if he made it up himself just to impress him.

What fired Sammy's interest though was why were the only ones missing adults and not kids. Does the Nanek Beast have a soft spot for minors? He wondered about these things as he continued to hear out the rest of Mick's intriguing report.

"You might think that the kids are lucky because they survived, but they're not! After their encounter with the Nanek Beast, each one of them has been reported to have recurring nightmares every night about the monster. It's like it's haunting them and there's no escape wherever they go!"

"Still, they're lucky to have lived, won't you say?" argued Sammy, sounding impetuous. "Better alive than not, like they say."

"One wasn't as fortunate as the rest though," somberly imputed Mick, shuffling over to the door leave. "A boy two, three years older than us... his friends simply called him 'Chunk' because he was a large... piece... of something. I don't know what, dude. But he was my cousin. And now he's gone, like all the other teachers."

Hearing the sadness in Mick's voice, Sammy wanted to offer his condolences and try to cheer him up. He stood from his seat and positioned himself beside him, waiting for the right moment to say what he needed to say. As he did so, however, Mick began feeling self-conscious around him, so much so that he stopped in his tracks, didn't walk out, became shifty-eyed, and started fiddling with his thumbs.

"Dude, something's wrong with your shadow." Mick then said, after a bout with the awkward silence that had unexpectedly wedged itself between them.

The blood in Sammy's veins chilled when he heard this, and his normally light brown complexion suddenly became pasty. He reluctantly lowered his head to see the fiasco for himself, but shut his eyes at the last minute.

He knew that his shadow arrow was there, right down on the floor and in front of him, for everyone to see. Otherwise, Mick would have told him that he was missing his shadow.

But how come? Why now? It had never appeared indoors before. It had always been considerate when it came to these things. How could it do this to him?

"Seriously, dude. Look."

He was right about ready to do an about face to hide his shame, when Mick suddenly slipped and fell forward, smashing his chin hard on the tiled floor. The force of the impact knocked his glasses right off—and a tooth—both of which flew under one of the desks. The pain of losing a molar must have been so intense and excruciating that Mick ended up wailing and bawling uncontrollably—like a baby.

"Are you okay, man?" Sammy inquired, bending down and leaning over close, as he forgot all about his shadow arrow making an unwanted appearance. "Your chin's bleeding and you lost a tooth, but otherwise, you'll be okay. Just chill, alright? I'll help you up if you like. But if you can't stand up, tell me now and I'll go get the nurse."

Being the nice guy that he was, Sammy's initial reaction was to console his injured classmate, then help him back on his feet. Mick, who was lying flat on his chest and flopping on the floor like a fish freshly plucked out of water, was inconsolable however.

Despite Sammy's best efforts to calm him down, Mick's tears continued to stream down his moistened face, just as the volume of his already loud screams got turned up several notches to an ear-splitting pitch.

"Please tell me what to do?" Sammy then asked, getting desperate as he couldn't make heads or tails of why Mick wouldn't stop crying. He figured that the boy probably has a very low threshold of pain, which explained a lot about his condition. Then, he turned his head, like he always planned to, and—lo! And behold!—tightly coiled around his right leg was a rather large boa constrictor. It was sinking both its fangs into the soft flesh of Mick's thigh, when Sammy made eye contact with it.

"WHOAAA!!!" exclaimed Sammy as he quickly retracted

from its biting radius and retreated to a corner. As he made a mad dash to safety, he accidentally struck a keyboard, which crashed onto the floor with a noisy clunk, alerting the reptile to his presence. Sensing him nearby, the snake immediately withdrew its teeth from its victim's leg, confronted Sammy, and hissed at him.

"Two birds, one stone… must be my lucky day."

10

The guttural snarl didn't come from the constrictor, although Sammy almost wished it did.

There was someone else in the room. And whoever he was, he was most probably responsible for the vile serpent sharing the air that they breathe. Summoning whatever courage he had left in him, Sammy forced his eyes to scan the debacle that was Mick's livid leg, which was a sickly purple overripe eggplant riddled with red dots—calling cards of the serpent's drunken binge.

His incisive observation did not end there. Lifting his eyes—slowly—he followed the scaly, elongated body of the snake all the way up to where its tail dangled limply from. As it turns out, it was hanging out of a black robe, the type monks dress in. It was levitating in the still air without any feet beneath it to anchor the invisible body that fitted into it.

As if one arm wasn't gruesome enough, the other was its exact twin, equally flexible and equally ill-tempered. This one, however, preferred to hiss at him from a distance.

"Leftie here's taking a liking to you, boy! He wants to make your acquaintance, just like Rightie over there became best pals with your bawling buddy."

Smooth as its sarcasm was, the voice remained throaty and scowling. It was unpleasant, and it belonged to an unpleasant face that sat above the collar of the floating robe.

For starters, it had a bulbous head, like an octopus. Circling it was a crown of pliable tentacles that swayed to and fro as if submerged underwater. The face itself was as hideous as it could get—reptilian with cavernous eyes and razor sharp teeth—only steam roller-flattened. Whenever it opened its mouth, it not only exhaled clouds of green toxic fumes; it also shot out and extended a forked tongue that disgustingly flapped in the air.

"Took you a while to spot all of me!" it cheerfully ribbed Sammy, although the delivery of its formal greeting left much to be desired, especially since it came off as sounding menacing. "Now that you've seen me in all my—ahem—bone chilling glory, be free to scream all you like, until your lungs explode!"

The dialogue was wooden and cheesy. Had Sammy been elsewhere but in the scene, he would have been laughing instead of thinking up ways of how to save his life.

"This is awkward, isn't it?" added the monster, its gutsy bravado now tempered into a more sensitive façade. "I'm used to people screaming the moment they feast their eyes on me. But you're no screamer, so this all feels pretty strange."

Time stood still as Sammy watched and listened to the

monster talk. He was like a deer caught in the headlights of an incoming car. Tried as he wanted to veer away, he couldn't. He was just frozen in place, breathing slowly and waiting for the inevitable to happen.

"I can tell that you're afraid of me, but you're mind's still pretty sharp, like a blade fresh from a grindstone. You've got composure, but your nerves are on edge, probably because you're trying to devise an appropriate escape plan on the fly. That's understandable. But nobody's ever gotten away from me, so sorry you need to know about that."

When his legs got their strength back, Sammy sprung towards the door. He grabbed the metal handle like his life depended on it and pulled. After that didn't work, he tried pushing, but that too resulted in nothing. He was getting more and more desperate, like an animal trapped in a cage looking for a way out, when he felt something scaly and damp wrap around his waist.

"Nobody's ever escaped from me, and I'm not going to have you be my first!" the monster angrily rebuked him. "Besides, we haven't properly introduced ourselves yet. I'm Rular, by the way, although the entire school knows me as the Nanek Beast. You should ask me why I'm called that because I will be glad to dignify your question with a spritely answer!"

"What do you want from us?" distraughtly interjected Sammy, shortly after the other serpent, Leftie, lassoed him around the waist and yanked him violently over to her master's side. Feeling her cold, crusty body wrap itself around him—and tighten—the boy quaked in fear as he had never done before.

"Just like all the others, how droll, eh?" growled Rular angrily, blowing thick smokes of toxic fumes into the boy's frightened face. "They see me, they fear me, they go mad! I was hoping to get a different reaction from you, but I guess, that would be expecting too much. If only my boss would let me kill you, little fleshlings, my life would probably be more exciting while I'm on his leash."

As soon as the Nanek Beast blurted this out, the serpent's grip on Sammy's waist tautened, like a vise. He was in excruciating pain and close to passing out, so unlike Mick, who was already unconscious since a couple of seconds ago. That boy was lucky. Sammy kicked and screamed, as he frantically tried to loosen the whorl on his hips, which was coming close with every passing second to fracturing his very bones.

"How does it feel to be helpless?" sneered Rular as he dangled Sammy in front of him like a favorite plush doll he was playing with. "Squirming in the hands of another, trying desperately to escape, but finding it difficult to impossible to do so? Believe it or not, I know how you feel, for I too am helpless. I am no more than someone else's attack hound. I move only when my boss bids me to. So you see, we aren't that different, you and I."

Rular was rambling. Sammy couldn't make proper sense of what the monster was trying to say, especially since he was in a world of hurt and, at the same time, completely focused exclusively on trying to escape its steely clutches. Unless a miracle somehow happened in the next couple of seconds, he was bound to snap—into two, like a twig.

"Then again, perhaps we are different after all. You are a mere fleshling insect like my boss, and I... I am a jinn-mera."

When Sammy's relentless efforts to slip out of the serpent's suffocating knot proved futile, his base survival instincts took over. Without intending to do so, he threw a blind punch—a wild punch—and somehow, it found something soft and supple to bury its balled fist into.

It connected with Rular's left eye, pushing it deep down into its large, gaping socket!

AAAAAAH!!!!

It didn't take long before Sammy realized what he had done. Scared out of his wits that the monster's retaliation would be swift and inevitable, he tried to retract his arm from the stiff hole it was interred in... but it was stuck! He struggled to pull it out with all his might, but it wouldn't budge. He was about to give it another go when Leftie, the boa constrictor that had him securely fastened in its grip, slithered treacherously to bite him in the shoulder.

AAAAAAH!!!!

It tried injecting its sharp fangs into his sweater, but they broke off before they could even tear the fabric. Rushing to help its injured reptilian sibling, Rightie, the other boa constrictor, quickly uncoiled itself from Mick's tattered leg and flew straight into Sammy's back like a missile dead on target. When Rightie tried to do what Leftie failed at, she suffered the same fate—two broken fangs and blood gushing all over the insides of her mouth.

AAAAAAH!!!!

The robe that hosted Rular's unseen body started convulsing as both serpent arms went down for the count, striking the floor hard one after the other. Sammy hit the floor, feet first, with his arm still deep to the elbows in Rular's hemorrhaging eye socket.

"Curse you, fleshling, let go!" barked the monster out loud, which shook and lurched back feverishly, as it attempted to free itself for the Nth time from Sammy's invasive reach. The boy gave it a strong pull this time around. He yanked as hard as he could and—wallah! His arm was finally free! And clutched tightly in its hand was an eye the size of a baseball!

"My best eye!" squealed Rular as he drew back to a corner, dragging his two flaccid arms with him. The monster wanted to say more, but something whizzed past Sammy's ear—a black blur, straight and swift.

It was the boy's shadow arrow.

When its pointy end skewered Rular's left arm, the monster released a terrible piercing shriek, the kind that rattled the soul and left it remembering it. In the next instant following this, both Rular and Sammy's shadow arrow just up and vanished in a cloud of purple smoke that quickly dissipated as fast as it appeared..

"No," whimpered Sammy, distraught over the thought that he may have finally lost his shadow arrow for good. "Please come back." He begged it and begged it to return, even pleading aloud so that he may be heard. But nothing came back.

"You beat it, Sammy. You really beat did."

Mick was sitting up on the floor, nursing his injured leg, which was still as purple as ever and peppered with red dots. He had found his missing glasses, as well as the molar he had misplaced. After flashing an appreciative smile at Sammy, she attempted to stand up with the assistance of a nearby desk. This proved to no avail. Her pain was agonizing and almost unbearable. Every time she moved, even an inch, it was like a saw teeth were eating through her shin.

"Are you okay?" Sammy asked concernedly, bending down again to be at eye level with his hurt classmate. "I'm sorry about your leg, Mick. I really am. You wait here, while I go get help, alright? You need to be taken to the hospital right away."

"It's Mickayla. I'm a girl, dude."

Words completely failed Sammy the moment he heard the shocking news break. He didn't know what to say. He was speechless. He had no idea how to respond to what he just heard. All her could do was listen, and listen intently.

"I know you're thinking that I'm some cross dresser or something," she added playfully, removing her glasses to wipe them on the hem of her Hawaiian shirt. "That's perfectly fine.

I can't blame you. What can I say, I like pretending to be a boy. It's like wearing a mask, you know. When you have a mask on, you're someone else completely. I find that sort of thing very liberating."

Her sentiments echoed Sammy's own. Without being aware of it, she had struck a raw nerve in the boy, who empathized with her tragic plight of trying to flee the hell of her own individual identity. Like Mickayla, Sammy wanted to be someone else more than anything. He loathed himself for living an accursed life, marked by constant pain and suffering. If he could just leave his own skin and trade it for someone else's, he would have grabbed the opportunity long ago. But he knew only too well that a chance like that was nothing but pure fantasy. In the harsh reality of his world, there was no escaping his horrid fate—not even by putting a mask on.

"Tell you what, dude. Since I know all about your little secret, and you know mine, what do you say we make a deal?"

"What kind of deal?" asked Sammy, suddenly jumpy over the prospect of entering into a contract.

"The 'you don't tell, I don't tell' kind of deal."

Upon learning what Mickayla had in mind, Sammy's fears were immediately allayed and he relaxed more. He glanced at the young girl's mauve colored leg, and realized right away that she may be out of commission for some time. For just how long, he had no idea.

"Deal."

"Wonderful, Sammy! I guess, I'm ready for my close up now."

They smiled at each other and shook hands. Outside, the sound of quick approaching footsteps drew nearer and nearer. They were finally coming, Sammy thought to himself. And not a minute too soon.

11

It was a bad precedent missing an entire class on the first day of school, but Sammy Tsunami had no choice. He was held up in the computer room for almost an hour. His alibi? The door was locked from the inside, and he and Mick couldn't get out. Worse, Mick developed a severe allergic reaction during their incarceration, so much so that he almost died while help crawled to the rescue.

When the teachers who freed them became skeptical, however, about their bogus story, all Mick had to do was threaten to sue the school for negligent child supervision, and all was right.

Nobody argued with him when he skillfully pointed out that the school should have assigned an adult on duty at the computer room during the lunch break hour. They even excused the two boys for not attending Mister Sandover's trigonometry class. That meant no detention, no demerits, no trouble whatsoever.

Although getting the very first hall pass of the year made him the envy of the entire school, Sammy was deeply troubled, and his haggard face reflected this as he quietly sat in Mrs. Galactrix's class in a trance. He worried about Mick—who was actually Mickayla, a girl pretending to be a boy—especially since learning that she had to be transported to a hospital for medical treatment.

Although his thoughts dwelled on his hopes for her speedy recovery, he mourned for the loss of his very own shadow arrow, which bravely sacrificed itself earlier to save him and Mick from that monster. Every now and then, he would look at his feet to check if it had returned. And every time he did, it was not there.

"Breaking news, boys and girls!" skittishly announced Mrs. Galactrix, who was reading something off a computer tablet clutched in the palm of her hand.

"Mick has officially dropped out of school, so he will no longer be coming to class anymore. If you don't know who he is, or haven't heard of him, then that's okay. This is the first day of school, you know. I don't know him myself actually, except that he's in your class. For those who have an idea who this person is, just so you know, he's in the hospital right now. He got hurt, I'm not sure, I don't know, I don't care. Anyway, that's that!"

Immediately after the news broke, the entire class got talkative. Chat groups quickly formed. Some students even got off their seats to gossip with groups across the room from them. The hot topic of their various discussions centered on Mick being the first victim of the Nanek Beast this year.

All the tell-tale signs were there—the abrupt exit from school, the mysterious injuries—sure indications that it was the monster that done it, and not anything else.

As all this hustle and bustle was going on, Sammy snapped out of his forlorn haze and began noticing some of his missing classmates, particularly the ones he personally knows. On his right, Oleta wasn't by her desk, nor was Timmy on his left. Nark was gone too. His chair in the center of the front was empty as well.

"Settle down, class, because you don't wanna see my mean old game face now, do you?" lightheartedly ordered Mrs. Galactrix, making a funny face as she did.

It wasn't long before everyone returned to their seats and quieted down. The teacher was about to put in another word to officially begin the lesson, when the sliding door whizzed open and in walked Nark and Timmy, both looking worse for wear like they were in some sort of fight. Timmy himself was wearing a patch over his left eye, looking like a pirate, and a bandage tightly wound around his left bicep.

"Explain yourselves for being late," Mrs. Galactrix commanded, folding her arms across her chest and staring them down, just as they took their seats. Her sudden mood change frightened the class. One second, she was this cheery, vivacious spirit. In the next, she was cold, despotic and steely.

Although she gave the boys dirty looks, they gave her no answers. They were both silent as a mouse, and seemed indifferent. It was as if she didn't exist in their eyes.

"Do you, two, have a hall pass? Speak now or be the first names on my blacklist this year!"

When Timmy heard the teacher say Sammy's name out loud, he turned to him and ogled him menacingly with his one good eye. Then, he picked up a sharp number two pencil from his desk, and in front of the boy's scandalized eyes, ate the whole thing!

Speechless and stunned, Sammy watched the bearded giant chew up the wood and lead in it with curious fascination. As splinters and toothpicks grinded into dust inside Timmy's mouth, Sammy thought that it was quite the coincidence that his seatmate was wearing an eye patch over his left eye, just as Rular—the Nanek Beast—had lost his. In fact, that missing eye ball was safely tucked inside one of Sammy's pockets, a souvenir of their first and last encounter.

"If you, two, are ignoring me—and disrespecting me—then march out that door right now and go straight to the principal's office."

Sammy then caught Nark, glancing at him over his shoulder. He had the same mad expression on his face, like when he saw him in the parking lot earlier at lunch time. Sammy was scarfing down the sandwiches Annie gave him, when Nark suddenly appeared in the rain. Could he be angry with him because he didn't share with him his food?

"Alright!" angrily yelled the teacher, straightening up and planting both hands on her hips. "Out, you two! Out of here!"

A church-like silence swept across the classroom . Everyone ducked for cover in their seats as they anticipated the showdown to escalate—Mrs. Galactrix on one corner, and Nark and Timmy on the other.

As the two students slowly rotated their heads to face front and make eye contact, the rest of the class bit their lips and closed their eyes. Soon as they did, Mrs. Galactrix let out a loud, deafening scream. The sound waves it generated rocked a couple of desks and seats, and even knocked some pencils on to the floor.

"Was that your best shot, maestra?" defiantly challenged Nark, training his baleful eyes on his teacher, as he casually reclined on his chair and calmly reached into his side pockets. "Well then, here's my rejoinder."

The atmosphere inside rapidly became heavy and electrically charged. Sammy himself became aware of this unnatural change in the air when he had to yank his bare hands off from his desk because of the static discharge the wooden surface emitted.

He felt as if his heart had skipped a beat when the zap suddenly startled him. This was nothing though, compared to what happened to his fiery sapphire hair. His split ends literally separated from one another, making him his head look like a ball with needles sticking out of it.

SOMEBODY PLEASE!!!

The shrill cry for help emanated from Mrs. Galactrix herself. She was covered from head to toe in a raging pillar of bilious purple smoke that had her coughing incessantly and gasping for air. In her terrified and confused state, she ran out the sliding doors, but before she could advance any further beyond the fixated gazes of her class, she suddenly vanished into thin air before their very eyes, leaving only misty traces of mauve to mark her mysterious passing.

****

"Relax, relax, relax!" Mister Dojo told the unruly rabble of children in front of him. He said it in a very soft spoken voice that struggled to be heard amidst a cacophony of howling, babbling and weeping. Although he even smiled his most angelic smile to show his sincerity, no one took him seriously. In fact, he was largely ignored. When he tried again to placate his inattentive young audience, a shoe flew right in his face.

"Now that does it!"

Chaos reigned in room fifty-two after students there witnessed the grisly end of their teacher, Gailforce Galactrix, officially now the first adult casualty of the Nanek Beast this year. There was widespread screaming, there was widespread panic, and there was a lot of belted out bawling in between. Students expressed their grief, their shock and their anguish by rioting and basically going nuts. Desks were overturned, seats were thrown to the wall, and even the substitute teacher himself was tackled!

"Get off me, or get detention!" snarled Mister Dojo, the substitute teacher on duty, who was assigned the daunting task of quelling this particular uprising of eleven and twelve year olds. "No student gets to manhandle a teacher, especially inside school premises!"

"All we want is for you to open the doors, so that we can leave!" snapped back Nark, who had the old man in a headlock, while burly, hairy mute Timmy pinned his arms and legs down. "You have no right locking us in, like this! After what just happened to our teacher, we all need trauma counseling! Not a lesson in figures of speech!"

"I am the grammar teacher for this period, and I will teach grammar, come hell or high water!" stubbornly vowed the old man, as a group of students started hurling their seats at the sliding doors to break the glass. "You will all sit down, you will all behave, and you will take the pop quiz that I will give you! That's right, children! A pop quiz!"

His eyes widened as if afflicted with some insanity-inducing disease. As his eyelids peeled and peeled, the old man's handlebar moustache began to twitch frenziedly. It seemed like it was going to fly out from under his nose and strike his enemies down, like a remote controlled shuriken!

"Hands off, Nark!" demanded Annie, jumping into the scene of the scuffle from out of nowhere, and armed as usual with her abrasive self-righteous posturing. "That's a teacher you're assaulting! I hereby place you under arrest for violating Article three hundred and two, paragraph twenty-two, section bee of the Great Beagle School Code of Conduct!"

"You don't understand, Annie," Nark began to explain. "He

not only locked us in here… He gassed us! The toxins went airborne and circulated the second they came through the air-conditioning vents. Aren't you wondering why everybody in class is acting… strange?"

Annie swept the room with her sights, and all she saw was unbridled, embarrassing mayhem, courtesy of the people she used to lovingly call her classmates.

Even her gentle-spirited sister was not spared the madness that had sickened everyone. Along with a couple of others, Ruby had been hard at work trying to smash the plexiglass on the sliding doors, hurling chair after chair at it with a cyclical rhythm.

"Talk, dirtbag!" she pluckily ordered the pinned down substitute teacher, after having a sudden epiphany. She was so angry at the treacherous lout that she even pointed a trembling finger at his bloated red nose.

"Okay, okay, alright!" gave in the old man, deciding to cut his losses. "I made a mistake. I was supposed to use something that would calm you down and relax you. That was the plan. Unfortunately, there was a mix up. I may have put something else in into the vents. I think it's the one that brings out the wild animal in every person… the one that makes people slightly crazy."

"So it's your fault then that we're like this?" Annie pressed on, continuing with her interrogation, as both boys tightened their grips around the portly frame of the old man. "Speak!"

"Yes," ruefully admitted Mister Dojo, letting out a sigh.

"But the good thing though about this is that this gas erases your memories of this incident. After you wake up—that is, after you pass out, something that's bound to happen any minute now—you won't remember any of this. Come to think of it, I won't have any recollection of this either myself! That's too bad!"

"I take it that, since we won't remember anything, there's no use threatening you with reporting your actions to the principal, so that the school board can strip you of your teaching license!"

"That's right!" confirmed Mister Dojo, seeming rather proud of this thought. "Besides, even if you reported me, the principal wouldn't fire me. He and I are close, tight-knit, fused to the hips! And tell you what—I don't have a teaching license! That's right! I was hired to teach in this school even though I don't have a teaching license! In fact, I don't think that I ever graduated from high school."

The slits of Annie's eyes narrowed as she brought them closer to Dojo's. Instead of breaking out a nervous sweat as the girl's face loomed closer to his own, the old man closed his eyes and puckered up his lips.

"We won't remember a thing, right?" Annie said flatly, turning to Nark and Timmy whom she both nodded too. "Boys, she then added, cracking her knuckles. "Weapons free and bash at will!"

12

The trail was hot for a few minutes, then went cold. When it did, Sammy Tsunami found himself inside the indoor gym, right in the middle of the basketball court. The bleachers beside the entrance were vacant, just like everything else in this spacious place, except that they shouldn't be.

This was where Sammy lost Mrs. Galactrix—at least, her shadow.

Twenty minutes ago in the classroom, everyone thought that they lost her. Mrs. Galactrix disappeared in dramatic fashion in a billowing cloud of purple smoke before the scandalized and traumatized eyes of her students. In a flash, she was gone to no one knows where. And before everybody could pick up their dropped jaws from the floor and get all the way back to reality from their respective dazes, Mister Dojo had slipped in with the announcement that he would be substituting for their 'absentee' teacher.

Two red flags went off right away, prompting Sammy to exit—and immediately. First, there was the gas. It came down surreptitiously and stealthily from the vents in the ceiling, misty and clear and almost undetectable. When the boy sniffed a whiff of the poison, he knew it wasn't just cooled air, but something else entirely. This alone had the boy squirming in his seat uncomfortably, but the one that got him springing out of there and through the door was the second one.

Nobody noticed it either, but him. It was hiding in plain sight, just outside the door, looking in and wondering what just happened.

When Mrs. Galactrix departed the world abruptly, she left behind a shade of herself on the wall, by the fire extinguisher locked inside the glass case. Sammy knew it was her because of the distinctive outline of the shadow and the peculiar nuances that attended its every small movement. The idiosyncratic hand gestures alone, like a maestro conducting a symphony, easily gave her away.

Her shadow didn't linger long, however. The second Mister Dojo faced the class to present himself, it just up and left, right about the same time the sliding doors were about to close shut.

"Excuse me, sir, but I need to go to the restroom!" Sammy said out loud, raising his hand for the teacher to see as he quickly shuffled his feet towards the exit. Before the old man in front could breathe a word, the boy had whisked himself outside, half a second before the doors locked and the gas seeped into everybody's lungs inside the classroom.

That was twenty minutes ago.

Since then, Sammy had been tailing the shadow of Mrs.

Galactrix—from the hallways, to all the way down to the lobby where it slid through the entrance of the gym, and vanished completely upon reaching the bleachers.

"Please let me help you!" he called out aloud, his echo bouncing back to him several times before totally fading beyond the reach of his hearing.

As expected, he got no response—at least, for some time, and not in a way that he ever anticipated. There, on the top of the bleachers behind a fat crack in the wall, Sammy noticed someone peeking at him. From where he stood, the only thing he noticed was a silhouette of a person's head. Strangely, it neither had eyes—or a face—for that matter.

"Wait!" he cried out. He ran as fast as he could up the narrow flight of stairs next to the bleachers. When the ghost sensed Sammy's quickening approach, it immediately retreated back into the darkness behind the wall and vanished.

"No, no, no!" Sammy begged it. By the time that he arrived at the zenith, the ghost was gone. But that didn't stop the boy from going after it. Losing no time, he peered through the hole in the crack and called out to it again to come back. Just like before, there was no answer, only a mocking silence.

****

The other side of the peep hole was a dimly-lit small room, empty and dust-smitten, with threadbare splintered hardwood decking the floor. Its concrete walls were creased with heavily shaded cracks that seemed together to form a black and white mural of a lightning storm.

Foggy and smelling too of burning candle wax, Sammy immediately got the impression that the place was haunted, and he was spooked. When several gray, translucent figures— with no faces—emerged from the shadowy corners and started to amass and congregate in the center of the space, the boy confirmed his worst fears about the place. Scared though he was of the apparitions that were materializing out of thin air right in front of his eyes, he couldn't veer away. Just like a deer caught in the headlights of an incoming car.

"You are safe now," whispered one shadow to another in a soft, bloodcurdling voice that sent shivers running down Sammy's spine. "The monster cannot reach any of us while we are in here. This is a haven."

"Are you sure we're okay, Mister Keck?" asked the other one in an equally gentle, but chilling tone. The voice was unmistakably a woman's, and it belonged to none other than Mrs. Galactrix herself. Sammy immediately recognized it from the get-go. Even the semi-distorted shape of the shadow, much faded now as if water washed, was hers. That much too, he was certain of.

Poor Mrs. Galactrix is now but a shade of her former self.

"Positive," curtly replied the shadowy male figure she was conversing with. "No harm will ever befall you here, Mrs. Galactrix. Welcome."

The name, Mister Keck, was terribly familiar to Sammy

for some reason that eluded him. He thought about it, and thought about it for a while. Then, after some hard pondering after some time—eureka! From brute memory, he retrieved it, as clear as it first formed. The upper classmen gossiping at the lunch room earlier mentioned him as one of the teachers, who had mysteriously vanished, and this was why it had stuck in Sammy's head like a song playing on the radio.

"Hurry!" urged yet another shadow, this one a small child and the only one in the group. "The monster's right outside! We have to get downside—and quick!"

The show they unintentionally put on for Sammy was over in an instant. The light in the small room had gone out, covering the entire area in total darkness. By some strange coincidence, the gym on the other end of it was dimming as well, but not for the same reason. Shadowy profiles of leafy vegetation crept from one corner of the massive building to another, sweeping across the basketball court itself and the bleachers to completely drape the enclosed surrounding with the familiar shades of vaulting trees and wild shrubbery.

Sammy couldn't tell whether he was imagining it or not. It seemed so surreal, so unreal.

Whatever it was, the boy distinctly heard leaves rustle and the slushing of snow, felt the biting cold wind chill him to the bone, and caught the distinct scent of moist forest pine after the rain. These were things he knew and knew well, since the time he and his family started taking up residence in the woods. He wondered how it was possible that he was experiencing them right now within the warm confines of his school. It was eerie—eerie, eerie, eerie.

Abandoning the hole in the wall, Sammy made his way down the steps towards the exit. As he did so, he consciously tried to imagine his shadow arrow, now forever lost and gone, leading the way just like old times.

He was halfway through the stairs, when he saw an enormous formless silhouette lumbering behind the trees, cracking their boughs and rattling their snow covered leaves, as it squeezed past them. In his rough estimate, he assessed that it was probably over fifty feet tall, which was ridiculous, looking back on hindsight. The elevated ceiling of the gym wasn't that high to begin with. For all Sammy knew, this was an illusion of some kind playing tricks on his eyes.

"Don't look at it."

A woman's voice blurted out this warning, not his teacher's but familiar nonetheless in a vague sort of way. Before even attempting to flip through the files stored in his head to identify whose it was, the boy did the practical thing—find out where it came from.

All he needed to do was twist his neck and have his head face left, and there he saw, standing in a distance right across from him, the shadow of a woman he had seen earlier that morning in the lobby. The one that was stalking him. He tried to examine her face, only to be reminded that she had none, just a blank gray outline of a head.

"Who are you?" Sammy dared to ask, trembling in the cold. "Why have you been following me?"

The second he completed stating his questions, he heard a loud hiss behind him. Acting on instinct, he whirled around to see, and what he saw was the shadow of a very large snake slithering by his feet, its fanged mouth wide open and ready to snap at his leg.

Surprised and startled by the sight of the serpent's shade, Sammy stepped back and lost his footing on a step. And fell.

He would have cracked his skull upon impact, but someone caught his back in the nick of time. "Sammy Tsunami! I didn't see you in class today!"

The boy spun around, taking greater care this time to maintain his balance on the narrow step he was standing on, and found Mister Dojo there.

"Sir!" Sammy exclaimed in astonishment. "What just happened?" He was still trying to properly process what just happened, when he noted that the gym had returned back to its normal, drab self. The shadows were gone, so have the bitter cold and the smell of wet pine. Everything was exactly how it was prior to the time he peered through the crack in the wall. It was like waking up from a dream.

"You happened," replied the old man, hardly opening his stiff lips. "You cut class, you played hooky and now, you pay the price for your missteps in judgment. But that can wait. I have something for you."

He handed over a wrinkled article of clothing to Sammy.

It was a bandana, the very same one Oleta Teytata wore, the one with the eyes of Horus printed on it.

It was stained with blood.

13

"You promised me that you'd never tell! What good is "cross my heart and hope to die" anymore?"

Ruby was agitated and seeing red. So much so that she broke down crying in her own arms. They were folded across the reading table in front of her when she dunked her head on them and let out a whopper of a wail. She was in the library that fateful afternoon with Sammy and Annie, who could only cover their ears and watch her have her ugly meltdown.

"Quit it, Ruby!" reproached her panicked and edgy sister, as her eyes nervously twitched and shifted around, taking quick mental notes of both the stunned and irritated reactions of the people around them. "We are in the library where people are supposed to be quiet AND MINDING THEIR OWN BUSINESS!"

She yelled her last words out loud until her throat actually hurt, hoping to dissuade bystanders nearby from being fixated on their backs and wondering what mischief they were up to. Noting that her plan didn't work, she quickly tried another approach.

"NANEK BEAST AT 2:00!!!"

Invoking this taboo wonderfully yielded both instant and favorable results that Sammy couldn't help but be impressed and embarrassed at the same time. No sooner did Annie holler these words into the hallowed halls did people vault right out of their seats and rush for the nearest exits, like lemmings. Once the library had been cleared and emptied, Annie then turned to her distraught sister whose face was still completely buried behind on the cushion of her meaty arms.

"Come now, Sis," she said in a softer voice with a milder tone. Although Annie despised demonstrating any show of affection to her sibling, she made an exception this time around by placing her hands—albeit reluctantly—on her wide back where a large white number nine was plastered there on her green jersey. "It's just Sammy, and we're all good friends here. And I promise, promise, promise to never breathe a word about this ever, ever again to anyone as long as I live—cross my heart and hope to die!"

Hearing her refer to him as a good friend made Sammy's heart strings soar. His day was already pitch-perfect as it is when Nark earlier called him "buddy dude." Now, he was on a roll of sorts and his collection of friends just kept growing and growing and growing. Although he was flattered to have learned Ruby's secret when Annie personally confided it, he felt awkward about the two sisters squabbling over him. Guilt stricken and ashamed, he wanted very much to intervene in their private dispute and help them resolve their differences right away, but decided not to at the last minute after entertaining second thoughts.

"Okay, okay, alright!" ranted Ruby as she emerged from seclusion, sprouting back to her feet with renewed vigor and steadfastness. "I'm a two-time repeater of the sixth grade! There, I finally admitted it! Annie here is two years younger than me. She was in the fourth grade in elementary school when I first came to Great Beagle. Now, we're classmates, and I had her swear not to tell anyone from our class this dark, dark, dark secret of mine… because I don't want to be judged for my life choices."

"This isn't a life choice," insolently interrupted Annie, correcting her sister once again as she circled her like a vulture preparing for a strike. "This is a life error."

"Why do you always do that?!" Ruby exploded, nearly strangling her sister, who was able to recoil away in time at the first sign of danger. "I've nearly had it with you! Just because you're smarter than me doesn't mean you can run all over me like that!"

Sammy finally stepped in between the two. He grabbed Ruby's trembling hand and tried to calm her down with some soothing words, which he whispered secretly in her ear. In no time, she was relaxed and had backed away. She was also blushing and holding back a very girlish giggle when she retreated to her corner to ruminate—a turn of events that genuinely surprised Annie who didn't know what to make of her sibling's strange and sudden change in behavior.

"Smooth!" she coyly teased Sammy, appreciative of how well he defused the tense situation between her and her sister. "You better ask Ruby now about the place you wanted to go to before she actually changes her mind again and flares up."

Sammy almost totally forgot about that one himself. He wanted to know where the back of the school was because of the note that Mister Dojo slipped him in the gym, the one hastily scribbled in black felt marker ink on the back of Oleta Teytata's bandana which had blood stains on it:

MEET ME AT THE BACK OF THE SCHOOL AFTER CLASS AT AROUND 5 P.M. OLETA'S IN GRAVE DANGER. UP TO US AND ONLY US. YOUR BUDDY DUDE, NARK.

He initially thought it was a childish prank and laughed it off. His impression changed, however, when Mister Dojo snatched the bandana away from him, licked the blood stains on it before his shocked eyes, and confirmed to him that it was, indeed, blood.

"I know the taste of blood better than a vampire!" the old man haughtily declared to Sammy as he thrust the bandana back into his reluctant custody. "This is blood without a doubt! Oleta's blood!"

When Sammy quizzed Mister Dojo later on as to how he came into possession of the bandana, he told him that he found it on Oleta's empty seat after class ended. Not one to take the law into his hands, Sammy then pressed the old man to do something about the situation, like alert the principal or call the authorities or something. To this suggestion, the old man simply replied:

"I'm just a substitute teacher here. I don't get involved in murder investigations. I teach math for goodness sake!"

****

"Are you, okay?" Ruby's voice was like a cold splash of water, like the ones his mother usually washed him with whenever he ended up sleeping too long. It snapped Sammy out of his blank stare and languid haze. "You wanted to ask me where the back of the school is, right?"

"Yeah," Sammy tersely replied, wiping the cold sweat that trickled down his brow. "Would you know where it is by any chance? It's important of sorts."

"Honestly, I don't know where it is, and I've been to, like, everywhere in this whole entire school. I heard that there's really no such place, but then again, I could be wrong. There are rumors about it, and I know some students like to make up stuff and all, so it could just be a hoax…"

She then paused for a second, suddenly self-conscious and feeling ashamed. "I'm being wishy-washy, right?"

"You've been very helpful," Sammy said to her politely before standing up to go. Without being aware of it, he ended up sounding patronizing, which he only realized after their conversation ended. It bothered him a bit brushing her off like that. Seeing the slightly pained look on Ruby's sheepish face made him hate himself even more.

"I've got to, ladies. Thanks a lot for your time."

More than anything, he wanted to set the record straight and tell them both the real reason why he was making all these inquiries. In the end, however, he resolved not to because he didn't want to get them involved in his troubles. Specifically, he didn't want to put them in harm's way, just like what happened to Oleta.

"Maybe you should try asking the janitor," Ruby suggested timidly as she shrugged her shoulders. "He or she would probably know best. Just saying"

"Why, the janitor?" Sammy shot back, intrigued.

"The janitor probably knows every nook and cranny in this place. I heard that there are even secret rooms here with traps and stuff!"

"That's ridiculous!" strongly disagreed Annie, who had grown bored and tired of listening to the two yak and yak. "That's an urban legend! There's absolutely no truth to that!"

"Some urban legends are true," Ruby countered defiantly. "The Nanek Beast is an urban legend. And we all saw what it did to poor Mrs. Galactrix this morning."

Never one to lose to an argument gracefully, Annie felt slighted by Ruby's unexpected show of prowess in debating. Instead of throwing in the towel, however, she rose up to the challenge and prepared a full sermon in her head to chastise her rebellious sister and put her back in her place. She was ready to open fire and charge into battle, when her cell phone rang.

"We have to go, Sis," she blandly said to Ruby after reading the text message on the small screen of her handheld device. "Dad's picking us up right now in front of the lobby. You know how he hates it when he's kept waiting. Ciao, Sammy Tsunami!"

"Yeah, see ya tomorrow, Sammy," Ruby added, bidding her friend goodbye as she got up from the desk together with her sister. "I'm looking forward to reading your school paper piece!"

That was his alibi. He told the Pastrami sisters earlier that he was looking for the back of the school because he was writing about it for the school paper. When he told them his intentions, he didn't know that the school even had a school paper, let alone that it was named the "Daily Froogle."

****

Left alone now in the library where a funereal silence pervaded the still air, Sammy brooded over why he needed to do what he needed to do. *Was Nark still his friend, or wasn't he anymore?*

He remembered Mickayla, and the compelling case that she made about Nark being involved in the unsolved disappearances of the teachers and the sudden departures of several students who had close encounters with the Nanek Beast. Although he didn't want to believe it at first, the appearance of Rular in the computer room changed all that.

Then, after barely surviving an attack by the monster itself and losing his shadow arrow in the process, he caught Nark and Timmy returning to the classroom together. Both were giving him dirty looks, as if to tell him that he did them wrong. *What wrong was that exactly?* Curiously, Timmy had a patch over his left eye, which got him to thinking about Rular whom he had just blinded—by ripping out its left eye!

Even more suspicious than all of these was what happened to Mrs. Galactrix. After telling Nark to leave the classroom, she mysteriously combusted and vanished into thin air. *Could Nark have had something to do with this?*

And just when he began discovering that there are ghosts living in the gym, he gets Oleta's blood stained bandana with a cryptic message from Nark written on it, telling him to meet him at the back of the school after class so that they can team up and save Oleta from God knows what.

So what is Nark trying to pull here? Is this a prank of sorts?

In the end, he was certain that it was all just a prank, all the way down to the marrows of his bones. Notwithstanding this, however, he decided to go anyway out of curiosity. Besides, he thought that it would be fun. Glancing at the clock, the time read 1:58 p.m., which gave him three hours or so to crack the case of where exactly was their rendezvous place. As he shuffled his feet towards the exit, he got a fleeting look at his shadow stalker again.

It appeared to be staring at him from behind one of the shelves in a far corner. When he tried approaching it, it ran away, disappearing into one of the thicker shadows nearby.

"If you want to come with me, I don't really mind," Sammy told it, shortly prior to walking out of the library. When he had gone and closed the door behind him, it quietly emerged again, this time moving more cautiously than it did before by tip-toeing its way towards the exit the boy left from.

****

The back seat of the white sedan was wider than it looked on the outside. It was spacious and comfortable enough to seat both Pastrami sisters—Ruby and Annie—and keep them as far apart from each other as possible.

Not that they had a quarrel or anything. It was basically because of the snacking—Ruby's snacking. The red haired girl with the stout figure just couldn't get enough of her potato chips, her after-school comfort food. It had only been ten minutes since she got into the car, and she was already attacking her third family size bag.

"How can you stuff yourself like that?" irately asked Annie, disgusted at her sister for shamelessly pigging out. "At the rate you're going, you're gonna choke yourself to death if you keep shoving those chips down your throat!"

"Don't bother me," brushed off Ruby, spitting out crumbs unintentionally into her sibling's sour face. "I'm concentrating here. I need to focus on eating my food! I might choke!"

"Sheesh," groaned Annie as she wiped off the crumbs from her face using a moist towelette she pulled from her purse. "I can tell that you're stressed, because you eat whenever you're stressed. The first day of school just ended, and you're stressed! Why is that? It's not like we have an exam tomorrow to worry about or anything."

"I'm worried about Sammy," Ruby eagerly confessed after munching down on a handful of barbecue flavored crunchies. "He was looking for the back of the school. I wish we could've been more helpful to him."

"You like him," teased Annie, getting sly and naughty. "Well, he's probably younger than you, around my age, so I don't know how he feels about dating an older girl."

CRUMPLE!

Immediately after she heard her sister's negatice comments, Ruby squeezed the foil bag she was eating out from. Chips flew out in every direction around her when she did, littering the carpet of the vehicle below. She then turned to Annie with teeth clenched, and glowered at her.

"Do you like him too?" Ruby snapped back with unbridled fury blazing in her eyes. "A classmate of ours, I won't mention her name, told me a while ago that you hugged Sammy during lunch hour. You even gave him MY bag of sandwiches as a present. I was going to ask you about this when we got home, but I think I'd like to hear your explanation now, please."

Annie's porcelain white complexion reddened, then she

balked. Her eyes and mouth broadened, and her breath thinned and cooled. She shivered as Ruby slid over to be by her.

"It isn't like that!" Annie fretfully clarified, as she scrambled for words in her head to try to appease her livid sister. Annie was small compared to Ruby, who was not only a full two inches taller than her, but several pounds heavier. Personality-wise, however, Ruby was the daintier and more feminine one, while Annie was tomboyish and bossy.

Under normal circumstances, Ruby would have been pelted with insults by her brainier sister and verbally subdued into obedience. But the present situation was anything but normal. Ruby couldn't be told what to do in this case—not in matters of the heart.

"Then please enlighten me, my dear sister?" impatiently pushed Ruby, leaning forward into her sibling, who shrank back at the sight of her smoldering gaze.

The white sedan turned a corner, and a light rain began to fall outside. *Pitter-patter, pitter-patter, pitter-patter.* It then pulled up into a driveway flanked on one side by a wall, and on the other by a grass covered yard. The garage door then lifted off the ground, inch by sluggish inch, as a low mechanical hum played in the background.

"He was hungry, okay?" Annie finally blurted. "I felt sorry for him because I heard his stomach growl. That's why I gave him your sandwiches!"

"And why did you hug him?"

"Like I said, I felt sorry for him. Hugging him was a reflex action really. I couldn't help myself. You know how I am when it comes to charity cases, like those rain soaked puppies the other week. Did you see how skinny Sammy was? He was practically a skeleton! No meat on the bone! He was like… a puppy."

Ruby's fierce expression softened up. In no time, she was back to her cheerful self again, all smiles and giggly. "I believe you," she said with a sigh. "Well, I guess, there's nothing else left for us to do then, except to make more sandwiches!"

Annie groaned. She was expecting a long, laborious evening ahead of her.

14

The back of the school was impossible to find. It didn't exist on any map-not officially, of course—nor did anyone have an idea of where it was exactly. Sammy found that out the hard way when he scoured for clues, asking anyone he bumped into.

With the adults, it was a rumor that got talked about every now and then during coffee breaks and around the water cooler. Seventh and eight graders, on the other hand, knew a couple of urban legends about the place, most of which had something to do with ghosts of long dead teachers and students haunting the grounds. Whatever the source of the information was, one fact was unanimously undisputed—no one has ever, ever set foot in there. This got Sammy to seriously thinking whether Nark was just pulling his leg.

At least, that was how he felt until he accidentally caught Mister Dojo, the bus driver-slash-lunch lady-slash-substitute teacher, cleaning one of the toilets in the boys' bathroom. The old man was slumped over a toilet inside one of the stalls, briskly scrubbing the deep end of the bowl with a tooth brush that he used alternately to clean the tiled floor.

"Isn't that unsanitary?" Sammy asked, surprising the old man who banged his head on the door of the stall, causing a bump to instantly sprout on his nearly bald head.

"There's nothing wrong if people don't know, right?" he answered back, mustering a sheepish grin. "So you caught me at my other job, so what? It's a good living and it helps pay the mortgage on the house that my blood sucking ex-wife took from me in the divorce. That's why I live in a school bus now—your school bus, by the way, which I make sure to spray with air freshener every day before I go pick up, you kiddies. So don't look at me that way, like you're judging me for the job I love doing with all of my heart and soul. There's a lot of money to be made, kiddo, if you're not afraid to get your hands dirty in pee and poop. Lots of people don't think this work pays anything, but you'll be surprised, I tell you."

"So that's why you live in a school bus," sympathized Sammy, who was about to turn and walk away when Mister Dojo grabbed him by the arm with his dripping wet hand.

"I live in a school bus because I don't want to commute to work every day. Just think of it this way, kiddo: I wake up and there I am at my work place. Convenient, right? I don't have to deal with the hassle of taking the bus or the train or dealing with jerks in my car pool to get to work. It's that simple. I can't think of any other reason more to justify it. It makes perfect sense to live where you work. Of course, I would rather live inside the school and sleep in the classrooms, if only the school district didn't dispatch roving security guards at night to make sure no one was loitering around here or quietly eating dinner and watching T.V. inside the faculty lounge."

Seeing the desperation in the old man's blood shot eyes, Sammy smiled warmly at him and nodded. He clearly understood what Mister Dojo wanted to convey, and decided not to press on, not even with cynical jabs or wisecracks.

"Don't worry, sir," he assured the old man, as he gently pulled himself away from his soggy clutches. "I'm not telling anybody about your secrets."

"Thank you, thank you, thank you, Sammy Tsunami! You're a good man, and for that you get ten gold stars come class tomorrow."

"But this is Middle School, not kindergarten. Who gives out gold stars as a reward anymore anyway?"

"I do," empathically declared Mister Dojo, showing off his gold teeth with pride to Sammy as he rose to his feet. "That's because I am different and special from any other teacher who teaches in this great school. I am a substitute teacher, who cares for every student here with every fiber in his body. There's no better way to say you did a good job than with gold—gold stars, gold teeth or gold anything. That's why I had all my chompers made golden. It's my reward to myself for doing an excellent job at what I do. It also makes me look incredibly attractive to the ladies. Every time they see my smile, they immediately think that I'm rich, that I'm successful and that

I have it made—although I'm still working on all three. These twenty-four karat babies in my mouth get them all the time, but for some reason I cannot understand, they leave me as soon as they find out that I live in a school bus! What do they have against a dude who lives in a mobile home, I don't really know."

Sammy was cringing as the old man said these words. Not because of anything except for the fact that Mister Dojo's breath was extremely bad. For a while there, the young lad thought that he would pass out at the first whiff.

"Oh-kay," said Sammy as he tried to politely exit out the door and ultimately escape from the one-sided conversation that they were having. "I need to go now, sir. I'm meeting someone at the back of the school."

As if those words had triggered a switch inside Mister Dojo's head, his expression turned from defensive to contemplative in a micro-second. He planted both drenched hands this time on Sammy's shoulders and gawked at him with his left eye twitching uncontrollably.

"What did I just hear you say? You're meeting someone at the back of the school? Well, kiddo, let me tell you straight, alright? There is no back of the school! It's a rumor, it doesn't exist, it's old wives tales! So get over it!""

"But I'm supposed to be meeting someone there right now, sir," meekly interjected Sammy, who was slowly shrinking as the old man's head pushed closer and closer to his. "Didn't you read the note on the bandana you gave me? It's... It's right here!"

Sammy tried yanking out the bandana from his pocket, but it was stuck there, squished between the inner lining and Rular's clammy eye.

"I don't read letters that are not addressed to me," the old man declared with self-righteous spunk. "So who is this someone that you're meeting with?"

"Nark," disclosed Sammy, somewhat embarrassed to mention the actual name. He was playing along with the little charade of the old man, who had allegedly confirmed to him earlier that the bandana had been smeared with real blood. Personally, he thought it was a load of crap.

"Narky Boy, eh? The Batoo-toot who cracked a horse whip on me on the bus?"

"What's a Batoo-toot?" implored Sammy, his curiosity piqued.

"You're too young to know things like that," Mister Dojo dismissed him, turning his head away as if to say that the subject is closed from further discussion. "So I had to bleep the rest out. You'll know what it means when you get older."

Mister Dojo let go of his hold on Sammy and started rubbing his forehead, unmindful that he was getting some of the toilet water on there. He looked tired and spent. When he closed his eyes to contemplate the boy's words, Sammy attempted once again to slip out, but was caught right away by the old man who angrily slammed the door shut with one, decisive push.

"Very well, Sammy Tsunami! A favor for a favor then! You keep my secrets safe with you, and I trade you with the location of that place which you seek. But know this, a warning if you will! Those who go to that forbidden area of the school never return—and I mean, never return! If you still want to go where not even the bravest of the brave dare to tread, then go to the principal's office right this second and talk to the principal himself. He is a very good natured and extremely handsome man. Not to mention, funny and soft spoken. Only he knows the way!"

After telling his spooky story with such clarity and conviction to unnerve Sammy, Mister Dojo retreated back to his toilet stall to continue cleaning up the toilet bowl. As he swaggered away from Sammy's sight, the boy was filled with much conflict as to whether he should heed the old man's cautionary tale or not. A part of him was convinced that he was insane, while the other part gave him the benefit of the doubt. As he pondered, he heard a series of loud knocks on the bathroom door.

"Open up in there!" rang another lad's voice from the other end. "It's open," Sammy replied. It was then that he saw the lock securely fastened. To his recollection, he didn't remember ever bolting the door shut. Then, it hit him. Mister Dojo must be responsible somehow.

******

The principal's office was on the top floor—the third—and it was at the end of a long, winding corridor that started with a double swinging glass door between Rooms thirty-six and thirty-seven.

"This is a surprise!" remarked Sammy, who was more shocked than merely just astonished. "You're the principal of this school too!"

Mister Dojo was in a glamorous grey checkered suit and tie this time around. He was seated on a plush leather upholstered swivel chair behind a wide brown wooden desk that had all sorts of papers and clutter on it. He lifted an eyebrow at Sammy, as if to send a message to the boy that he was really the big kahuna in the school—not just some bus driver, substitute teacher, janitor or lunch lady. Seeing the confused expression on Sammy's face, the old man decided to drive the point home even more by reclining in his chair to show how comfortable he was with the power that he wielded. As soon as he arched his back into the soft cushion, he fell off and tumbled on to the floor—once, twice, thrice… until he crashed into the garbage bin in the corner by the curtains.

"You didn't see that!" he gestured to Sammy as he crawled slowly back into his seat, gathering his lost poise and composure along the way. "This chair doesn't like me, Sammy Tsunami. I've farted too much into it over the years, and it has never forgiven me for doing so. One of these days, I'm going to send this miserable piece of furniture to the back of school where it will rot for all eternity! But not today though. The school doesn't have the budget to buy a new one for me. And as you know me well by now, I'm too cheap to reach into my pockets to personally spend for something like that. So what can I do for you?"

"You told me in the bathroom to see you about directions to the back of the school."

"No!" furiously cut in the old man, throwing his arms in the air then lowering them down again in dramatic effect. "The janitor told you to see the principal, and that's me! Do you see the janitor sitting before you, kiddo? There's no janitor here, only the all powerful principal! Bwa ha ha!"

There was no argument from Sammy there. Flashing a sheepish grin, he nodded in agreement and took one of the seats across the table. Noting that his guest has retreated from what he perceived to be a hostile stance, Mister Dojo's mood lightened up and he gave out a loud, extremely annoying cackle before buckling down to business.

"Very well, seeing as I cannot stop you from pursuing certain doom, I will generously instruct you with directions to the back of the school… only because you asked me nicely, Sammy Tsunami. There is one condition though."

Sammy's expression soured when he heard about the amendment to their earlier agreement. He knew there was a catch somewhere because things were going too smoothly for him that they were too good to be true. In his mind, Sammy Tsunami has long resigned himself to the fact that he was an incorrigible hard luck case. Nothing good has ever happened to him, and nothing was about to. He was mad at himself for believing otherwise for a second there.

"What condition is that?" he asked calmly, crossing his legs and smiling. "I was of the impression that all I had to do was keep my mouth shut about your… secrets."

"No, no, no! It's nothing like that. This is for your own good!"

The wily old principal then produced a ball of blue yarn from one of his desk drawers. Before handing it over completely to Sammy, he tied one end to the knob of that very same desk drawer, as tightly as he could knot it.

"What is this for?" inquired Sammy, even more puzzled now than before. "You want me to sew you some clothes?"

"No, no, no, kiddo!" Mister Dojo began to explain. "You take that with you on your way to the back of the school. If you need to ask me something, just wave at any one of the video cameras around the campus, and I will communicate with you via loud speaker. I'll be able to monitor your movements from here and talk to you, thanks to this wonderful machine."

He was referring, of course, to the very same elaborate device that he was patting lovingly like an obedient docile cat. It was on his desk to his right, and it looked more complicatedly cheap and defective, rather than expensive and sturdy. The contraption was basically a small T.V. set connected by cable to what looked like a radio box with a large microphone wired to it. It had a sticker on the side that clearly read "KARAOKE KING."

"Now, listen closely to what I have to say, Sammy Tsunami: go down to the lobby and exit through the east gate. You'll know how to get to the back of the school from there."

"It's really that simple?" Sammy remarked unflatteringly, finding it hard to believe that nobody in the school knew the location of the place he was seeking, although it was just a matter of walking through a door that lay in plain view. "Why do you need to make things complicated in order to believe that they are real, kiddo? Life is simple. Don't complicate it."

"Alrighty then," agreed Sammy, getting up to leave. "Goodbye, sir," he then said, as he dragged himself towards the door, musical sounding words that rang to the delight of Mister Dojo whose grin stretched from ear to ear.

"Not so fast!" called out Mister Dojo, stopping Sammy in his tracks as the boy was about to slip through the door. "There are a few more matters I wish to speak with you about. Please... sit."

15

The yarn unspooled and unspooled and unspooled. Everywhere Sammy went, it unspooled, leaving a winding trail of blue thread.

Although the ball had been secretly tucked away inside one of his pants' pockets, it didn't stay secret for long. The elongated fibrous evidence it spat out and scattered on the floor couldn't help but attract a lot of attention from the many bystanders and passersby that loitered around the campus. Before he knew it, Sammy had a curious band of stalkers following him merrily around.

"The things I do… the things I do…"

He was mumbling something underneath his mouth as he casually made his way across the lobby, pretending to be oblivious to the train of people that had formed on his tail. He sounded like he was complaining, and who could blame him for doing so, given what he had to put up with. Although he consciously tried to maintain a snobbish profile and a stone faced expression to go with it, there were some who pestered him with question after question after question. He didn't allow himself to be distracted though, for he knew only too well that he was under the watchful eye of Mister Dojo, the principal, who observed him closely from the monitor perched on his office desk.

And from that lofty position, the old man was seeing things he did not like.

"What's the dealio here?" asked one of the teens shadowing Sammy, a lanky young fellow in a blue hooded sweatshirt. "I mean, is this like a school project or something?"

Before anyone else could follow through with another similar bonehead question, the deafening voice of the principal rang through the speakers that hung in the ceiling, like the voice of God come to announce something important.

"Don't harass Sixth Grader Sammy Tsunami, children!" Mister Dojo ordered in his usual gravely tone through the mike. "The business that he is carrying out right now is official and sanctioned by the office of the principal himself! Me! So keep your distance from Tsunami, alright? Thank you, children, for your cooperation."

After Mister Dojo signed off, the mushrooming band of casual followers started getting agitated. Their initial reaction was to collectively lift their heads up, and spot where the voice was coming from. As the train disintegrated into a confused crowd, dispersing in all directions, Sammy set his eyes on the east gate, which was nothing more than a humble archway leading to a rose red double door. Heading there as briskly as he could, the very same lanky boy, in the blue hooded sweatshirt, intercepted him and began stirring up trouble. He picked up some string from the ground behind Sammy's back, then turning to one of the video cameras dangling above, he yelled out rebelliously:

"And what if we don't? What will you do if we don't?"

Suddenly, without the slightest warning, classical music started piping out of the speakers, filling the entire lobby. As it turned out, Bach's Concierto Number Seven proved to be extremely excruciating to the delicate ears of Sammy's stalkers that they all collapsed to the floor screaming in pain and begging for it to stop.

"Feel my wrath, children!" vengefully announced Mister Dojo through the speakers, as the musical piece played on even louder. "Feel the wrath of your Beloved Principal! Bwa-ha-ha!"

****

Dismayed as Sammy was that he wasn't able to extract any useful information from Mister Dojo, he did however comply obediently with his ambiguous order—to the letter.

As instructed, he exited out the double doors that led to the east parking lot, all alone this time around without the colorful parade of folks trailing behind him. Once there, he had to pause a while to appreciate the spectacular view of the ginger mountains that rose up from behind the forest greens in the distance. Their jagged peaks seemed to beautifully disappear altogether under a herd of rolling clouds that were migrating west.

It was the mid-afternoon and the sun was high up, blazing at it utmost zenith where it relentlessly baked everything that happened to be lying or grazing around in the sweeping vacant expanse. Two minutes outside, and Sammy started to sweat like a pig. As he started his run, he wondered what he needed to do, remembering the words of the principal that he would know once he had stepped outside. The moment he looked down at his feet, there was his answer, right in front of him, ready and raring to go.

"I don't know how, but I'm sure glad you're back!"

His shadow arrow was a welcome sight the second it materialized on the hot, simmering asphalt. He thought he had lost it forever, when it shot into the air and buried its pointy end into the heart of that monster, Rular, a while back in the computer room. Now that it has returned, he couldn't be happier.

"Take me to the back of the school. We have business there with a friend of ours."

It dragged him along the side of the building where there were several shaded areas to get out of the punishing heat. Tempting as it was for him to take a break from the oven and cool down, Sammy stayed on the scorching path where he could keep an eye out on his shadow arrow. It led him north for miles, all the way up. To no real surprise, it was empty too—not that it was any consolation to his nerves, which were on edge for some reason.

Glad as he was to have his shadow arrow back to keep him

company and point him in the right direction, Sammy remained paranoid and jittery. He took a second and third look around before bursting into a sprint every few yards, leaving nothing to chance. There was nothing but wide open spaces, of course, although he already knew that. There were no prying eyes, no curious stares, no… people. He was completely alone beside the long, gray shadows cast by the east wall, except that he didn't feel that way.

While the thought that someone out of the blue might catch him on the run with an oddly shaped shadow at his twelve o' clock, this didn't bother him as much as the thought that he was being hunted. Someone or something was tracking him down, and he was pretty sure in his gut that it was coming from the shades.

"There's something following us," he whispered to his shadow arrow, as it banked a hard right heading west. "I'm going to have to speed up to outrun—*AAAAAAHHH!!!*"

From out of a stretch of shade, a wild spook rocketed into the air, startling Sammy into nearly fainting. As its panther-like body descended elegantly to the ground, its clawed paws almost grazed the boy's forehead, nearly tearing a deep gash into it.

"No, not again!" said Sammy to himself, breathing heavily as he tried to regain his composure and mount an effective retreat. When the beast landed on all fours a mere few inches away, it immediately staggered forward to attack. Although it had no eyes in the swirling vaporous mist that passed for its head, it seemed to lock gazes with the boy, who flinched at the sight of its dagger-like incisors snapping viciously at him.

"Help me out here!" he called out to his shadow arrow, which was facing northwest on the roasting tarmac and quietly ignoring his pleas for assistance. Sammy was hoping for a last minute rescue, recalling back how it saved him from Rular in the computer room not too long ago. He wanted it to fly as it did then, and spear the wild spook right in the torso, taking it out of the equation.

Much as he willed it to, however, it didn't take off. It didn't even budge. It just stayed put where it was, insisting that he follow it across the great expanse of the vacant parking area towards northwest. The boy wanted to wait, thinking that it needed more time to make up its mind, but there was no time to spare. It was either run now—or be chewed up!

Opening its wide jaws, the wild spook sprang at him. Quick as it was though, Sammy was nimbler. Weaving his svelte frame to the left with perfect timing, he was able to dodge the frontal assault with ease. The monster shot past his shoulder like an arrow.

"I had a fun time at the petting zoo," Sammy joked nervously, losing no time fixing his scarf to make sure that there were no loose ends of the red fabric dangling out. The last thing he wanted was another wild spook sinking its teeth into it and removing it from his neck. If that ever happened, he would lose his head—literally!

"Let's do this again next time, okay?" he then put in with

a reluctant smile, as the wild spook prepared itself for another go at a pounce. "Then again, maybe—never!"

He was out of there the next moment. With a spurt of explosive speed, he blew northwest like a bat out of hell, tearing the blacktop new road lines. His shadow arrow, which led him on at his helm, directed him at a walled enclosure a few miles down a narrow dirt road that began from the edge of the parking lot. The bricked structure had no windows of any kind, no signs posted, and no drainage of any kind visible on its façade.

It did have one door though on the side, which was all Sammy needed to know.

The door was metallic, with a rusty silver coat of paint. It had no knob of any sort on it, and appeared to be locked from the inside, probably bolted, although Sammy couldn't really tell from afar. Though Sammy worried about how he would get in, he tried not to think about it too much. It would be a bridge he would cross when he got there. For the time being, he just wanted to embrace the moment and enjoy the exhilarating run that he was on, no matter how brief it was going to turn out to be. Never did he feel so free in his life—like he did now.

"Time to hit escape velocity!" Sammy bragged out loud as his line of vision melted away into a wild kinetic light show of luminous flickering streams rushing at him again and again, over and over. "Escape velocity, here I come!"

Then—*BANG!*

The next thing he knew, he was hurting all over and lying flat on the ground with a view from below of an open door. On the other side of it was the dirt road, still cloudy from the dust his heels had kicked up from his last run. Through the fading mist, a silhouette emerged—a large cat of some kind, running on all fours towards him, only that it did not have a head.

Just a ball of dark vapor with teeth floating in it.

By the time he was up again on his feet, the wild spook had hurled itself at him again. And it would have most certainly pinioned him to the floor and gouged his face—had someone not closed the door shut at the last second and kept it out.

16

"You!"

"Hand over my bandana, Tsunami. I bought that at a yard sale for five bucks. Best five bucks I ever spent."

Oleta Teytata was leaning on the wall beside the fire exit, chewing gum and looking every bit her usual lethargic self. She winked at Sammy with one of her striking ocher eyes when he came up to her with gnashed teeth. As soon as the boy was close enough, he turned over to her what she had asked for, pulling it right out of his pocket.

The same pocket he kept the damp eyeball of Rular in.

"Thanks," she said with a naughty smirk, casually picking up her printed bandana before taking her sweet time wrapping it around her blonde head where it belonged. "What's with the string by the way?"

"None of your business," Sammy boorishly riposted, stroking the ball of yarn inside his pocket to make sure he hadn't lost it. It had shrunk considerably since Mister Dojo gave it to him, probably just a third now of its original size. Its blue string stretched out from his pocket, all the way to and under the metal door where Oleta stood next to.

"How rude! And here I thought you were very fond of me."

"Don't fool yourself!" snapped Sammy, reddening with rage. "You were toying with me in the lunch room! What are you? Some kind of… Femme Fatale Lolita?"

"Just so you know, I only did it for the money," teasingly explained Oleta, not the slightest bit remorseful. "Nothing personal, darling. Nark paid me twenty bucks to lure you over here. Mister Dojo helped out a bit as my accomplice, and got two dollars for his troubles. He calls it his other part-time job, whatevers. Anyhoo, Nark thinks you're in his way so he wants to get rid of you. I think he's jealous of you, or something."

"He wants to get rid of me?" Sammy shot back in disbelief, too shocked and too stunned to say anything else.

"Yuppers," Oleta obliged, swaggering close to Sammy to get in a whisper or two into his ear. "I know you don't believe me because I lied to you earlier, but you can talk to the man himself and he'll tell it to you straight. He's behind that door right across from us, waiting for you at the back of the school."

Betrayal most foul! In the secret places inside Sammy's head, he was saying these words again and again, over and over. Although he entertained certain doubts about Nark, he didn't take him for a Judas who would orchestrate such a dastardly scheme to polish him off. Oleta's revelations, coldly honest and brutal as they were, had opened his eyes to the truth, and yet, blinded him with a vengeful rage.

"He really wants to get rid of me?" Sammy repeated himself, unable to process and accept the new status quo that had been suddenly handed over to him. His muscles tightened and tensed. He was eager and anxious to leave and go through the main entrance that led to the back of the school. More than anything, he wanted to set the record straight with Nark. If Oleta was spinning a lie to drive a wedge between the both of them, he wanted to know. He needed to know.

"You're upset, I can tell," cooed Oleta, planting a soft kiss on Sammy's cheek. "We should go on a real date sometime if you ever get out of this mess. I personally think you're cute. Make sure to save a lot though. I'm very high maintenance, and there's nothing I like better than a guy who likes spending his money on me. Ta-ta!"

****

Once through the door, Sammy found himself on top of a windswept narrow wooden staircase that curved all the way down to what appeared to be a sprawling and elaborately constructed labyrinth.

From his lofty perspective, he could readily tell that the angular concrete walls forming the maze were at least twenty feet tall in height, with each one was thick enough to stop a bullet cold. They appeared to be weather beaten and stained by the elements. With the help of the sweltering sun that kept vigil overhead, vines and all sorts of clinging plants grew and thrived on them, hanging like torn and shredded emerald drapes on the stone slabs and giving them an "ancient" feel.

"Now this is something that you don't see every day," commented the boy, astonished by the unusual discovery that he had made. "The back of the school must be on the other end," he then concluded, taking his cue from where his shadow arrow was pointing. "I better hurry before the sun sets. I sure don't want to still be in there come night fall."

With a quickened pace, he descended the stairs, each step old and rickety, sounding off a yawning creek every time he pressed his foot down. None of the wood broke though, thankfully, and soon enough, he was safely down below where the ground was rock solid and baked to stone perfection in the humid heat. Traction there was even good, which assuaged Sammy's fear that he might accidentally slip and crack his skull on the floor.

"Time to get to work then," he told himself, checking his pockets to make sure that he had the ball of yarn in the right, and Rular's eyeball in the left. He also made certain that his shadow arrow was where he needed to see it. After being satisfied that he had everything he needed for the adventure ahead, he proceeded onwards. From the foot of the stairs to the entrance of the maze itself, it was only a quarter of a mile, nothing Sammy couldn't handle, exhausted and parched though he was.

One gap in the wall was all there was—one narrow gap.

Although the breach itself was thin, Sammy was pretty sure that he could fit through there with no problem at all, considering his slender physique. The problem was, the closer he got to the way in, the farther it got. It was as if it was moving away, pulling back into the distance.

Wanting to test out his theory, he sprinted straight for the entry way, throwing caution to the wind. Not only did the wall where the gap was recoil upon his imminent approach, it even slid sideways towards the right!

"The door is… getting away?" he remarked as he picked up more speed. It was right about to disappear behind a wall perpendicular to its own, when Sammy jetted through it without a second more to spare. It closed shut with a loud thud, trapping part of the blue string between two stone slabs.

"Oh, no!" he fretted, noting the opening to the labyrinth gone. "I guess the principal will have to do something about that wall. Maybe, introduce it to Mister Sledgehammer."

KA-KLACK!

Something activated somewhere, that much he was sure of. Soon the wall was active again, shifting back in the direction it came from. He spun around to see where he was going, and was startled to see all the walls in the maze moving about, realigning and reconfigure themselves until new doorways emerged, then disappeared, only to reemerge again in a different place.

"So many choices to choose from!" observed Sammy as he

watched intently as five new openings appeared out of the blue. "Lucky me, I have you!"

His shadow arrow directed him to the left. He followed it through a crack, and was nearly clipped by a swinging wall. It led him here and there, through the twisting, winding corridors as walls traded places and folded unto themselves, slamming and scraping each other at a restless pace.

While the walls were being skittish about where to position themselves permanently, the sun was setting in the orange sky, casting long shadows over the labyrinth—to Sammy's mortification. He needed to hurry and improve his pace. His shadow arrow, sprightly as it was in avoiding the slithering darkness, was quickly losing light to move in through.

As if that dilemma wasn't bad enough, Sammy also had to deal with the undesirables that were surfacing one by one from the blackness. He saw teeth, sharp ones and lots of them, all probably wild spooks in his opinion. Not that he was looking forward or anything to finding out. Soon as he spotted the exit, he was out of there in a flash! *KA-KLACK!*

"Made it!" he cried out loud when he crossed the finish line, which was an actual red line painted on the ground a few yards away from another rusty metal door—a double door this time. As soon as he was on the other side of the line, the shifting walls stopped their shifting, and stopped cold in their tracks. The corridors were now defined and "stringed" together in blue. If Mister Dojo wanted to follow, all he need do was follow the trail of the blue string.

"Do you know the story of Theseus from Greek Mythology?" Sammy remembered Mister Dojo asking him this when he insisted that the old man tell him why he needed to bring the ball of yarn. "Theseus was given a ball of string by Ariadne when he entered the labyrinth to kill the Minotaur. Because he left string behind along the way, he was able to retrace his steps and exit the maze after he had done his job."

Thinking back to this, Sammy looked back at where he came from, and hoped that the shadows would be gone when he gets back. He worried too much, especially about the wild spooks that had by now emerged from their hiding places. They were hunting now, he was sure of it. In fact, one just reared its ugly vaporous head from a distance. It didn't see Sammy, fortunately, and went on its way. "I hope all this trouble you've gotten me into is worth it, Nark," he said to himself before entering through the doors. "I hope."

17

The sky traded an inflamed orange hue for a dull gray by the time Sammy arrived at his destination. It was late in the day and the sun had already retired. Everything was dipped in shadow as far as the eye could see. Even then, it wasn't hard to tell how horrid and filthy the place was. The foul stench alone easily gave things away.

The back of the school smelled like it looked—a mass grave of junk and all sorts of refuse rotting in the open air. One whiff of the effluvium here, and noses were dead, murdered and even mutilated.

As difficult as it was not to breathe, Sammy still gave it a whiff, summoning all of his mental toughness to overcome what he merely dismissed as a stink. He failed miserably, of course, ending up vomiting all over the garbage and collapsing to his knees.

His lungs burned from the sulfurous toxins in the oxygen that he inhaled, and his eyes were bloodshot. As if things couldn't get any worse, a head-splitting migraine suddenly set in, reducing him into a shivering mess. It was a no man's land that he had found himself in. He had a choice though. It was either leave right here and right now, or stay to become part of the rubbish that surrounded him to no end.

"Welcome to my lair!" rang a sinister sounding voice that came from across the dump. It belonged to none other than Nark the self-styled Shark himself who was perched atop a mountain of garbage, striking a triumphant pose like a fool in the departing orange light of the setting sun. He had cast a long shadow over Sammy, hard as it was to imagine, from the humble ends of his dwarfish frame.

"What are you, some kind of animal who lives in a lair?" Sammy's snappy come back, which was actually meant as nothing more than witty banter, knocked the wind right out of Nark's sails, so much so that the small boy immediately lost all desire and interest to continue on with his rehearsed monologue. Like a bad sport, his face crumpled up and frowned, but this sullen expression would only prove to be brief and short-lived. Reining in his explosive temper, the scantily tall lad managed a weak smile to the surprise of Sammy, who was sure of himself that Nark would blow his top like a bomb in his face.

"Witty, but not so," coolly remarked Nark, the slits of his condescending eyes narrowing.

With some effort, Sammy lifted his head up to meet the small boy's piercing gaze, which was framed by the exultant expression that glowed radiantly on his tiny face. It was then that Sammy, under the thin glimmer of dusk and the soft glow that emanated from the golden diamonds knitted on the front of his sweater, noticed the intricate network of wrinkles and the globular sacks under his friend's eyes, badges of age that were so clear when so near. Seeing that Sammy had discovered his facial imperfections all on his own, Nark smirked with approval, then casually reached into his pocket for something.

The second he laid his eyes thick on Nark, Sammy felt a rippling anger coarse through his muscles. He was twitching and tensing up simultaneously, his hands even balling into tight fists. Never in his life did he feel so incensed with any one person. If he could smite Nark down, he would have certainly done so already.

But he was hesitating, falling back, mainly because he wanted all his questions answered. He wanted to have all his doubts erased. Deep inside, he wanted it to be all just a misunderstanding. He didn't want to lose his friend. He wanted Nark back by his side, like when they were headed together to class in the morning. Although he knew what he wanted, he knew too that it was all wishful thinking on his part. Something in his gut told him that it would never happen.

"I look old, don't I, my friend?" he said without the slightest bit of difficulty breathing the foul, disgusting air. "I am not a child like you, young and vibrant and stupid! But I am not an old man either, in spite of the wrinkles that you see around my face. I am seventeen years old since five days ago, would you believe? Just a little older than you. No thanks to a genetic gland disorder, I have stayed a midget my entire life, and have looked like a wretched grandfather, my youth notwithstanding. Worst of all, I am dying, slowly and inevitably from whatever mysterious affliction that ails me now. That's the awful secret that I've kept. Now, you know."

After listening to his dwarfish friend's moving confession, Sammy's anger melted away as quickly as it had built up. He genuinely felt sorry for Nark for the misfortunes of life that had befallen him. Suddenly, he didn't feel so bad about himself being poor and wretched. In fact, he counted himself lucky that he wasn't walking in his friend's shoes right now. It was a blessing to be thankful for.

"You're a smart boy, buddy dude," Nark carried on, feeling something in his pocket which Sammy suspected was a stone of some kind. "I bet that you found out, as well, that I'm not a first time sixth grader either. It's my shame really. This is my sixth time at it—my sixth time as a sixth grader. I tried and tried, you know, but somehow, I just can't advance. Everybody laughed at me for being stupid, my classmates and my teachers. And then I found this, and my fortunes changed drastically overnight!"

Out from his pocket, the imp produced a crystal-like rock, which was no bigger than an egg, amethyst purple, and jagged around the edges but not so much as sharp that they could cut whoever held or touched it. Nark held it up to Sammy to behold, but instead of gazing up at it in awe, the boy let down his host by vomiting. It had been the noxious air that was poisoning his lungs to no end. He tried holding his breath, but when that didn't work, he attempted inhaling it to get accustomed to his malodorous new environment. Unfortunately though, it didn't work out so well.

"This is the reason why I rule this pitiful school!" bragged Nark, brandishing the tiny gemstone shamelessly in front of Sammy, who struggled to not pass out from the reek that stayed thick in the air. "This is the Nanek Crystal, an alchemystic stone forged in the Ghostwells, and passed on to me by its previous owner as a gift for a great favor I have rendered him! I have been its master for quite some time now, as well as the beast whose soul it is tied to."

"So you used that crystal to dispose of those teachers then?" Sammy accused, keeping a brave face about him as the fetid smell of the dump continued to overwhelm him. "And you frightened those students too into dropping out of school with that monster on your leash! The very same one you sent to kill me!"

"I do not deny these things," admitted Nark with a menacing grin. "They offended me, so I got my revenge on them. No one laughs at me—not even you, Sammy Tsunami! Those who do, pay a price, a steep one!"

Before Sammy could break in another word, Mister Dojo had burst through the door, holding up an aerosol spray can. He was still dressed in a suit and tie, and was staring up at Nark on the mound with vengeful eyes. Pointing the spray can straight at the small boy, he boisterously announced through gritted teeth:

"I told you that you'll get your comeuppance, Narky Boy! Prepare for the principal's payback! But before I do so, give me the ball of yarn, Sammy—and fast as in pronto, arriba-arriba!"

Without asking why, Sammy took out the big blue ball of yarn from his pocket and swiftly slipped it into Mister Dojo's coat. Appreciative of the gesture, the old man nodded at him with a laconic expression on his face before jumping back to business.

"Good work, kiddo. It's been a while since I've been here, and my memory's no good anymore, you see? I never would have found this place again if not for the thread that you left on the floor, so tee-why. Now, step away. I'll be handling things from here on."

Pressing the button on the top of the canister, Mister Dojo released a wisp of freshly scented chemicals into the air that wafted gently into the noses of the two students. He giggled when he caught their confused expressions, and began to dance like a fool on a pile of steaming garbage.

"I just cleaned up your act!" he shouted out loud at Nark, so much so that he hurt his throat and lungs. "How's that for a comeback, you naughty child!"

Nark responded in kind by shaking the Nanek Crystal in the air. The small gem glowed with a dim purple light, just enough to draw attention but insufficient to illuminate. Mister Dojo was watching it twinkle in the small boy's hand, when a dense cloud of purple smoke swept over his entire body. In a blink of an eye, he was gone, done, vanished and lost. All that was left to remember him by was his faded shadow, which quickly fled the scene for parts unknown.

"I disposed of all the adults in this manner," pointed out Nark, looking pleased with himself. "I could have done the same with the kids who dropped out, but I chose not to. Call me a softie. As for you, my friend, I have something else in mind planned."

Timmy emerged from behind a mountainous pile of compost, festering in the dying heat with a halo of flies circling its conical peak. He still had a patch over his left eye when he stepped out, and bandages wrapped around his left shoulder. As soon as he met Sammy's probing gaze, he immediately stripped away the patch on his hardened face to reveal a gaping hole where an eye once belonged.

"If you're a bright lad, Sammy Tsunami, then you've already figured out who this crazy looking, one-eyed gentleman really is."

"That's Rular," Sammy answered back confidently, absolutely certain of his response, "the Nanek Beast himself!"

"Bingo!" happily concurred Nark, ecstatic with what he had just heard that he almost leapt into the air in jubilation from his precarious roost. "You've got a good head on your shoulders, buddy dude!" he then praised Sammy generously as his malicious grin widened even more like a red gash across his face. "He's not in his working clothes right now, but he soon will be. Just to make sure you know, this is what makes his gruesome transformation from a retarded old creep to a hideous octopus-snake monster possible—the Nanek Crystal!"

The thinly glinting trinket was displayed again for all creation to behold, and Sammy couldn't help but be filled with the urge to just openly criticize Nark for the tedious routine he was torturing him with.

"See what you've done to my friend," pointed out Nark afterwards, parading the bearded man in front of Sammy, who winced at the sight of Timmy's mutilated face. "He was a king and a sorcerer once. When he died, his soul was grafted on to the corpse of a demon offspring of a leviathan and a hydra. Thus, he became a lich—an undead aberration of immeasurable power. Unfortunately for him though, an alchemystic bound his spirit to this tiny stone which I hold now. As such, his man talents are mine to command now. He is my personal genie, my granter of wishes."

Sammy's blood curdled and his face was drained of all the rosiness of life. He knew where his horror story was heading— with him, the victim, dead at the hands of the supernatural fiend. He wanted to reason out with Nark, but a stark raving madness had afflicted him.

"What have I done to hurt you, huh?" Sammy passionately inquired, just as a thick fog of amethyst purple suddenly engulfed Timmy from out of nowhere, smothering him completely in its churning vapors, until every vestige of his humanity was gone—all replaced by the monstrous effigy of Rular, no less!

"I sentence you to die, my friend!" vowed Nark, the crystal in his hand blazing more brightly now, as the Nanek Beast eagerly prepared itself for its grand revenge on the boy who plucked out its eye and stabbed it through the shoulder.

"You have become a thorn on my side, which I must now take out!" added Nark, zealously waving his glimmering crystal in the air with triumphant confidence. "You and I could've been great together, but you broke my heart, Sammy, with your lies and betrayals! Now… I break yours!"

Before Rular could lay a serpent's scaly touch on the boy, his shadow arrow flew swiftly to intercept. It entered the snake's forehead with ease, puncturing it through and through before exiting out, killing it instantly. Then, just when everybody expected it to follow through with this feat by striking Rular down in the face, it hit the crystal in Nark's hand dead on, shattering it into smithereens and destroying it completely— along with itself!

NOOOOOO!!!!

From the smashed pieces of the crystal formed a plum colored whirlwind, which quickly swallowed everything and everybody in its destructive path—from the trash mounds that were scattered around the lot, to Sammy, Nark and Rular themselves, who were all quickly overwhelmed by the suddenness and power of its voracious appetite. Before they knew it, they were twisting and turning inside the tornado itself as it spun death with every turn of its mindless devastation.

18

When Sammy woke up, he was somewhere else entirely… somewhere drained of life and color…. somewhere dead.

The first thing he saw was the sun, which was nothing more than a white stain on black sandpaper sky. Its lackluster brilliance swathed the world with a gray, dull radiance that struggled desperately to sustain itself in the midst of intensifying shadows.

In the deep snowy woods where he found himself alone and confused, this tussle between light and dark was never more evident than in the movement of the restless shades themselves.

They would come alive all of a sudden and sweep across the denseness of the forest, obscuring every inch of their path, only to be beaten back thereafter by the soft, weak, shimmering glow of the sun—a victory that would shortly be lost and won again in an endless, cyclical tug-of-war.

"Where are you?" echoed a familiar voice inside Sammy's head, just as his eyes were getting accustomed to his drab and colorless new reality. Sure that he heard it, he immediately searched his monochrome surroundings for its source, seeking out shrubbery, tree trunks and rock for a recognizable face.

He had forgotten about the thick snow he was slouched on seconds ago, which now hampered his every effort to advance. Although his boots did their best to stave off frostbite from his feet, it did little to keep out the cold itself, which was the same thing that could be said for the rest of his clothes.

"I'm over here!" Sammy hollered into the freezing air, defiantly braving the creeping onslaught of hypothermia as he continued to scamper through the woodlands. "Follow the sound of my voice! I'm heading to you now! Meet me!"

He tried his best to pick up his pace, to run, knowing only that it was his best chance of finding her. With his lungs hot, his breath short and his feet buried above the ankle in the snow, it seemed impossible to even try.

The longer he delayed reaching her, however, the greater the chances of her going or continuing in the wrong direction. That meant that her voice would eventually fade from the range of his hearing, and once that happens, she would be lost to him. If only his shadow arrow was around, it would be easy, but it was lost again like before, probably for good this time.

Much time passed after that first strange encounter, but still he waited. With bated breath, he waited on for the voice to announce itself again. While he did so, he kept himself preoccupied by plodding across the winter brushed lands with a savage relentless that stemmed from an impatience that needed to be quenched. A conquering spirit drove him on, undaunted by the perilous climate that sought to murder him in cold blood in his tracks.

"Tell me where you are!" he commanded the cold as fatigue treacherously set in, inflaming his already inflamed muscles. Like before, the only answer he got was the whistling of the wind and an icy draft clawing at his bare skin. "Please!"

Stopping for a while to properly breathe and rest his aching joints, Sammy stumbled upon a phantom—small, glinting and almost too inconspicuous to notice. It appeared to be a crystal shard with an amethyst purple shade, roughly the size of a cockroach. The strange thing about it was that it flew through the air like a whimsical bird, taunting Sammy to catch it.

"Are you the one calling out to me?" he asked it plainly, immediately realizing how foolish he was to have assumed that it had been. Losing interest in it as quickly as it had piqued his curiosity, the boy trudged on through the snow, but not before he caught the shard fly off high into the sky.

Not that it was the only one to do so. Sammy saw several others take to the heavens, some near and some far. They raced across the sandpaper skies like shooting stars, twinkling as they floated beyond the boy's sights.

Where are they headed to? he wondered. He was curious enough to try and find out, when the one he had been earnestly waiting for rang for him again. "Where are you?" the voice in his head repeated itself. Sammy sensed her nearby, no farther than half a mile north. She was close and over there. The only problem was, there was a lot of "there" over there to cover.

"I'm coming!" Sammy yelled out loud, the echo of his words returning to him thrice fold. He struggled to do more than just wade across the moist, white ice. If he could fly, he would have. "If you can follow my voice and come to me! I'm trying as fast as I can to reach you! Keep talking so I know where you are coming from! "

He was beginning to sound like a broken record, saying the same thing over and over again. But changing his one trick pony act into something with a bit more variety was the least of his worries. His heel lost traction all of a sudden, which meant that the solid earth underneath his feet was gone. The second he lost his footing, he was swallowed whole by the snow. Everything happened so fast that there wasn't time to even let out a scream.

As it turned out though, Sammy had stumbled into a hole on the ground that opened into a rocky slope. There, he fell and he fell and he fell, bruising and cutting himself as he rolled down the uneven edges of the stone mound. When it was finally over, he lay flat on his back on a hard, snow covered floor, barely conscious from the pain that had taken over his wracked body.

"Where are you?"

"I don't know," he feebly answered, looking straight up at the sharp, conical stalactites that dangled overhead from the dense black ceiling. Having deduced he was in a cave, he rolled his eyes from side to side to check if the coast was clear. Finding the cavern walls equally painted in pitch-blackness and the enclosure within them empty, Sammy ventured to continue speaking with the voice that had yet to give him a response to his last communication.

"Are you there?" he then said, as he attempted to lift his head up from the ground. To his dismay, it would only budge just a little, an inch and no more. "I really need your help. I think I'm hurt. I... fell."

For a while, he heard nothing, then a couple of growling and some snarls.

His heart beat faster when it became apparent to him that he was no longer alone. Rolling his eyes again to his left, he caught the faint image of an animal, black as night and big, creep out from the right under the shadows on four hind legs.

It didn't approach him right away. It circled him menacingly, and then was followed by two others. They closely followed its lead, playing a dangerous game of musical chairs with Sammy as the prized seat in the center. The boy trembled feverishly as their crooked gaits got closer and closer.

"Where are you?" called out the voice once more, but Sammy didn't answer this time. He kept quiet and very still, arching his head up to get a better view. His neck muscles worked just fine now, although the same couldn't be said of the rest of his body. Flat on his back and unable to rise, all Sammy could do was wait patiently for the inevitable to come. It was then that he noticed something different about his appearance.

He had color, unlike everything else in his new pale and shadowy reality. And that color was going to be all red soon, that much he was certain of, unless a miracle abruptly happened soon.

When he finally got a good perspective of things, he spotted three wild spooks in his immediate vicinity, encircling his stretched out, paralyzed body, like vultures going for the kill. Their full set of serrated teeth was on display for the boy to see, floating inside the swirling dark clouds that protruded in lieu of their missing heads.

Their panther-like bodies moved with a beautiful, hypnotic elegance-not beastly at all. They were probably waiting for Sammy to make the first move before they would attack. As such, the boy didn't indulge them. He pretended to be a statue, frozen and motionless.

Somehow, however, the plan backfired and one wild spook broke from formation and pounced on Sammy, who recoiled as fast as he could. It would have certainly sunk its jagged incisors into his leg had it not been beaten back, thanks to a swift blow to its temple that sent the creature flying and reeling on its side to a corner of the cave.

"Mom?"

The silhouette of a woman stood between Sammy and what remained of the pack of wild spooks. It was tall, slender and shaped in all aspects like his mother, even down to the dress, only that it was completely featureless.

It didn't move like his mother though, because this strange

figure was agile, graceful in its movements, and impressively quick. When the two wild spooks decided to do a double team attack, she dodged one and finished the other off with a hard blow to its stomach that knocked the wind completely out of its lungs.

"No," it replied to Sammy, turning its head briefly for him to glance over its faceless, pitch-black face. "I am not your mother."

"Watch out!"

Sammy's warning came too late. The last wild spook had already thrown its hefty feline body over the waifish frame of the dark phantom, knocking it down to the snowy floor and pinning it there. Immediately upon seeing this horrifying sight, Sammy sprung into action, leaping to his feet then placing a series of uncoordinated kicks into the side of the beast in the hope that it would release his brave savior.

"Get off her! Off!"

It obliged. Whirling around towards Sammy, it made a slashing movement with its paw, clipping the boy's scarf in the process—and taking it partially off! Although the creature didn't land a nail on him, Sammy collapsed on the ground as the searing pain in his neck rose sharply second after passing second. The thick exposed wound that bordered the edges of his head and neck began to glow ruby red, as he scrambled desperately to find the missing fabric lying in the snow to hide it away.

ROARRR!!!

It wasn't Sammy's stomach, but the wild spook this time around. It growled its loudest, as it maliciously stepped on the other half of Sammy's red scarf, which the panic and pain stricken boy had been groping for. Placing its full weight on the cloth, it had nailed it to the snow covered earth with a claw, effectively removing it from the boy's feeble reach.

Watching his last glimmer of hope slowly fade away, Sammy resigned himself to his dark fate, just as the will in his soul had left him after one final attempt to get a hold of that lost piece of his scarf had failed.

19

As he lay dying under the foul, hot breath of the wild spook, the ghostly silhouette of his mother materialized out of nowhere and buried the sharp end of a baby stalactite deep into the creature's torso, slaying it instantly. When that deed was done, it quickly took the unfurled end of the scarf from its icy resting place, and tied it around Sammy's neck. In no time after she accomplished this did Sammy's pain and suffering subside, returning him back to his normal, health self.

"Thanks," he gratefully told the silhouette that couldn't smile at him even if it wanted to, for lack of a mouth. "You were the one following me back in school, right?"

To this, it simply nodded in the affirmative.

"And the voice inside my head a while ago in the forest, correct?"

Again, another nod in the affirmative.

"Who are you?"

"What am I, is the more precise question," it replied, sounding every bit like India, Sammy's mother. "I am one of your mother's shade. She sent me after you when you left for school this morning. My purpose is to protect you, if you ever run into trouble of this sort."

"Shade?" inquired Sammy, as he got back to his feet with the assistance of the silhouette. "What's a shade?"

"A shadow doppelganger. We are natives to the Ghostwells, this world that you find yourself in now. Here we stay, until we are summoned to the human world by our masters, the alchemystics. In the human world, we are nothing more than wayward shadows to your eye, belonging neither to anyone or anything."

"And what about those wild spooks that you took care of over there," Sammy interrupted, cautiously observing the dead bodies of the creatures that earlier assaulted him, now scattered around like discarded garbage on the cavern floor. "Are they native to these parts too."

"That is correct, Sammy Tsunami," pleasantly replied the silhouette, leading him gently by the hand to the exit of the cave, which was a few paces ahead. "Only here, they are not called wild spooks… but something else."

"I don't want to know," cut in Sammy, as his eyes slowly shifted away from the corpses of the beast to the mouth of the cave that opened into a small clearing in the woods, where a dull, gray glow bathed the area and warded off the grainy darkness that clung to the towering trees that encircled it.

"They chased me on my way to school earlier," Sammy continued, walking into the drab light that fell softly on his colorless complexion. "They almost took off my scarf, but I managed to outrun them somehow. That was a close call, like when you saved me earlier."

"Ah, yes. I did try to stop them from catching up to you as best I could. But you were too fast for me. Embarrassed as I am to say, I cannot match your ridiculous speed even with my best time. You're just too, how do you call it, super silly fast!"

When he heard it say the words "ridiculous" and "super silly fast" to describe his speed, Sammy almost forgot that he was not talking to his mother. It had the same inflections, mannerisms and choice of words as her that it was hard to tell her shade apart from her. Still, it managed to warm Sammy enough to bring out a smile on his haggard face.

"So if my mom is your master, and your masters are alchemystics… that would make her an alchemiystic as well, right?"

"Correct."

His words outraced his thoughts, so much so that the stark realization of what they meant only hit him shortly afterwards. It was like a surge of electricity had streamed throughout his entire body, leaving all his motor functions completely paralyzed for the duration of the few minutes that his brain needed to process things.

"I can't believe that my mom is more than just a grocery clerk!" Sammy maintained, throwing his hands in the air as he tried to make eye contact with the eyeless figure in front of him. "All she knew was how to punch in numbers on a cash register! She said so herself! Her very words to me: *All I know in life is punching numbers into a cash register!* And I quote!"

"Apparently, she had a secret hobby you didn't know about."

In his mind, Sammy was starting to like his mother's shade—and a lot! Not only was she dependable in a fight, she even shared the same off kilter sense of humor his mother had.

"This could all be a dream," Sammy retaliated, playing along, "and you could be nothing more than a figment of my over-active imagination whom I don't think I will even remember when I wake up… which should be pretty much soon."

"This is no dream, Sammy Tsunami," it replied back, taking on a serious tone suddenly. "This is the Ghostwells. You came here through the portal opened up by the alchemystic stone known as the Nanek Crystal. That's how you and your friends got here in the first place."

"My friends?"

"The dwarf boy… Nark… the wielder of the Nanek Crystal. Him and everyone else he banished to this place, as well as the monster whose life force is bound to the Nanek Crystal, the jinn-mera calling itself Rular."

"Jinn-mera?"

"A genie that's actually a chimera. Chimeras are creatures that are a combination of other creatures. In Rular's case, it's snakes and an octopus."

He was taking it all in as it telepathically streamed these into his thoughts. All the same, Sammy's ears couldn't believe what it was hearing. Everyone Nark had exiled to this place was here somewhere, and all Sammy needed to do was gather them together, including Nark and Timmy, then escape together— assuming, that is, that there was an exit somewhere.

"Can you take me to my friends?"

"Of course. And I will do you one better. I'll even escort you out of the Ghostwells. That was what you had in mind, wasn't it?"

The smile on Sammy's face couldn't be wider if didn't have ears. He was just loving the fact that it was anticipating whatever he had in mind, so much so that he wanted very much to give his travelling companion a proper name.

"Shadow Ranger, that's your name," he told it with a straight face, tongue in cheek, and with arms folded. "We're right in the middle of the forest, you're my guide, and you're shady… so it fits!"

The shade was silent for a moment, pondering how best to react to the awkward situation Sammy had put it in. Before it could do so, however, Sammy had slapped it on the shoulder and motioned it to follow him. The boy hobbled when he took his first few steps, still hurting from the fall into the cave.

He was being courageous about it though, not complaining about the painful stings his cuts and bruises gave him. Seeing him limp forward, dragging his injured leg, prompted Shadow Ranger to rush to his immediate rescue.

Without so much as even asking Sammy for permission, the shade threw his sagging arm around her shoulder to help him walk. Appreciative of the gesture, Sammy simply nodded to her to show his approval, not caring whether she could see it for herself, or not.

20

"You've been awfully quiet, and with too many questions bottled up inside that pregnant head of yours."

Shadow Ranger had the accent down and the ornery tone. If Sammy didn't know any better, he would say that it was his mother trying to coax him to speak, and not this shadowy reflection of hers which propped his injured body up as a crutch would.

Since leaving the clearing to head on back into the thick of the forest, he has had his arm around her, while leaning in close into her limber form for support. Still in pain from the fall in the cave, the boy could barely manage to walk without the shade's help. It was a small consolation for him that she resembled his mother in every bit, except for the obscurity of her absent features. That way, he didn't have to feel embarrassed around her as she didn't look like any stranger to him at all.

"Do you know why people go insane?" she went on babbling as they made their way through a closely knit cluster of trees that barely allowed room for passage. "They go insane because their questions don't get answered. They think that questions eventually answer themselves, but they don't."

"Alright then," fired back Sammy, his tongue loose now with the grease of curiosity. "You know this, and I'm sure you do. That creature that attacked me and my friend a while back in the computer room, the one calling itself Rular, the 'jinn-mera' as you call him. Tell me everything you know about that monster."

"He was a sell djinn, a gimme gold genie, a mercenary peddling magical services… until he sold his spirit and had grafted it on to the alchemystical gem stone known as the Nanek Crystal, so named after the alchemystic himself who had created it."

"Was he always a fearsome looking jinn-mera?" wondered Sammy, suddenly recalling Rular's terrible countenance which had made an indelible impression in his mind. "I mean, was he ever human even once?"

"Once," replied Shadow Ranger, pretending to see Sammy as she turned her head to him. "He was a warlock and a king in an age long past, before becoming a jinn-mera. None of that humanity remains nowadays unfortunately."

A cold snap suddenly caught them off guard when they came upon across a grassy knoll that lay at the outskirts of the forest. Above, the dwindling sun was following them, casting as much light as it could to compensate for the darkening shadows that crept over the blades of grass, transforming them from a depressing shade of gray into a menacing black.

"It's freezing!" Sammy screamed out loud, as a flurry of snowflakes began to fall. "We need to get to shelter—and fast!" he told Shadow Ranger, who was huddled near him, still carrying his shoulder over hers.

"There's a house nearby, not too far away to walk to," Shadow Ranger assured the boy, turning in the direction of the wooded area ahead. "Just be patient and we will be there before sun-gone."

As if they were tempting fate by pressing on, the flurry soon deteriorated into a raging blizzard. Three limping steps in, and Sammy couldn't go on. He let his weight pull him down. Before he could do so, however, Shadow Ranger caught him and carried him on her back during the rest of the journey. Although the shade herself seemed unaffected by the adverse weather conditions, she hardly had the strength to lift the boy, let alone advance in the knee deep snow.

Be that as it may, she knew she had to hurry up. Otherwise, the boy would be stone cold dead from hypothermia. There was no time for rest, especially since the shadows themselves around them were quickly disappearing into a blustery whiteness of nothing.

"Live and endure!" she tersely directed Sammy before the boy passed out into unconsciousness. "There is so much to look forward to! You have to weather this, survive it! Everything will be alright thereafter! This is not to be your end! It is not to be your finish!"

Eventually, it didn't take long for them both to reach the

house itself, with Sammy suffering no more than a mild case of frostbite. The house—a rundown stone shed, no bigger than Sammy's own—hardly impressed in lifeless monochrome. What lay inside beyond its unlocked wooden door, however, was an entirely different story.

"Finally, somebody else in living color!"

Nark walked right across the small room holding a log of firewood in his hands. He easily stood out in color from the toneless canvass he was put in. There was something odd about him, besides the fact that he was cheery and all excited. He had ditched the gawky casual wear he previously had on, and was now appropriately dressed for the wintry weather outside in a whopping maroon parka with a furry rimmed hood drawn over his head.

As soon as he caught a glimpse of the shadowy interloper carrying Sammy, who was unconscious and hard of breathing, his elated and relieved expression immediately soured. In a flash of smoldering anger, he swung his club fiercely at the shade—one, two—but missed completely.

"That's my pal, Sammy, you have there, witchy thing!" Nark blurted out in heat. "If you've killed him, I'm going to have to avenge him! And that'll mean a cracked skull for starters!"

"He's not dead," coolly pointed out Shadow Ranger without any pretenses whatsoever. "He's hurt though, and needs healing."

"Oh," dryly remarked Nark, relaxing his weapon hand but

not letting his log go. "Alright, but if you try anything funny, I'm going to deck you, you hear? I'll give you this one chance to prove yourself, witchy thing! One chance and no more!"

Ignoring Nark's feeble threats, the dark phantom laid the cataleptic boy down on the limestone floor, then, proceeded to fire up the fire pit at the center of the small enclosed space that they shared. Directly above it in the ceiling was a chimney hole that sipped up all the smoke emitted by the lit up litter of wood. As the shade calmly worked on getting the flames burning, Nark snuck a curious glimpse at a slumbering Sammy, whose face was smothered with shards of ice.

"The blizzard out there caught you both with your pants down, huh?" he said out loud to Shadow Ranger, who crouched beside the pit, tossing firewood after firewood into it to stoke the blaze. "What are you supposed to be then... a ghost?"

"I am no ghost," the shade replied meekly, taking a handful of herbs from a wicker basket nearby and mixing them together in a metal pot. "I am his mother's shade. I was made with no name, but he gave me one. He named me Shadow Ranger."

"You certainly seem to know your way around this place," Nark then commented, impressed with the shade's familiarity with where to pick up stuff and things from around the house.

"This is a peasant's house," the shade rejoined. "There are many like this one in the village where I come from. I, myself, live in one, so I know where the herbs and the fire pit are at."

When he discerned the sincerity in her delicate voice, Nark

cast the log away by hurling it into the fire. He then sauntered away towards the lone window inside the premises, where everything beyond the glass was a dirty, glowing white.

As he kept himself busy watching the void outside from behind the pane, Shadow Ranger began boiling her ingredients. In no time, her herbal concoction that she made produced a sweet scent that filled the room. It was a pleasant calming aroma.

"So, witchy thing, is there a way out of this horrid place?" nonchalantly inquired Nark, striking conversation with the strange entity crouched a few feet away from him by the steaming pot. "I initially thought this was hell, you see, until you and Sammy came along, which was a good thing. I figured that since Sammy's a good guy, unlike me, this couldn't be hell, right? Am I right or am I right?"

Shadow Ranger gave him no answer. The minutes passed as the wind whistled outside as it blew sternly across the snow flurries. Eventually, the boiled mixture was done. Taking the pot from the center of the pit, the shade then emptied all of its contents out by hurling it straight at Sammy, who instantly woke up, literally steaming.

"What did you do that for?" furiously demanded Nark, who immediately rushed to Sammy's side to render whatever assistance he could. "Are you trying to boil him alive?"

"On the contrary," politely replied Shadow Ranger, "I am trying to repair him, mend his wounds."

Although he saw it himself, personally and up close, he

still couldn't believe it. Nark was carefully observing Sammy's contorted and pained face, when the cuts and bruises on them, including the frostbite, magically thawed away before his very eyes. He was so stunned and frightened by the sudden metamorphosis that he flinched away and retreated to a distance.

"How did you do that?" he insisted the shade answer him. "If you're no ghost, then you're certainly a witch for sure!"

"As I told you, I'm his mother's shade, nothing more. Being that, I share his mother's affection for him. For this reason alone, I can never harm him."

"What about me then?" quizzed Nark, who slowly staggered away from his corner to be close to Sammy. "Can you hurt me?"

"Do you want me to?" snapped Shadow Ranger, kneeling beside Sammy, who was wide awake now and sitting upright on his sleeping bag, watching the two bicker and argue. "Don't tempt me, little man. I know you tried to harm him earlier."

"Don't get so worked up there!" backed off Nark, realizing that further antagonizing the phantom would only work to his disadvantage. "We're all friends here, alright? This here is my home, and I have welcomed you both inside with open arms. And I mean that, even though I had a log in my hand earlier. As host, I am entitled to some respect from my guests, yes? Of course, you know that! You are a well bred witchy thing, aren't you, well aware of manners, am I right or am I right?"

Sammy had heard everything that was said, and was

particularly touched by Shadow Ranger's bold declaration of affection for him. In every respect, she reminded him of his mother, and of how fierce she was when it came to protecting him.

For all he knew, the shade herself was probably in the back of the school too when Nark and him had their little testy confrontation earlier. As he pondered this, his strength slowly returned to him and a healthy color formed on his cheeks, restoring him to what he was prior to his injuries. He was starting to feel good about himself again too, that is, until Nark approached him and greeted him with a ravenous smile.

21

"Whassup?" the boy said to his dwarfish companion out of common courtesy, the words sticking to his throat as he made an effort to expel them out.

"Whassup yourself?" Nark naughtily retorted, sitting himself down on his flat bottom next to Sammy, who pretended to busy himself tying his red scarf around his neck. He was also watching the blizzard outside, listening to it sing. It was singing an all too familiar tune of sadness and desolation.

"Nice coat. Where'd you get it?"

"It's a parka," corrected Nark, stretching his arms in it. "Found it here in this hovel. It was just lying around on the floor, so I thought I'd sequester it. Anyway, it's meant to be worn, not worn out on the ground."

A cold silence wafted between them all of a sudden. Stifling the urge to say something nasty, like reprimanding Nark for stealing somebody else's property, Sammy bit his lips. On the other hand, Nark, noticing how uncomfortable he had made his friend by disclosing how he got his parka, kept his mouth closed out of fear that he might make a bad thing worse.

Neither one budging, they waited for each other to break the ice, something that took quite a while to happen.

"You tried to kill me," started off Sammy with a blistering accusation, a deadpan but deathly serious expression washing over his face. "Not once, but twice."

"Oooh, that," Nark groaned, not wanting to be reminded of his earlier boo-boo. "You're still alive and breathing, aren't you? So what's the problem? No problem here as far as I can tell."

"You-tried-to-kill-me!" Sammy repeated himself, this time slower and more intense. "First you sent that monster of yours, Rular, to polish me off in the computer room. Then, at the back of the school, you sicced it on me again! Did you know that that thing really, really hurt Mickayla bad and---!"

"Who's Mickalya?" Nark rudely barged in, disrupting Sammy's outburst and train of thought. "I'm sorry, but I don't know anybody of that name who is a student in the school. And believe me, I know everyone one. And everyone knows me."

"You know… forget it," Sammy quickly backtracked, suddenly remembering his unbreakable pact with Mickayla to never divulge her secret to anybody. "Just forget it."

"So what are you so angry about?"

"You-tried-to-kill-me."

"Can we please let bygones be bygones?" begged Nark, scratching his head as he strained himself to laugh off his shame. "That's all in the past now. I'm totally over it, so why can't you? We can be buds again like we were this morning, if you like?"

There was nothing but silence again between the two, a more uncomfortable one than before. Seeking someone to back him up, Sammy's eyes drifted to Shadow Ranger, who was sitting quietly at his back, observing the wrangling from there. Much as he wanted to see the approval on her face, there was nothing to see, except for a pitch black slate where her countenance should be.

"So are we cool or what?" Nark then followed through, breaking the ice this time around.

"Yeah, we're cool." Sammy answered casually, exasperated a bit by all their arguing. "We're frosty."

"Doesn't sound like you've forgiven me," Nark impudently presumed, glaring at the boy as he handed him out an open palm that was as cold as winter's ice. "Let's shake on it anyway, what do you say? We're in a dire situation together, or haven't you noticed? If you want to play the blame game, that's fine. That won't get us anywhere, and you know it. You need to bury the hatchet, buddy dude. You have to face the stark reality that we are going to have to depend on one another if we are going to get out of this. We will need each other, like it or not. So are we cool, or are we cool?"

"I have her," countered Sammy, pointing a thumb past his shoulder to the silhouette crouched at his back. "Who do you have watching your back?"

One fleeting look at the faceless shadow by the boy's side, and Nark needed a moment to organize his thoughts.

Like Sammy, he awoke in the forest alone, with nothing but the clothes on his back and his wits to keep him alive. For a while, he searched the woods aimlessly for any kind of company he could find. In the end, he found no one to share his fears with, after endless hours of ambling through the clammy snow swept mud.

By chance, however, he stumbled upon a small stone house in a clearing and took shelter there. It was while waiting for something to turn up in his favor that the witchy thing entered the abode with the sleeping boy tucked in its grimy clutches.

The sight of Sammy alive made Nark sick to his stomach, yet still, he saw the boy's sudden reappearance as an omen—a good one. Finally, he had a friend in his midst, with a ghostly servant at that, who could help him execute his intentions.

It was a golden opportunity too good to pass up, and he knew it! If he was stupid, he would have clung to his foolish pride, and brushed Sammy off like the poor dope that he was. But Nark needed Sammy, more than the boy needed him. The dwarf wasn't about to let his last chance to get out of this sordid place just up and go. He needed all his cunning and craft to make this boy realize that he was more important than he actually was. He knew only too well that it was either that, or dying alone in this wretched wintry place.

"You need me, buddy dude." Nark maintained, attempting to fashion a passable grin on a face that had already gone sour.

"This is my mess you've gotten yourself into. And since it is my mess, only I can fix it. Only I can get both of us out of here."

"He's right about that," seconded Shadow Ranger, surprising the two to the extent that their jaws dropped out of sheer disbelief. "Nark over there is the undisputed master of the Nanek Crystal, one of a few lesser alchemystic stones in existence. One of its inherent powers is opening doors between your world and the Ghostwells, this place you are both in now. Only he can command it to open up an exit for you to get back, so it's best that he tags along. You will definitely need him if you desire to return home."

"See, the witchy thing is right about me," Nark delightfully stressed, his head held high and his posture brimming with confidence as a result of the unexpected affirmation.

He then stood up, strutted over to a door to wooden chest in the corner, flung it open, and rummaged through the sheets and linen folded and stacked there. He was tossing them out indiscriminately on the dusty stone floor, making a small mess of things, when Sammy cut him off.

"What are you doing?" asked the boy, picking up after his dwarfish friend, who carried on in spite of being clued in to desist.

"I'm stealing," was Nark's sharp response to the boy's query. "If we are going to go out there again, we need to carry some supplies. Otherwise, we won't last very long. You can either help me find what we need… or get out of my way, pretty please with lots of sugar on top. Thank you very much."

Upon hearing this request, Sammy reluctantly moved away to the side and let Nark conduct his business, taking with him the few bedcovers that he collected from the floor. He was about to place the sheets that he had back into the chest, when Shadow Ranger grabbed them all and proceeded to fold them into neat squares, to his surprise and appreciation.

"Hel—lo! What have we here?" Nark was pleased with his discovery. He had uncovered a large dagger by chance underneath the fabric inside the box. It had been sheathed in what seemed like a leather scabbard with the words *'GUT WEED'* written on it. In his small hands, it looked long and thick enough to be a sword.

Although it had been forged entirely in steel, it was not heavy at all to wield. Grasping the hilt, Nark swung it around—*WHISH! WHOOSH! SWOOSH!*—with a child-like playfulness that matched the wide eyed wonder in his eyes.

Had Sammy not interrupted him by speaking with Shadow Ranger in a loud and insistent tone, the dwarfish lad would have continued on with his sword game. Not wanting to disclose his treasured find to his companions, who seemed to be engrossed with each other's company, he secretly hid it away inside his parka which had a pocket big enough to hold both the scabbard and its blade.

"And where are we going to find this Nanek Crystal anyway?" Sammy quizzed Shadow Ranger, who kept herself busy stacking up the folded clothes on the limestone floor.

"The last time I saw it, it was in Nark's hand when it shattered into smithereens."

"Oh, that's right," recalled Nark, whose face suddenly turned pale as if he had seen a ghost. He then dropped what he was doing, rose to his feet and faced up to Shadow Ranger, who met his stare dead on with her eyeless countenance.

"There is no Nanek Crystal, is there?" he then said with stern conviction, tilting his eyebrows downwards. "The one that broke was the only one of its kind. It was unique, correct? With it destroyed, there is no way back for us, is there?"

"I cannot explain it, but I sense it here in the Ghostwells," Shadow Ranger revealed, pointing right at the window, where outside was a complete blank, a whiteout, courtesy of the snow storm. "As soon as the weather betters, we shall go to it. And then, you can both go home."

A sense of relief washed over Sammy, for he believed in his heart that Shadow Ranger's word was good. He was about to propound a few questions to her to clarify some other things, but Nark had beaten him to the chance.

"Rular's out there too, isn't he?" the small boy belted out, changing the topic to one that interested him greatly. Upon hearing this, Sammy's expression changed. He shuddered and the shivers swelled up within him.

"He's going to be gunning for my blood," continued Nark, tensing up as he pondered this idea the more. "I worked him as a slave for two years. I don't think that he will just forgive me for the indignity I caused him. He was a king after all before he became an undead oaf. That means, he's got a lot of wounded pride to nurse."

Sharing Nark's sentiments, Sammy thought back to the crimes that he committed against Rular. Not only did he pluck out its left eye and stabbed it through the shoulder—he also murdered one of its snake arms with his shadow arrow before it ultimately destroyed itself shattering the Nanek Crystal. Sammy was pretty sure the Nanek Beast would come for him too. That much he was certain of. On days like these, Sammy couldn't help but wish that he was somebody else. Somebody not him.

22

The trio embarked into the wilderness as soon as the blizzard subsided, and the lone star sailing the heavens returned back to its proper perch atop the black grainy sky. They headed east this time across the forest, following Shadow Ranger's lead. She always walked five steps ahead of the boys, egging them on to catch up every time they fell back. Although the weather had cleared, it was still bitingly cold, especially now that the snow on the ground had added on a few inches, thanks to the furious flurry earlier.

"You mentioned something about this place being called the Ghostwells," opened up Nark, trying to engage the shade in a little chit-chat as he was now bored with all the quiet marching that they have been doing. "Why is it named that?"

"This is where the ghosts come to be nourished," Shadow Ranger answered back, peeking briefly at Nark, who looked like a ghost himself with all the sheet and linen from the shed now wrapped around his parka to keep him warm.

"Living things in your world need water to survive. Unliving things, like ghosts and other spectral creatures, need memories to sustain themselves. A ghost lingers on in your world because it cannot let go of certain memories that it made when it was still alive. The Ghostwells are basically made up of these memories—a lot of them people and places long gone, like this forest over here and that peasant home back there. They're mementos of someone or something that had passed away. As long as ghosts cling to these memories, they can never move on to where they should go. The memories here keep them from further journeying on."

"And what if they are able to let go of all these memories?" asked Nark, pretending to sound interested as he tried to suppress a yawn. "What then?"

"Then, their memories disappear upon their departure, vanishing when they themselves vanish. When that happens, the landscape of the Ghostwell changes. Old memories are replaced by new ones, and such is the cycle of life here."

"And what about you?" inquired Sammy, jumping right into the conversation his two companions were casually having. "Are you a memory too?"

"No, I am a construct of your mother, given life by her alchemystic arts," clarified Shadow Ranger. "The Ghostwells may be a place where the memories of ghosts dwell, but they are certainly not the only ones that reside here. There are many immigrants from a lot of different places that have called this reality their home, myself included."

"So shades created by various alchemystics have formed a

community here of sorts, like your home village which you mentioned earlier, am I correct?"

"That is correct, Sammy Tsunami. There are shade villages, towns and even cities throughout the Ghostwells. There are a lot of us living here. This is where you can find us when we are not roaming your world as wayward shadows."

"And what about Rular?" Nark butted in, eager to find out about his. "He's out there too, right?"

It was the same question he had asked before in the shed, the one the shade purposely avoided answering. When he thought Shadow Ranger was giving him the cold shoulder when she announced that it was high time for them to leave, now that the blizzard was over—he didn't insist, not wanting to agitate his only chance at finding a way back home. This time, however, was different. Nark figured that, since the shade was in a very helpful mood, he should take advantage of its obliging disposition while he still could, and find out once and for all if what his gut was telling him was true.

"The Nanek Beast is, indeed, out there," sadly confirmed Shadow Ranger, opting not the sugar coat the bad news when she broke it. "And yes, he is looking for you, Nark. And you too, Sammy, for the eye that you took from him, among other things."

The two boys looked at each other, shaking like leaves from the cold and from the terror that was rising up in their stomachs. In each other's troubled faces, they saw their shared fears reflected at themselves, so obvious that it couldn't be denied.

"Is it possible to avoid running into that thing?" Sammy willed the shade to answer, his tone louder now and desperate. "We can take another route if it's tracking us, you know? It's not like we're in a hurry or anything. We just want to get back home alive, and I don't think that's asking for too much."

"There is… no other way but this," Shadow Ranger cryptically answered. "I can sense him around, not nearby though, but I don't know if he knows where we are, or where we are headed. I'm quite certain though that he's combing the land—at least, the area where you came in, which is within a radius of twenty miles, give or take."

"What kind of answer is that?" Nark exploded, fuming mad. "Are you implying that… that ugly octopus snake thing will eventually find us, no matter what we do? Are you saying that our doom is inevitable? What are you saying exactly, huh?"

The dwarf was ranting. He was shivering, more than all the others, despite of all the layers of wool and cotton wrapped around his diminutive figure. His stride wasn't nearly as long as his companions, basically because his legs were shorter. In order to compensate for this handicap, he had to double his pace in order to just pull alongside the rest of his party, which was tiring for him. The effort he put into this left him gasping for air and exasperated very often, so much so that he had to beg everybody to stop for a moment or two every now and then so that he could catch his elusive breath.

"I can carry you on my back if you want," offered Shadow Ranger, gliding towards Nark with an outstretched arm and an open palm. "Sammy has been deliberately slowing his pace, so that you can keep up with him. We need to move faster because it is getting dark. Please, let me carry you."

"Take your filthy hands away from me, you witchy thing!" woofed Nark, balking away from the silhouette which tried to cradle him into its arms like an infant. "I will walk like all of you! I may be smaller in size, but my heart is bigger than any of yours!"

"As you please," said the dark phantom, neither disappointed nor displeased with the brusque rejection. Turning around to return back to her position some five paces ahead, the shade noted the concerned expression on Sammy's frosted face. The boy looked as if he agreed with the shade, but said nothing because he didn't want to offend Nark, who was sensitive about a great many things.

"Let's go," urged Nark, starting to saunter forward again. "The sooner we are out of these accursed woods, the better. Too many eyes watching us from the shadows—too many hungry eyes."

Echoing Nark's paranoia, Sammy's hawkish eyes swept the trees and shrubbery surrounding them, particularly the long shadows that they cast. Hiding there in the dark, he found a couple of four legged animals, even one or two wild spooks, which were carefully observing them from afar.

****

"How long before we arrive?"

The forest behind them was shrouded in a cheerless black. There were gaps between the trees, wide ones and narrow ones, where all sorts of creatures lurked, some of whom eavesdropped. Most of these beasts weren't familiar to Sammy, but the wild spooks he definitely knew, especially since they seemed to be the most dangerous of the bunch.

There were two stalking them, one large and one small, probably a parent and her cub. Both had been following their trail for over an hour now, slinking quietly in the shadows, waiting for a chance to get near. Sammy had spotted them from the get-go, but he opted not to warn his companions of their presence because he didn't want to alarm them needlessly. The last thing he wanted was everybody panicking and people getting hurt in the process. The woods were treacherous, and he didn't want somebody like Nark running away into the arms of some unseen and greater danger.

"We are being watched," cautioned Shadow Ranger, who helmed the marching party, followed by Nark, and then by Sammy himself who brought up the rear. "No sudden movements."

"Two wild spooks at my eight o' clock," said Sammy in a

hushed tone, glancing behind to see whether the pair were still there on their backs.

"Wild spooks?" then asked Nark, wondering what the heck was Sammy talking about. "What are those?"

"He's talking about the two large cats with the cloudy skulls in the back," clarified Shadow Ranger. "They won't attack us, unless both of you start sweating fear. But they're not the ones we should be worried about. Look!"

Sammy trained his eyesight in the direction his mother's shade pointed at. There, behind a large pine trunk stood two gray figures that he immediately recognized. Annie and Ruby Pastrami were beckoning them to come over to them, but something seemed different about how they conducted themselves. Not only did they not have any color on them, unlike Sammy and Nark, there was an unmistakably sinister air around them.

"Don't go near them!" Shadow Ranger cried out loud, beginning to run. "We have to get out of this place—and quick—before these trick faces overwhelm us!"

"What are you, ladies, doing here?"

Nark didn't catch the shade's dire warning and broke off from formation, wandering away from the path like a defiant child. He tottered across the snow piles in the direction of the two girls, who giggled and laughed at his smug strut. With a big, sunny smile grafted between his dimpled cheeks, Nark good-naturedly hopped over to chat with the pair, who welcomed him over to their side with open arms.

"Nark, no!" implored Sammy, reaching out to latch on to his dwarfish friend's parka. As he firmly secured his hold on the back of the coat, the boy caught sight of his mother, India, who was sitting on a branch of a tree, smiling. Like Annie and Ruby before her, she was a colorless gray and ominous looking, devoid of warmth and as wintry cold as the wicked weather.

"Over here, Sammy!" she playfully hollered aloud before dropping feet first on to the ice below. "Give Mommy a kiss!"

He had jerked Nark back so hard that they lost their equilibrium. They both fell on the ground, snow flying all over the place as they clumsily tumbled all over themselves. Then, before Nark could turn around and give Sammy a scathing scolding for his rashness, the three shadowy figures came at them altogether—in halves.

"S-S-Sammy, w-what are they?" stammered Nark, cringing. "What's happening to their… bodies?"

Separating their upper bodies from their lower halves, which remained standing upright where they left them, the shadowy copies of Annie, Ruby and India flew at the pair of boys, eerily dragging only their torsos, arms and heads.

"I told you both to run!" Shadow Ranger reproached the two, who promptly complied and scurried off behind her in the opposite direction. As they went, the shade stood her ground to face off against the terrible half-bodied trio. "I'll take care of the trick faces myself!" she called out prior to charging into battle.

They didn't look back when they dashed right out of there, the shrill screams behind them notwithstanding. After running aimlessly for some time, fatigue finally set in, sooner for Nark than for Sammy. The small boy had to quit fleeing to get his bearings back.

"Don't stop now," pleaded Sammy, who kept vigil beside Nark while the shorter boy leaned over on a tree to catch his breath. "If you can't go on, I'll carry you on my back."

"No charitable hand-outs!" angrily shot back Nark, pushing Sammy away, while his other hand clutched at his chest which felt like it was caving into his heart. "Run away and leave me if you want! But I won't be treated like I have to be pitied!"

"This is no time to be fussy! We have to hurry up, or we'll both be finished! Please, Nark... come on!"

Squatting down to offer a ride on his back, Sammy extended a hand out to the impish lad, who hesitated for a while before sheepishly balking away. With the sounds of terrifying screams still going off in the distance, however, he quickly reconsidered Sammy's generous proposition. Swallowing his pride, he grabbed hold of the other boy's hand and was about to climb on to his back, when an ominous shadow got the drop on both of them.

"There you are!" said Annie's shadow copy as she surprised the two boys, who nearly fainted when she suddenly appeared out of the dark behind them. "I've been looking all over for you both!"

Before the trick face could get closer though, Nark whipped

out the blade he was hiding from under his parka, and plunged it into the creature's heart with eyes closed. Although he had been compelled by his instincts to strike first in self-defense, Nark did so without realizing who his target was. It was a blind leap of faith that he took when he went for the kill. It was only after he saw Annie's pale face turn even paler did he fully understand the full of extent of what he had done.

"N-Nark?" The last words of Annie's shadow copy left her the second her breath did. Her expression of horror and shock melted away quickly to one of peace and serenity once the life had ebbed completely out of her. It didn't take long before she disintegrated into a faint wisp of black smoke.

"No, please, no, don't die on me, please!"

He fumbled for words as he tried to wrap his free arm around her ethereal shoulders. She was gone before he could grab her, leaving him alone to wallow in the depths of his own despair.

"That wasn't our Annie," stressed Sammy to him. Instead of offering any consolation to ease his dwarfish friend's suffering and anguish, he rendered him a service by reminding him of the truth. Nark, however, did not appreciate the gesture at all, choosing to ignore him so that he can hold on to his grief a little longer.

"You killed it, my Lord Sword Shark!"

This was how Shadow Ranger congratulated Nark when she finally caught up with the pair of boys, just right before Annie's monochromatic doppelganger completely evaporated into thin air. Her obscure reference to Nark had them both scratching their heads as she glided over to their sides.

"What did you just call me?" Nark wanted know, dumbfounded, as the hand he held the hilt with continued to tremble.

"You're starting to remember," was the shade's terse reply, walking over to the small boy. Before she could say more, Nark tossed the short sword into the snow, then turned and left. Sammy, who was still reeling from what just happened, followed him closely, not bothering to pick the discarded weapon up and return it to his impish friend.

Noting the disinterest of the two in the abandoned blade, Shadow Ranger left it alone as well, although she did seem to regret her decision. "Pity," she told them as they marched on ahead, "that was genuine alchemy steel and no cheap imitation."

They lugged themselves across the snow for a couple more hours, not saying a word to each other about what transpired, before stumbling upon a breach in the trees that led them out of the wooded area. Outside the break, a hoary ghost land awaited them.

****

"We wouldn't be in this fix if my crystal hadn't broken," Nark said out of the blue, with much regret and melancholy. He stopped at the edge of the gray forest, right before the snow sloped down towards the bank of what appeared to be a stagnant body of water of some sort.

It was a walk of a few miles, not very far. The group, however, was tired and had no more strength left in them to go on. It was fortunate and timely, therefore, that Nark had decided to reminisce all of a sudden and pause in his tracks. It afforded them some breathing space and an opportunity to take a much needed break.

"The crystal has been my poison for years. I was drunk with the power it provided me. Anyone who ever crossed me, I either sent away or terrorized. And to think that all I've ever used it for, all this time, was to get the respect that I've always craved for in middle school. Had I been smarter, I would have been a wealthy person by now. All it would have taken was a single wish."

"I don't mind being rich myself," Sammy point-blankly commented, shrugging his shoulders. "Me and my mom have been poor all our lives, and it's the worst, dude, really. Our house is a small wooden dilapidated cabin located in the middle of the forest. We live out in the woods because we can't afford to live in the city. There, we're constantly surrounded by all kinds of wild beasts, and we're always hungry because there's never any food around. I have to go to school every day in the same clothes—these clothes—because my family can't afford to buy me new ones, even second hand or third hand ones. I've been wearing these rags since I made the third grade. If you think your life is bad, try walking in my shoes."

"Those clothes on your back are really all you got?" queried Nark, turning to face Sammy who was shivering from the arctic cold a short distance away from him. "Can't you, like, take the furs from the animals that you catch and make yourself some other duds from it?"

The boy gave his dwarfish friend a quizzical, contemptuous yet confounded look before answering the question.

"You want me to come to school dressed like a caveman, dude?" Sammy sardonically stated to him. "I get laughed at and teased because of the way I look. Now, you want me to put on a freakishly stupid Halloween costume so that the other kids can rib me even more! Some friend you turned out to be! First, you wanted to get rid of me by sending that monster after me—not once, but twice! Then, you trap me here with you in this black and white version of hell. Why do you do this, man? What have I ever done to you for you to hate me like this?"

"I thought we were cool," quickly reminded Nark, who was now on the defensive. "In the shed earlier, or whatever you call that dirty hovel back there, you told me that we were cool. And now, you're blaming me for all your troubles! I mean, what is this, huh?"

"You started it by getting my goat, dude!" accused Sammy, now flushed red with anger. "I had already let everything go, but you had to tell me to dress like a Neanderthal! Why would you do that? Are you trying to insult me?"

"No, buddy dude, no!" laughed Nark bashfully, as he mentally geared up for the forthcoming explanation he was going to give. "Look, I'm sorry for all the grief that I caused you earlier. I really am! It's just that, I did those things because I was jealous of you. There's this girl that I kind of had my eye on, you see—that tomboy with the braces... Annie. I saw her hug you in the lunch line earlier, and seeing you two together just drove me batty insane, so much so that I wanted to hurt you really, really bad. I flew off the deep end because you were my friend and that sort of betrayal on your part cuts really deep, you know."

"She gave me some sandwiches, alright, because she heard my tummy growl!" exclaimed Sammy, who couldn't believe his ears that the root of their falling out was actually something so trivial as a small misunderstanding. "Nark, she hugged me because she felt sorry for me. I hadn't eaten in two days, to tell you the truth. She probably figured that out somehow, which was why she did what she did. I'm not into your lady, dude. I'm just so into her sandwiches."

"You swear?" Nark was looking at Sammy with apologetic eyes when he asked him this. He then walked towards the boy slowly, dragging his little feet now weighted with guilt.

"Yes!" Sammy immediately replied with a sunny smile and without any hesitations whatsoever. "So are we cool again?"

"We're frosty cool," Nark beamed back, elated to no end. "You like that fat sister of hers anyway, right? That gal is so into you, it's so obvious and plain! That one has a lot of meat on her bones. If you ever go hungry again, you could just eat her and she'll fill your belly right up! Mmm... scrumptious!"

A sheepish grin formed across Sammy's face when he heard that last disdainful remark. He wanted to challenge Nark to teach him a lesson, but seeing his pal leave his side with a cheery grin on his puffy cheeks, he decided to go with a much softer approach to avenge himself.

"You know that you did stab her through the heart back there," Sammy fired back, reminding his friend about the fate of Annie's shadow copy. "Yes, I did," answered Nark. "But I'd never do that to the real Annie, be rest assured."

23

"This is not how I envisioned spending my evening," whined Annie as she reluctantly dogged her sister who was listlessly strolling a few paces ahead of her, and following the soft glow on the ground emitted by the flashlight in her hand. "You owe me big time for this, Roobs! Big time!"

"Quit your yapping already!" Ruby told her off half heartedly, her guilt over dragging Annie into her own mess twisting inside her heart like a knife. She glanced over at her sibling briefly, a quick two second head turn, before returning her eyes back to where they belonged—the long and winding blue string below her feet that seemed to go on and on in the direction they were headed.

The vast parking lot on the east side of the school was no place for agoraphobics, or people who fear wide open spaces. Empty and enormous, with no trail of any kind cutting through its wide expanse, the paved stretch of open land was a nightmarish landscape for anyone who was terrified of ending up mislaid out in the middle of nowhere. Luckily for the Pastrami sisters though, they didn't have to worry about this in the likely event that they ever got bored of their little adventure, or got too cold wandering around the outdoors.

All they needed to do in such a case was to simply make an about face and follow the string back towards the colossal edifice of their school. Once there, it was easy for them to return to where their dad had dropped them off—the exact same spot he was going to pick them up at precisely an hour from now.

"Aren't you glad we didn't need to break into the school, Sis?" painfully joked Ruby, trying her best to ease the tension that was steadily brewing between her and her sister who was all frowns since she spoke badly to her no more than a minute ago. "At least, Sammy left us something to go on with."

Annie rolled her eyes away snobbishly, and then folded her arms across her chest. She was trying to forget how Ruby had convinced their very accommodating and considerate father to drive them all the way back to school after they had supper. Things happened so fast that she didn't have time to stop her from executing her plan.

Her sister's alibi was simple, but effective. Ruby had told their dad that the track team was holding early try outs starting at around eight that night, and that she wanted to join this year, but needed to meet the minimum qualifying time in order to do so. She had been an athlete all her life, and even ran the hundred meter dash during last summer's junior Olympics that there wasn't anything even mildly suspicious about her excuse. Besides, their dad had a soft spot for her, especially after she had flunked sixth grade last year and had to repeat it all over again.

That traumatic experience not only took a heavy toll on her emotionally. Ruby ended up losing her slim and taut figure as well, the one she kept dieting herself to death for. She was eating more now, and growing stouter and stouter as a result of her spiraling depression over being held back. And now, here she was, chasing after a boy she had just met in school. Annie couldn't help but think that Ruby was doing this in order to compensate for her mild discomfort of being in the same class as her—her much younger sibling.

"Pay dirt, finally!" exclaimed Ruby, excited as she directed Annie's waning attention to her find. It was a metal door fastened to a walled fence, no more than a few yards across from them. The string trail ended there, right under the door. It was just like Oleta Teytata had said.

What Ruby was secretly keeping from Annie was the fact that she had received a call on her cell phone from this classmate of theirs earlier. They had met in school and became casual acquaintances behind Annie's back. Oleta rang her up shortly after she arrived home. She told Ruby that she had valuable information to share as to Sammy's whereabouts… that is, if she could pay her price. Steep as twenty bucks sounded to her, she immediately agreed to deliver the money to Oleta tomorrow in exchange for the information she promised.

"Follow the blue string around the east side parking lot to a door leading to the back of the school," her enterprising classmate then told her over the phone. "That's where he will be." Seeing now how right she was, sent Ruby's heart a flutter.

"This was what Sammy was trying to find—the back of the school!" she declared enthusiastically, almost jumping for joy.

"How do you know that, Roobs? For that matter, and I've been meaning to ask since we got here, how did you know that we needed to follow the blue string to this place?"

"Some of my former classmates, who are now in the seventh grade, told me that Sammy had been walking around campus leaving a snaking trail of blue string behind him sometime around late this afternoon. That's how."

She was lying through her teeth when she disclosed this, feeling no remorse whatsoever as she did. All Ruby cared about was walking through that door and gazing upon Sammy's handsome face again. Her heart was beating hard against her chest, pounding even, the second she grabbed the handle and pulled on it. She was conflicted about what she was going to say to him. Should she apologize to him for not helping him out earlier when he needed to find the back of the school? Or should she just scratch that thought out and ignore it altogether?

"This is it," she whispered to herself before taking a deep breath to psyche herself up. "Courage, Ruby, courage."

The door gave way easily, not putting up a fight at all, but neither one of them expected to stumble upon what lay behind it. Seven men, thinned to the bone with prickly beards and clad in soiled business suits, were standing in their path, looming over them with bloodshot eyes that gravitated downwards to where they had paused, paralyzed and speechless.

"Sorry to bother you!" quickly apologized Annie in a huff, bowing politely at the puzzled adults prior to backing away to mount a hasty retreat. As equally flustered as Ruby was, who was in the forefront and closest to the men, she held her ground. Instead of shuffling her feet out of there, she instinctively decided on an entirely different approach which was to engage the strangers in conversation. It was her way whenever she got scared.

"Well, hello there," she greeted them pleasantly with a disarming smile. "I'm Ruby Pastrami, and I go to school here."

"Are you out of your flipping mind?" scolded Annie, who was livid and deathly pale as she frantically rushed to her sister's side in order to lock arms with her so that she could yank her away. "You just don't give away your personal information out to complete strangers! They may be pedophiles—or worse, serial killers!"

"I knew a Ruby Pastrami from my biology class," finally belted out one of the men in the back, a short stocky fellow with a toothless grin on his bearded face. "She was one of my students last year. Unfortunately, she didn't make the cut, so I gave her an 'F' as her final grade. I'm fairly certain that, thanks to me, she got held back. If you're her, then you're still in sixth grade, girl."

He looked nothing like she remembered him, but there was no mistaking the sniggering voice or those beady eyes of his that shrank her down to size like some mad scientist's shrink ray. She knew his name just like she knew her own, for she had cried it out many times when she had wept, that time when her tears flowed out uncontrollably like a raging river. Soon as she had heard a rumor that he wasn't coming back next year to teach because the Nanek Beast had somehow abducted him, she felt as if a thorn had been removed from her side. Relieved, she was eager to move on with her life and head on back to the sixth grade in spite of the embarrassment and shame that had scarred her for life. The first day had gone pretty well without a hitch, and now this. There was no doubt in her head that he was back from the dead—the very bane of her middle school existence.

"I did get held back, Mister Tully," glowered Ruby, restraining herself as her eyes suddenly began to water. "I'm still in the sixth grade, thank you very much. And as for the rest of your companions... you're the Terrors, aren't you?"

It was supposed to be a private joke to be used only in certain circles in the school, never intended for their ears to hear. Students would talk about them behind their backs and call them all sorts of names. That much they were aware of, being students once themselves before becoming the educators that they are today. In their own time, they invented names for their teachers too—mostly ones that got a laugh from friends. Like those who had come before them, they had been given funny names as well by the kids in their classes. It was no big deal really, since getting ridiculed by despondent students came with the job description of being a strict, no nonsense teacher.

There was one term of affection though that they particularly enjoyed, for they felt that it perfectly captured the essence of who they were—seven teachers who had banded together for the sole purpose of upholding academic excellence in their middle school. Collectively, they liked being referred to as the 'Terrors' for it meant that they were to be feared and not to be trifled with. Also, it was a fitting homage to their work, which basically consisted of failing as many sixth grade students as they could, so that only the best of the best get to advance to the seventh grade. Before they had all up and vanished last year without a clue, they had flunked more than half of that year's sixth grade class, ensuring that a solid majority of them got held back.

Although Annie had never experienced the dark reign of the Terrors herself, she had learned about their notorious exploits through her sister, Ruby, herself a victim of their stifling machinations. Legend even has it that these seven men used to meet in a cave in the nearby forest after school, where they would sit around a camp fire discussing who were doing good in class and who weren't. The cavern walls around them were rumored to be filled with picture portraits of the students whom they intended to flunk because of their poor performance in class. Some would even have exes on their faces in red ink, while those who were doing well—like the honor roll kids—would have gold star stickers pasted on them. Those who gave them grief in the classroom and talked back to them, on the other hand, had their photographs burned by the seven in the flames they had gathered themselves around.

"Yes, we are the Terrors," proudly owned up the tallest of the group, a beanpole of a man with a sinister looking grin and a wide forehead that stood out more prominently than the split ends sticking out of his curly black beard. "Everyone presumed we were dead, didn't they? That's too bad. Anyway, we're back now. And if you please, can you kindly point us to the nearest rest room?"

****

Sammy Tsunami was thinking about his mother, India, and how much he missed her when he felt his neck scream out at him with an intense smarting. He had scratched a nagging itch underneath his ear shortly before the tyrant started urgently demanding that he do something about it. Reaching for the red scarf below his chin, he felt that it had unknotted somehow and loosened, such that the Adam's apple on his scrawny throat was now exposed to the elements. Carved across it was a wound that was slowly opening up like a blooming flower.

If he seemed desperate to cover it up immediately with his scarf, he certainly did not show it—at least, not to his two cohorts who were walking ahead of him. He had fallen back purposely to fix his problem, which he was pretty sure he had caused when his fingers must have inadvertently pulled down at his scarf upon removing them from near his ear. As he fumbled to tie the cloth around his neck, his vision started to double, such that, when he looked down to see his shadow arrow on the ground, it had spawned a twin of itself! Fortunately, the aberration didn't last long. Soon as his scarf was in place, his seeing returned to normal.

24

A small frozen lake stood between them and their freedom.

Flanked by the snow covered forest with the mountains in the background climbing high into the black sandpaper sky, the ice rink glistened in the faint rays of the shrinking sun. Diamond glitters danced all over its reflective surface as if to entice travelers to tread on it with no worries. They belied the hidden danger of thin ice and the certain doom of the arctic waters that waited silently underneath.

Here, the air around them was electrified—so much so that even breathing produced tiny sparks that popped, then fizzled out as quickly as they appeared. It was their movement, however, that burdened them. Every stride they took was punished unmercifully by bothersome surges of static electricity, zapping them bit by little bit, and sometimes all at once. They stung— and sometimes singed them—but never failed to startle. The shock they gave was so sudden and so strong that, even though they would be gone the next instant, they would stop their very hearts from beating albeit briefly.

The worst thing about the place was, they had no choice but to move slowly, like tortoises in the sand. Nark found this out the hard way when he hurled himself a few yards ahead of the group.

Wrapped up in all the linen and all the sheets that he purloined from the cabin, he was pretty confident that he had ample protection against the hostile elements. He didn't get far across the ice though. Sparkles started exploding all around him, and soon, they did more than just char fabric—they burned them. Soon, Nark was engulfed in flames and had to discard his make-do winter protection, leaving him cold, vulnerable and exposed.

"How far?" Sammy asked, turning to the travelling companion on his right. Shadow Ranger didn't answer his question because this was the eight time in a span of thirty minutes. The boy wasn't aware of it though, for he was walking with his thoughts drifting elsewhere. He was chilly, and it had become something of a reflex action for him to just blurt out the same things over and over again.

"How far?"

Nobody stopped and thought about how strange it was how charged the air was, considering that the lake was covered in ice for some miles and an arctic wind was blowing. The bottom line was, the cool air was supposed to be humid, not extremely dry like in an arid desert. It boggled the mind that these contrasting climate conditions were able to mix and match, and co-exist simultaneously. It was anything but natural.

When it finally hit Sammy, he was able to recall back the last time he experienced something like this. Although on a much smaller scale and not as pronounced, it was in the classroom earlier when Mrs. Galactrix just up and disappeared in a billowing cloud of purple smoke. Realizing this after connecting all the dots, he suddenly felt an overwhelming sense of trepidation seize him. Not only was he trembling now from the bitter cold, he was shaking copiously from the terror that was welling up inside of him.

"Over there!" hollered Nark, directing everyone's attention to a some kind of flat stonework structure in the distance, the only thing of sizeable significance for miles in the middle of the snowy steppes that was on the other side of the icy border. "It's some sort of shelter we can take refuge in! Come on!"

Brimming with excitement over his find, the dwarf picked up his pace. He didn't care about the sparks that popped and fizzled out all around him, nor did he mind their much larger siblings—the sparkles—that were trying to build actual fires on his clothes. All he cared about was a place for him to rest, for he was tired and hungry and couldn't go on any longer. Channeling all of his remaining strength into his short, aching legs and feet, he walked briskly, swinging his arms, just as he felt the moist ground beneath him rumble and shift. "Watch out!"

The brittle ice cracked—here, there and everywhere— sparing them no breathing room, no respite, and no chance of ever surviving. They were as fast as their feet would carry them. It didn't matter anymore that the air electrified them or the slippery surface underneath threatened to flatten them on their backs. It was a run of life and death, and for the slow ones, only an icy grave awaited.

"Pick up your pace!" telepathically yelled Shadow Ranger to the two lagging behind, who were trailing her by a considerable distance. "Death catches the slow!"

Although the ice all around them was shattering feverishly, creating smaller pieces out of even smaller pieces second after passing second, Nark and Sammy managed to keep their heads cool and maintain an even, cautious pace. It was a tricky tightrope to finish. While there was a pressing urgency for them to make it quickly across in the shortest possible time, the danger of falling on the ice-or even taking a dive into the subzero freezing waters beneath it, should it break—was something they couldn't ignore. Haste not only made waste in this case, it spelled death.

"Hurry up! There is no time! No walking! Run, run, run!"

She was right, of course. There was no time. Not long after she streamed these thoughts of hers into their stubborn noggins did the earth open up a gaping crater in the middle of the disintegrating rink. The force of the tumultuous upheaval that accompanied the thunderous explosion sent both Nark and Sammy hurtling through the air and crashing hard on the mound outcropping beside the vanishing icy fringes.

"Get up!" Shadow Ranger directed the two, who were still reeling from their hard fall. "Quickly now! He's here!"

From the deepest bowels of the crater rose a towering figure cloaked entirely in black and heart-stoppingly hideous. There was no mistaking who it was in Sammy's eyes, nor in Nark's—even though it had a gaping pink lesion on the top of one of its sagging scaly arms and a vacant eye socket on the left side. It was Rular, returned from the dead and massive as a mountain.

"My two favorite people, what a coincidence!" the giant contemptuously and disdainfully snarled, hunching his head downwards to see with his one good eye what tiny insects his foes had become from his lofty position scarping the skies.

"Nark, my former master, what a pleasure!" the monster continued with a toothy grin. "I've done your bidding obediently for years, while you've had my gemstone in your possession. I was a faithful and reliable genie, wasn't I? I would emerge from your magic lamp every time you rubbed it. But not anymore. Your magic lamp—the Nanek Crystal—is no longer within your reach! It is now gone—shattered! Such irony that it even turned on you and brought you here to the Ghostwells, my home and place of power. Here, I am a deity—a god! The elements in this world are mine to command! That said, it is truly unfortunate for you that you are now here, trapped in this place with me. You have no idea just how long I've thought about exacting my revenge on you; You have no idea just how long I will be exacting my revenge on you."

"Come on, Nark, we have to move!" coached Sammy, quickly rising to his feet where, without any spectacle or fanfare to trumpet its return, a familiar quiet friend of his decided to reappear again from out of the blue, to his astonishment and immense joy. "So you go off, make me miss you, and come back every time I'm in danger, eh? That arrangement suits me just fine, let's go!"

His shadow arrow prodded him forward, but he needed a minute to glance over his shoulder to properly marvel at how unbelievably tall Rular had become. He wanted to make sure that the monster was still missing an eye, the one that he took out. And it was. It even bore the wounds that his shadow arrow made—the gaping wound on the left serpent's body and the hole in the center of its still head, the one where the killing blow had been delivered.

Even in dull monochrome, the Nanek Beast lost none of its nightmarish allure. When it lashed out with its only good arm—the gigantic boa constrictor on its right—it practically shredded the atmosphere itself in a thunderous din. Seeing the black sandpaper sky ripped asunder, like crepe paper, paralyzed Nark, so much so that the small boy couldn't do anything else, but watch helplessly as the broken fangs protruding from out of the serpent's cavernous mouth rained down on him like a pair of fast hurtling meteors.

"No feeding the snakes!" hollered Sammy, as he snatched Nark away in the nick of time by the collar of his parka. By the time, the humongous reptile snapped its jaws shut to feast, his dwarfish friend was already hitching a ride safely on his back, and they were off behind Shadow Ranger who led from a few paces away.

25

"They're not going to make it!" hysterically observed a woman, as she helplessly watched two tiny figures advance in her general direction from a considerable distance. The three were crossing the blinding snow atop an elevated slope, tripping over themselves then getting back up again, scampering to get away. For behind them, hot on their tails but moving at a slow and steady pace, was a monstrous colossus the size of a modest skyscraper, roughly.

"We'll see," calmly replied the man beside her, as he raised his binoculars to take another look. By the time he saw them again through the magnifying lenses, they were falling down the slanted terrain, tumbling and turning, moving closer to where he was at—at a rapid, insane pace.

"They're on their way to us!" he then excitedly declared, tossing the binoculars aside as he left the woman alone on the rooftop, and rushed down the stairs. "We have to welcome them!"

****

Sammy Tsunami was at it again. He was cold to the very marrow of his bones, his muscles throbbed from the bruises and cuts that riddled his battered body, and to top it off—he was so hungry that he could hardly stand.

ROARRR!!!

He was alive though, which counted for something—even though his stomach begged to disagree. Seeing that Nark was too, just fast asleep beside him under a thin blanket of snow, Sammy felt relieved and grateful for the second chance that they both got—though it came at a high price.

Recent events that led to both of them being stranded in front of the entrance way of a granite building, right in the middle of a snow covered basin, all happened so fast that he was at a loss trying to reconstruct them all from brute memory in perfect detail.

All Sammy could remember was moving as fast as he could across the treacherous snow with Nark on piggyback. Right behind them and closing in was Rular, now a massive fifty-foot sci-fi monster in his humble estimate, getting ready for another attack. That was when Sammy had the brilliant idea of distracting him by throwing him something he might want to catch, something important to the monster and stolen from him.

That 'something' that he had in mind was the eye the boy plucked out earlier from the Nanek Beast's eye socket back in the computer room. He took it out of his pocket and was about to hurl it away, when Shadow Ranger feverishly pulled alongside him and shook her faceless head at him—profusely.

"Don't waste that!" she cautioned the boy, who hesitated then backed down. "That's your ace up your sleeve! Save it for later!"

After she said this, the next thing Sammy knew was that they were all rolling down the side of some steep hill. It was a long, endless fall that got them many souvenir injuries along the way, cuts and bruises and other whatnots. In the hurly burly of it all, he dropped the eye somewhere he couldn't remember. It just slipped out of his grip.

"Are you both alright?"

Shadow Ranger was a welcome sight to Sammy's eyes. She stood over him like a sentinel, tall and slender and strong. In his eyes, she was larger than life itself.

"I lost the eye." Sammy confessed sullenly. "It slipped out of my hand when we were tumbling down the slope. Sorry."

"You mean this eye?"

She tossed it over to him, but he never caught it, tried as hard as he did. That was because there was really no eye. And Shadow Ranger standing in front him was only a figment of his imagination—never really there. Realizing this, tears streamed out of Sammy's watery eyes as he thought back to the actual recent events that *really happened.*

"Don't waste that! That's your ace up your sleeve! Save it for later!"

When Shadow Ranger said these words to him after pulling

alongside of him on the run, it was already too late. Sammy had already hurled the eye into the distant plains, hoping that the enormous creature after them would be distracted and would go after it.

It didn't take the bait, probably because it couldn't see the tiny white ball hurtling through the air. Too small and too inconsequential, it was invisible to the line of vision of a giant. What the monster did instead was go for the kill.

Diving through the air at breakneck speed straight into Sammy and Nark, the large boa constrictor widened its already gaping mouth to prepare its venomous incisors, chipped as they were, for the bite. It was dead on target, and the two boys would have most certainly bought the farm where they stood motionless and stupefied—had Shadow Ranger not shielded them away from the serpent's poison-soaked fangs!

NOOOOOO!!!!

Sammy was screaming at the top of his lungs as he lost his footing and his balance. The snow covered surface beneath him had just collapsed, taking him and Nark down a slippery slope of hard and sharp ice. The last image Sammy saw before he blocked out from the pain was the serpent aiming its snout straight up at the black sandpaper sky as it ravenously swallowed the limp body of Shadow Ranger—the torso first, then the legs.

****

"Get inside—quickly!"

The next thing Sammy knew was Mister Dojo dragging

him through the main entrance of the building, while Mrs. Galactrix followed closely, carrying the unconscious body of Nark in her arms like a rag doll.

They were both in color, like Nark and himself, standing out from the black and white backdrop which meant that they couldn't be any of one of those shapeless evils that they encountered in the woods earlier. Knowing this gave Sammy some mild relief from his emotional discomfort.

Before the great wooden door behind them could swing to a close, Sammy managed to catch a couple of disturbing images outside that soldered themselves into his mind forever.

A wild tempest now raged above the elevated fringes of the basin. Snow, hail and rain beat down hard, combining together to form a massive curtain of some sort. Although it wasn't nearly thick enough to hide away the enormous outlandish silhouette of the Nanek Beast itself, it was tough enough to repel even the monster's most aggressive advances—acting like a shield somewhat against its every attack.

Tough as it was though against its relentless poundings and hammerings, the earth did still quake inside the basin, so much so that the building itself in its hollow center quavered feverishly with every strike the monster fiercely landed.

"You're both safe in here!" Mister Dojo hastily declared as he let go of Sammy's arm. "This is a haven. That thing out there can't get past the alchemystical defenses in place outside… at least for now."

"But not for long though," Mrs. Galactrix playfully cut in,

shortly after laying Nark down gently on the cracked stone floor that was littered with rubble and all sorts of debris, "which is why we all have to make our escape—with not a minute to lose, boys!"

Although she looked like she had been through hell, with the dirt smothered face, the soiled clothes and the disheveled hair combining to eclipse her natural beauty, Mrs. Galactrix still managed to maintain an air of respectability about her. She kept her good posture and her imposing stance, not to mention her signature cheerful flair which was refreshing for Sammy, who desperately needed a ray of hope he could believe in, especially now that the world all around him was going to pieces.

"And we certainly will in a while, Gailforce," Mister Dojo happily concurred before setting his sights on Sammy. "You'll be pleased to know, Sammy, that all the missing teachers that have been exiled to this drab and dull dimension have all since returned back to our vibrantly colorful world. They're all perfectly alright and safe. Mrs. Galactrix here was kind enough to stay behind to make sure that you two got out safely as well. It's a good thing for you too that you will all be able to return home and very soon."

"All thanks to Mister Dojo over here!" proudly proclaimed Mrs. Galactrix, beaming like a beauty pageant winner with her full set of sparkling pearly whites on display. "He saved us all, he did. He opened a doorway leading back to our dimension.

It's located down in the basement. Let's all go there right now, shall we?"

Although she said it with such winsome charm, her words were urgent. Behind the pleasing smile and sunny disposition, there was an unmistakable aggression in her tone and intonation. If she could just twist their arms to make them leave with her right now, she would have. But she was much too nice a person to resort to actual physical violence.

"It was nothing really," Mister Dojo laughed with false humility, tickled pink by the generous praises openly bestowed upon him. "When I got here, I had your ball of yarn, Sammy, tucked in my pocket. The string didn't break when the portal that brought me here closed. The doorway just shrank around the thread, enough to strangle it but not cut it."

Like Mrs. Galactrix, Mister Dojo has seen better days. Although his clothes were definitely in a more ragged and tattered condition than hers were, his round mug looked equally as sullied and stressed. In fact, it even seemed almost gaunt, as if he had dropped a few pounds or so.

"I was able to expand the doorway again so that it could admit one person through at a time. Unfortunately, it won't stay open for long. Once it shrinks around the string again, I won't be able to enlarge it anymore because the wielder of the alchemystic stone can only do it once and only once in his entire lifetime, and no more."

"Are you saying that you have the Nanek Crystal in your possession?" earnestly asked Sammy, genuinely surprised but still highly doubtful of the old man's preposterous claim that the gemstone was in one piece. More than this, he was struggling to come to grips with the old man's alleged powers of opening up inter-dimensional doorways. "But I saw it shatter before my eyes! How is it possible that it has been remade?"

"Alchemagic," tersely explained the old man, beaming as he flaunted what looked like a tiny, poorly cut amethyst for the boy to behold. There was no doubt in Sammy's mind the moment he saw it that it was the Nanek Crystal itself, just that it no longer appeared to be its original, undamaged self. Appearance-wise, it looked as if its broken shards had been haphazardly glued together by cement adhesive. As such, it was no longer smooth, but rough hewn with a lot of sharp edges jutting out here and there.

"That's just wonderful!" Sammy then sounded out, relieved to see the alchemystic stone in one piece, although it was more like several pieces made into one. For a while there, he was worried that it may have lost some of its potency, given its damaged condition, but after recalling what the old man said about using it not too long ago to reopen the portal that would get them back home, those anxieties that troubled him just quickly dissipated.

"We really should be off, fellows," she insisted, maintaining a gleeful expression on her gaunt face. Shortly after appealing to them to leave, a violent earthquake rocked the very foundations of the school, stirring everyone to a mad panic.

While Mister Dojo scampered for cover, terrified that

the roof might collapse on his head, Sammy busied himself catching his homeroom teacher, who lost her balance the second the floor split into two. She was right about to crack her cranium on the hard surface below when he managed to grab a hold of her.

"Are you alright, ma'am?" he asked her politely, tenderly putting her down. Although the tremors quickly subsided, she was shaking like a leaf from the fright. "I'll be fine," she replied, still traumatized from the shock. "The string… where's the string?"

She was in a stupor when she uttered those words. Hunkering down, she combed the floor for any trace of what she was looking for, searching every rubble-cluttered corner. When she found a short gray thread extending from right under a collapsed wall, her expression switched from distressed to chipper. Pulling at it, she was shocked to discover that the other end from beneath the wreckage was cut.

"I'm sorry, Gailforce." With a sullen expression on his wrinkled face, Mister Dojo discarded the ball of yarn in his hand by setting it down on the floor, the end of its string likewise cut and practically useless now. Immediately after seeing this, Mrs, Galactrix stared at the piece of thread fastened between her fingers, the very same one she extracted from underneath the wall, and let out a bloodcurdling scream. At exactly that moment, the ground shook fiercely again, rattling the building. Unlike the previous one, this aftershock was much stronger, such that the ceiling itself had partially cracked open.

"The exit's been blocked and the string's been cut!" she hysterically blathered out loud, her eyes bloodshot and her heart racing. "Even if we take another way, we won't be able to retrace our steps, not without the string trail on the floor! This place is like a maze, or did you conveniently forget that fact?"

With all the rubble lying around and the walls themselves close to being rubble themselves, Sammy couldn't tell whether the ramblings of his teacher about the quake ravaged structure were true or not. The interiors were too dimly lit and a mess to tell for sure.

"Calm down, Gailforce, please! We need to think our way out of here. Panicking won't get us anywhere."

"For your information, if it isn't plainly obvious yet," she told him off sardonically, "this place is collapsing as we speak, so we don't have the luxury of time to think!"

They were blathering something to each other that Sammy wasn't sure of, when still another quake came out of nowhere and knocked them viciously on their backsides. Not only did their sudden fall hurt them, it also cost them the Nanek Crystal which fell from Mister Dojo's sweaty grip and into a narrow crack on the floor, disappearing into it like a flame snuffed out.

"Don't worry," pledged the old man after witnessing in shock the loss of his precious crystal gem. "We don't need it anymore! As long as the doorway stays open, we'll be fine!"

"Assuming that we can get to it in time!" countered Mrs.

Galactrix, trembling at the secret thought she held in her head.

She was yelling something else out loud at the top of her voice that it was like thunder rolling indoors. Sammy tried to appease her by telling her that everything would be alright, but she ignored him deliberately. Too engaged in her heated exchange with the principal, there was no stopping Mrs. Galactrix from firing her mouth off. Fed up with all the quarrelling, the boy decided to brusquely interrupt the adults, when someone else from out of the blue unexpectedly did his own dirty work for him.

26

"What are you two babbling about?" irately asked Nark, still a bit sleepy as he stood up and rubbed the sand out of his drooping eyes. When they finally widened and saw the pair of teachers arguing next to Sammy, he instinctively recoiled out of a strong sense of self-preservation, almost losing his balance in the process as he scrambled for a wall to lean on. His face turned pasty white and his breath chilled. The second they turned their attention towards him, he was paralyzed from the waist down.

"I thought I killed the both of you!" he shrieked, as the earth under him rumbled and shook. "I willed my Nanek Crystal to send you away, I did! How is it possible that you are both standing here right now?"

"So this is all your fault then!" snapped Mrs. Galactrix, goose-stepping her way towards Nark, whom she promptly lifted up by the collar with both hands to bring him closer and to eye level.

"You did me a grievous wrong, Nark! I flunked you in algebra for three consecutive years in a row because you couldn't grasp the basics of the subject matter! It's downright embarrassing because you don't even try! You got held back because you refused to study and learn your lessons—not because your teachers are out to get you, you paranoid little scoundrel! Now, send me back home or else you're going to get something far worse than a time out or a detention from me! I'm going to recommend you for immediate suspension and possible expulsion! How's that sound?"

Nark mumbled something inaudible, then shifted his sights to Sammy and Mister Dojo, who were quietly by themselves in a corner. The earthquakes were getting stronger and stronger now, that the ceiling and the walls were shaking off more dust than ever before. Noting this curious development, Mister Dojo approached Mrs. Galactrix casually, clearing his throat first before attempting to say anything.

"I'm not going to approve any of those recommendations," Mister Dojo adamantly announced as he watched Nark squirm in her clutches, his small feet dangling a couple of inches above the dirty floor. "I'm sorry again, Gailforce, but no can do those."

"But, Mister Dojo, you're the principal!" Mrs. Galactrix pleaded, turning her head to him and away from Nark, who was silently motioning Sammy in secret to come to his aid. "Surely, this naughty student deserves some sort of harsher punishment!"

"Yes, he does, Gailforce. I completely agree with you. But I can't punish myself. I just can't!"

"What do you mean, Mister Dojo?"

Mister Dojo stared upwards at the cracked ceiling and got pelted with flecks of dust on his tomato nose for his troubles. He exhaled a heavy sigh before finally facing off with Mrs. Galactrix, who carefully scrutinized him with much bewilderment.

"He's me, you see," he began his explanation calmly, "me from fifty years ago."

****

"What?" snapped Mrs. Galactrix, reeling from a state of shock as she dropped the dwarfish lad on the floor like a sack of rocks. "This is some kind of joke, right?" she pressed on, convinced that the old man was playing a prank on her. "You certainly have quite a sense of humor there, but please be serious for a moment."

"I tell you no lie," wistfully assured Mister Dojo with a somber expression written all over his face. "I'm a time traveler, you see from fifty years from now. If I punish Nark like you'd want me to, I'd be messing with the whole space-time continuum and all that."

"So not true!" crossly protested Nark, cutting off Mrs. Galactrix right before she could tell Mister Dojo that he was full of crap. "How can I possibly grow up to be... you! For one, we don't look alike! We don't have the same nose, for starters!"

Nark's nose was wide, somewhat squished, and unpleasant

looking. Mister Dojo's, on the other hand, was hefty, reddish, tomato-like, and even more unpleasant looking.

"A large flying orange insect did this," the old man was quick to point out, fingering the tip of his ginormous nose. "It happened when I was around thirty-five years old which you will be too, soon enough, a few years down the road. I was hunting for game in the rainforests of Kancel when I stumbled upon this curiously shaped colored egg. As soon as I touched it, it immediately hatched and the newborn inside flew out and stung me. From that day forward, it never really quite healed. I think it looks better though compared to your flattened nose, Narky-boy, won't you agree?"

"I'm not stupid like you to have my nose bitten by some insect! You're just plain too dumb, old man!"

"You keep complaining about dying because of that disease you have that rapidly ages you, and now that you've seen yourself still alive fifty years from now, you have the nerve to say that it's not good enough!" Mister Dojo angrily scolded Nark, bursting a couple of blood vessels in the course of his blood-racing lecture. "You're a stupid boy, Narky-boy! A very, very stupid boy!"

"Well, at least, I'll be smart enough not to turn into you," Nark quickly chucked back conceitedly. "Turning into you is far worse than dying young!"

"Why you, ungrateful piece of flaming poop! You'll get your comeuppance, Narky-boy! You'll get your comeuppance!!!"

QUIET!!!

If Sammy could applaud Mrs. Galactrix for silencing the two, he would have. But his hands were tied trying to pry open a locked door his shadow arrow was pointing to. He had been hard at work at it while his three other companions bickered among themselves and passed the blame around for getting stranded in this nowhere place…

CLICK.

"I opened it!" proudly announced Sammy, throwing the door wide open for everyone to see. "Come with me," he quickly added before prodding everyone with a wave of a hand to follow.

As soon as he said this, they all turned to him, tongue-tied and astonished by his achievement. They were about to ask him if he thought that this was the right way to go, but before they could do so, a series of violent tremors brutally rattled the building, one after another. They were so alarmed by this dangerous development that they decided to skip the question and answer portion, and just go wherever Sammy led them.

****

"This way! Hurry!"

Tremor after stronger tremor rocked the very foundations of the building, sending bits and pieces of the ceiling raining down on them in clouds of sawdust. Soon, whole sections of walls crumbled around them, sometimes collapsing altogether like dominos. This prompted them from time to time to make detours every now and then, here and there—all at the expert direction, of course, of Sammy's shadow arrow which pointed the way.

As they scuttled across and around the winding and twisting corridors in search of the portal that Mister Dojo opened and left behind, they skirted a corner to arrive at one last narrow hallway which had a rather inviting fire exit at the very end. Curiously, the ceiling overhead in this area looked like a jumble of slabs loosely sewn together. Noting its dismal appearance, there was no doubt in any of their minds that it was close to caving in at any second now, which meant that they had to hurry if they were ever going to make it across safely.

"Over here!" hollered Sammy, gesturing to the others to hurriedly come to him as he flung open the door of the fire exit. As soon as did, Mister Dojo sped past him and everyone else, moving like a blur. In his excitement and haste, the old man ended up diving, head first, through the gaping entry like it was a pool of water. As a result of his devil may care, throw caution to the wind, mindless stunt, the old man found himself toppling down a short flight of stairs.

"You should be more careful!" Mrs. Galactrix sternly chastised him, while Nark burst out into gut wrenching laughter. "You are the principal, and you're setting a bad example for the children!"

She then shunned him and went on her way, Sammy dogging her as soon as he was done helping Mister Dojo back to his feet. The old man didn't follow the two, however, letting them trudge on ahead so that he can have a quick word with

Nark alone. He dusted himself off, and gave his much shorter younger self a castigating stare for the rudeness he displayed so openly beforehand.

"You're gonna feel that years from now, Narky-boy."

"But I'm not you right now, am I?" Nark said with a mean chuckle. "And don't you worry about me making the same mistake because I won't! Trust me... if you're really me, that is."

Instead of snapping back, the old man let out a hearty bwa-ha-ha-ha to the point that he was driven to tears. "So you've finally accepted the truth that I'm indeed you fifty years from now, eh?" he said triumphantly prior to sticking a finger into his mouth, reaching deep down in there. "Ngood Ngoo Ngow."

PTUI!

From out of Mister Dojo's lips and into his open palm, a blood drenched *gold* tooth was forcefully spat out, a molar of considerable size and weight. It glinted in the soft white light as the old man lifted it up for Nark to see. There was little doubt in both their minds that it was precious and expensive. The small boy himself couldn't help but be dazzled by its radiance and magnificence.

"Lost a tooth," he declared proudly, tossing it over to his impish companion who caught it immediately in one hand. "Keep it or sell it, it's up to you. That will bring you a pretty price, that's for sure. Or better yet, hold on to it for good luck for a little while longer! Nothing brings good luck like gold!"

Mesmerized by the golden trinket that he cupped in his stubby hand, whose pricey color stood out most gloriously in their drab and monochrome world, Nark didn't mind at all that it was all stained in inky black blood. It was his, a present given to him, and that was all that mattered.

"I should push you down the stairs more often from now on," Nark joked, hiding his prize away in his pocket. "Either that, or I'll use a pair of pliers to pull out all those gold teeth of yours."

Soon as he finished ribbing the old man, another nasty tremor shook the building, this time more vicious than the ones that came shortly before. They had to hurry as fast as they could to get to the lowest part of the structure—which they barely did and in just the nick of time! One second too late, and all three floors of the entire building itself would have come crashing down hard on them, flattening them like pancakes.

"That was close," Mrs. Galactrix exhaled, the air streaming out of her lungs cold as ice, as she surveyed what was left of the roof which was now hanging mere inches away from the top of their heads.

While everyone else, including Sammy, couldn't veer away from the remnants of the catastrophe that was dangling treacherously over their imperiled heads, Mister Dojo headed over alone to a nearby corner where a gleaming crack on the floor beckoned him.

It radiated a soft lavender glow that thinned and waned, as the hole itself shrunk by a few centimeters with each passing second. Sticking out of it, like a tongue, was a shadowy thread that slithered a few feet across the broken floor before ending behind a small pile of rubble next to what remained of a stone wall.

"Everyone come, except for Nark," Mister Dojo urgently instructed as he ushered Sammy and Mrs. Galactrix over to the bright, shimmering purple gash on the floor.

"Hurry, before it closes! And you, Nark, you stay here."

Nark himself wasn't listening, his mind elsewhere. The thing that had him captivated so much was the unnatural breach of light lying on the ground. Purple was the only other color, other than gold, that had enthralled him so in this bland, pale and gloomy reality. If he could only covet his plum discovery for himself, like he did the gold tooth, and slip it also into his pocket, he would have certainly done so already.

"Why can't Nark come with us?" inquired Mrs. Galactrix, unable to accept Mister Dojo's capricious and whimsical decision to abandon behind one of her students. "He can't stay here. It's a dangerous place."

"Because he needs to finish some unfinished business, Gailforce, that's why," answered back the old man, as he picked up the end of the shadow thread from the stony surface. "Besides, by the time that he's done with what he needs to do, the doorway will still be open to take him back to our world."

"You want me to die here?" furiously complained Nark, throwing his face at the old man in a show of defiance. "I thought you said that I was you in a bazillion years or so from now. If I get killed out here, there won't be a you, you know? I hope you realize that!"

"True," agreed Mister Dojo, who led Mrs. Galactrix gently down the breach with the assistance of Sammy, who kept mum as he overheard the confrontation between the two unfold with quiet disinterest. "But although my memory is quite faulty right now, I distinctly remember beating that monster out there—all by myself. So you should be good."

"Regardless of that, Nark should come with us," Mrs. Galactrix grimly asserted, still not quite restored to her normal congenial self. "Nobody should be left behind in this awful place—nobody!"

The old man mouthed something inaudible as he ambled over to a nearby gutted corner. He needed a moment alone because he was at his wits' end on how to properly explain himself. He was right about ready to begin composing what he needed to say in his head, when Nark returned to the fore with a few more things on his mind.

"So you want me to stay, so that I can go out there and trash that thing, am I right?" Nark clarified, looking peeved and petulant. "Are you crazy? It's suicide! That thing killed Sammy's shadow maid, and she had more skills than I do when it comes to handling these sorts of crazies!"

Strong feelings of deep sorrow swept over Sammy when his ears caught Nark mention Shadow Ranger. For the longest last couple of minutes of his life, he has tried his best to keep it together and block out all thoughts of his mother's shade, now fallen and lost. As the still fresh memories of her sudden and tragic passing surfaced again, no thanks to Nark's callous reminder, his chest tightened and his breath became thin and sparse.

"Nark should come with us even though he's been naughty," Mrs. Galactrix demanded before her legs slipped through the lustrous purple portal, which was now half the size of what it was and still shrinking. "Please, Mister Dojo," she begged, as she slowly sank into the shining orifice, "He's just a boy and we all saw what that monster out there is capable of."

"Trust me, Gailforce, it'll all be fine," Mister Dojo reassured her, before nudging her in. As soon as she was through, a horrifying thing happened that left him suddenly cold and deathly pale.

Without warning, the opening suddenly contracted to a close, completely vanishing into thin air until only the string that hung out of it remained. Although it appeared to have been cut, it really wasn't. The end of the thread remained suspended over the floor at the exact place where the portal was, still anchored at the other end of the sealed rift by some unseen rock.

"That's not good," The old man remarked wearily, turning afterwards to Sammy who was tugging feverishly on his arm. "What is it, kiddo? Are you just as worried as I am that we will never get out of this godforsaken place?"

"Nark's gone!" the boy told him with a whimper. "He fled while you and Mrs. Galactrix were conversing."

27

Finding a way back up wasn't easy—supposedly. With the entire building nothing but a smoking burial mound right now, everything breathing beneath all three compressed stories was either a corpse… or as good as one. Those slim chances didn't stop either Mister Dojo or Sammy though from getting out of there alive.

"If Nark didn't scuttle off like that, we would probably be gone from this gloomy place right now," whined Sammy as he cheerlessly scrambled out a pipe hole, clearing the obstructing debris along the way. "Why did he have to do that? Why did *you* have to do that?"

He was rebuking Mister Dojo for his past blunder, assuming that he was indeed Nark in his childhood. Although Sammy found this difficult to believe, he also found it hard to embrace the esoteric concept of alchemysticism or the fantastical shadow realm that he was trapped in called the Ghostwells.

"H-he n-needs t-to," stammered the old man, sounding like a lump was stuck in his throat. He emerged right after Sammy into the white emptiness of the basin, limping, breathing hard, exhausted—and cold. The last thing he expected was crawling up a freezing metal tube for several yards to get back to the surface above. Had he known earlier about the glacial conditions of his crawl space, he would have tried to persuade Sammy to take some other... warmer route.

"If you're really Nark, then you must have known that he came this way," stressed Sammy, fingering out the small footprints in the snow leading away from them for miles.

Sammy was anything but happy with the old man, especially with what just happened down there in the basement. As bad as it was that the purple glowing doorway had closed shut, trapping them in the Ghostwells forever, he also has to endure his enigmatic temperament, which was slowly driving him insane. It didn't help at all either that he was missing his mother gravely. Knowing that he will never see her austere and saintly face again, he resigned himself to his abysmal fate as the sidekick of Mister Dojo.

"He did come this way," confirmed the old man, stepping beside Sammy who had already began following the faint trail of footprints he was certain Nark left behind. "His strides are short, so we won't have any problem catching up with him."

As they moved together at an accelerated pace, Sammy thought back to how they managed to escape the deathly stone coffin that was the basement of the earthquake flattened building. He recalled the events clearly, which started with the doorway closing up before its expected time. Shortly after that happened, a dense darkness swallowed them up whole—but not before Sammy spotted Nark crawling under a crack in the wall and alerted Mister Dojo to his escape. Fortunately for both the old man and the boy, the golden diamond prints on Sammy's black sweater emitted a faint light that enabled them to see where they were going—and more importantly— Sammy's shadow arrow. It guided them down a number of snaking corridors prior to ultimately leading them into a flooded room, much larger than the basement that they came from, with several large open drain pipes depositing melted snow in small trickling quantities into the stagnant pool.

Unfortunately, Sammy's shadow arrow was averse to water. As such, it turned shy and immediately evaporated the second Sammy waded his feet into the pool, which was cold as death itself. Without a clue as to where to go next, he consulted Mister Dojo for answers. To his dismay, however, the old man gave him none.

"You're supposed to know where to go, right?" he grumbled in frustration to Mister Dojo, who could only scratch his bald head and smile sheepishly back. "I don't remember, which pipe to take," the old man replied with great embarrassment. "My memory's not as good as it used to be! That's why I had to insist that you take the ball of yarn with you. Without the string trail that you left behind, I wouldn't have made it through the labyrinth to the back of the school. As for this particular case, hmmm, the way up back could be any one of these darn pipes!"

Infuriated as he was with Mister Dojo developing selective

amnesia at such a crucial time, Sammy soldiered on, investigating each and every one of the pipes for signs that Nark had gone through them. After a thorough and exhaustive search—that had him enduring the freezing waters of the inundated area for over half an hour or so—he eventually found two that had handprints and footprints on their icy surfaces. Figuring that his dwarfish pal had crawled up either one, he tested out a pipe candidate to see where it led. Luckily, it took him straight up to the basin, which is where they were now since five minutes ago.

****

"I knew he could do it."

Pride swelled in Mister Dojo's heart when he saw his younger self from afar plodding through the snow and clambering up the slopes towards the tempest that raged at the summit of the basin. Nark had quietly abandoned the rest of the party, while they discussed him among themselves, in order to get a head start on what he meant to do. It was clear from the direction he was headed in that his intent was to face his former genie alone—the Nanek Beast itself, which stood like a dark tower on the periphery awaiting for his arrival.

"He's going to get himself killed!" grunted Sammy, strutting off after Nark at a furious pace. "Can't you at least be worried?"

"He'll live," promised the old man, catching his short breath as he tried to keep in step with the boy, who quickly put ten paces between them both with no effort at all. "Hey, wait up over there! Let's walk together, okay? My legs are shorter than yours so give this old dude a break, kiddo!"

"So Nark's really you, eh?" Sammy stopped and waited for the old man to catch up. For someone of his stumpy height and advanced age, he was no pushover in the brisk walking department. His gait though was like a duck's, funny but not funny enough to merit a few laughs.

"Right-a-mundo you are, kiddo!" Mister Dojo corroborated, not annoyed at all that Sammy continued to doubt him. As soon as he pulled alongside Sammy, the boy started shuffling his feet again.

"The tremors have stopped," Sammy observed, stating the obvious in the hope of goading the old man into answering him why they just did. He had an inkling that Rular had granted Nark safe passage, so that they could properly meet and talk and probably kill each other—with the odds favoring the fifty foot behemoth as opposed to the four foot dwarf who was bravely making his way to the slaughterhouse.

"Out of respect, he stopped," the old man calmly confirmed, alluding to the monster. "See the tempest over there!" he then pointed out, shooting a stern finger right at the fogged up sky that had much storm activity raging on behind it. "It's all over the basin, but we're not wet, see? Do you wonder why it's not snowing or raining or hailing in here?"

"Why?" routinely asked Sammy, although he already had an idea what the answer was. The last time he was outside the building, he never really bothered to look behind him or up. Now that he has had that chance to do so, he was amazed to discover that the basin was enclosed in some kind of glass dome that conveniently kept the elements out—and Rular himself out as well.

"The tempest is an alchemystical creation designed to protect this sanctuary from attacks launched by shadow adversaries like our gigantic friend over there," the old man explained enthusiastically, while keeping both his hawkish eyes peeled and concentrated on Nark's back, which was moving up the precipitous snow blanketed landscape faster than he expected it to.

"It creates an alchemagically charged electromagnetic field—a force field, if you will—that repels all those native to the Ghostwells from entering. I know you mourn your mother's shade, Sammy, but it wouldn't have made it through here with you. I'm sorry."

How Mister Dojo could have possibly known about Shadow Ranger stirred up a lot of mixed feelings inside Sammy, foremost of which was a profound sense of admiration. In the short spell of time that he had known the old man, he thought he was a joke, a laughing stock students could take a jab at whenever they needed some levity in their lives.

When he first met him earlier that the morning, the old man was nothing more than an inept bus driver, who had a tendency of dozing off at the wheel and driving like a maniac on the road. As the school day progressed, however, Sammy discovered that the old man wore many hats. He was the lunch lady at the cafeteria, the substitute math teacher, the janitor, and even the principal himself! Although Mister Dojo played each of his previous roles as a ham and comic foil, he certainly wasn't one now—at least in Sammy's eyes.

"Yeah, she died a hero," Sammy proudly remarked, referring to Shadow Ranger who had made the supreme sacrifice to save his life. The mere mention of her depressed him so much, that the boy needed to change the topic—and quick! The last thing he wanted was to dwell on her recent bereavement and wallow in despair.

"What's with the string by the way?" he then said, steering the conversation away to his favor.

It was wound securely around Mister Dojo's hand with one end free, extending all the way back to the back of the building. Shadowy gray in color, it appeared like the shadow of some other stretched out, elongated thread which didn't exist. Flaunting it at Sam my, in response to the boy's quizzical query, the old man brandished it proudly as if it was some prize he had won.

"Seriously, what's with the string? The doorway's closed already, so it doesn't have any use."

"That's where you're wrong, kiddo," Mister Dojo lobbed right back. "Think of the string as a copper wire which you can coarse electricity through. Now, since the string is still 'anchored' to our world, which is the one that's generating all the 'electricity' in this case, we can open up a doorway back… on any point on this string! Neat, huh?"

There was a madness behind the old man's spacious eyes that spurned Sammy. He wanted to remind Mister Dojo, who had probably gone senile, that the Nanek Crystal has been lost, and that, even if it has been recovered, it would do them no good since it could only be used once in the lifetime of its wielder—which, in this case, was Mister Dojo, the Nark of fifty years from now.

"This is very convenient for us, Sammy, because we're not required to open a new doorway at the exact site where the last one closed. That means we don't need to go back down to the basement to open a portal. It's just a matter of getting the 'electricity' from our world to surge on to the string, specifically, to that point on the string we want our new doorway opened!"

"You are aware that the Nanek Crystal is gone, right?" slyly retorted Sammy, unable to contain his disdain for the old man's far-fetched plans. "Even if we had it, you said yourself that it can only be used once in the lifetime of its wielder to open a doorway back."

"I did say that, didn't I?" good-naturedly responded the old man, fiddling with the ends of handlebar moustache again. "Don't worry yourself much, kiddo! An alchemystic always finds a way out of a bind, and you're travelling with one right here!"

If the old man was aiming to instill some optimism in

Sammy, he had failed miserably to do so. That was only because the boy was cynical by nature. Even then, he was also incurably curious. And being curious, he sought knowledge—knowledge that the old man had in spades.

"So you're an alchemystic, huh?" Sammy grilled the old man, keeping his sights to the fore like him, where a small distant figure was scaling what seemed like a mountain. "My mother was one as well, I was told," he grappled to add, not wanting to brag. He only said this to keep the conversation going. Hopefully, if he could manage to steer it well, it would eventually lead him to some answers he was seeking.

"I know your mother," Mister Dojo disclosed, gladdened to hear the boy mention her. "She was the best botanical alchemystic I've ever known. Her herbal transmutations skills are by far without peer. Did you know that she could turn poisonous mushrooms into cure-fast elixirs? That woman could transform any plant, no matter how deadly, into elixir medicines."

"If only her skills at cooking were any good," jested Sammy, just as his stomach grumbled to be fed. Now that he was done digesting Ruby's sandwiches, he needed another gastronomical handout—and fast—to quell his hunger pangs.

"She's an awful cook, I agree," the old man conceded, serious in his mood. "Her cures are awful tasting that you'd think they were poison themselves! If she was my mom, I'd probably be as pencil-thin as yourself, no offense there!"

He burst out laughing maniacally, to Sammy's displeasure.

Although the boy did not contest the old man's assessment of his mother's culinary talents or lack of them, he did feel slighted about him taking a potshot at his dear parent. Upset as he was, he tried his best to stifle his feelings of discontent and chuckle at least, if only to keep Mister Dojo still interested in his poor company.

Their tête-à-tête was sputtering, and he needed to keep it moving before it ran its course. There were things he needed to know, and only the old man knew them. One way or another, he was getting it out of him.

"So what is an alchemystic exactly?"

It was a straightforward question that required a straightforward answer, no beating around the bush. The boy came up with it at the top of his head, and was surprised himself that he didn't ask about it earlier, being so basic and all. Perhaps, it was because he had an idea already of what it was, and didn't need to know more.

"An alchemystic is somewhat of a cross between an alchemist and a mystic—two professions whose disciplines appear to be complimentary to one another, but are actually worlds apart. Alchemy is a science, specifically the science of transmutation, transforming things like lead into gold, or a pebble into a mountain. Mysticism, on the other hand, is literally concerned with only pure magic. It is a high and exotic art, and when combined with alchemy's scientific workings, both produce nothing short of... miracles of miracles!"

"Wow!" raved Sammy, pretending to be impressed as he

kept his eyes transfixed on Nark's clambering shrinking form, which was now close to the brim above. "And how does one become an alchemystic then? Did you attend a special school to learn these skills?"

"Don't be preposterous!" hammed the old man, scratching his bald head which now had a nice toupee of frosted snow cutely laid on top of it. "There's no school out there for these sorts of arcane crafts. You either start out as an alchemist or as a magic-user, like a wizard or a sorcerer, before learning the other trade. There's only quite a few of us out there because there aren't that very many who want to become 'multi-skilled' as I call it. It takes a very long time to hone one's talents—decades, scores, half centuries—in both the science and the art."

"And once you've mastered both the science and the art, what then?" pressed Sammy, all fired up by where their little chat was headed to. "I take it that you could make those little gemstones, like the one Nark had, the one that could summon Nanek Beasts to dispose of people that have offended you in some way."

He had positioned himself well, and was quite pleased with his modest accomplishment of auspiciously manipulating the conversation. *Maybe, he thought, the old man will finally show him the Nanek Crystal itself—that is, if he had it!*

"The Nanek Crystal is an alchemystic stone as you already know," began the old man, who felt a sudden sharp pain on his right cheek the second Nark stumbled over his crossed feet and fell. A small scar miraculously appeared there soon after, a remnant of Nark's carelessness on the slopes. The small boy did get up though, and trekked on—ultimately reaching the summit, to the old man's relief.

"Sorry about that." Mister Dojo apologized, referring to his momentary distraction. "Like I was saying, it's an alchemystic stone. These things start out as nothing more than ordinary objects—a gem, a rock, or a *tooth* even! They only become extraordinary after they have been imbued with alchemagic. You've heard about the alchemist's obsession, right? You know, the philosopher's stone?" To this, Sammy nodded. "Well, an alchemystic stone is similar to that, but its powers are not limited only to transmutation. Why, you can even use it to trap a jinn-mera, like Rular over there!"

"Because of what these stones can do, they have been called 'insanity stones' and even 'god stones'. Whatever you call them, they are always, in most cases, quite powerful."

****

28

Time crawled sluggishly by as Nark inched his way up the fattened snow. As he trudged on, his mind gallivanted back to his time in the woods not too long ago. He recalled being initially smitten and enchanted by the resplendent splendor and the quiet serenity of the grey forest. The beauty of nature, however, quickly lost its petty appeal on him after a couple of hours, going the way of the dinosaurs during the last ice age, as soon as fatigue seeped into his overworked body. He had become bored out of his mind, like he was now with the climb which seemed to go on and on without end.

By the time Nark reached the top of the basin, he was spent. His arms and legs screamed in agony, his lungs burned with cold and fire, and he was woozy. In addition to these ailments, he was also frostbitten, so much so that icicles had started forming on the ends of his hair, ears and chin. Exhaustion and pain overwhelmed him. He was going to die.

Slumping down on the snow on his flat belly, he thought back to how he got to this accursed point. After leaving the group in the basement of the collapsed building, he slithered his way back up somehow to the surface of the snow covered basin. There was a blizzard raging in the skies by the time that he got there, and it was raining cats and dogs, although strangely, none of that precipitation ever penetrated the insides of their quaint sunken tract of wintry land. It was as if they were under a force field of some kind in his modest assessment. As soon as his feet were planted firmly on the snow again, Nark immediately headed across the vast expanse towards the steep edges of the basin, located some several yards or so away. Above the elevated icy rim, he saw an enormous ominous shadow standing vigilantly on the crest. Undaunted by the sight of this eerie apparition, he courageously scaled the precipice itself, taking forever on his part to do so. Now cold and dying on the pinnacle itself after an arduous climb, and stuck in the middle of an unrelenting tempest, it was taking him forever now to meet his maker.

"I didn't think you had the guts to face me again, boss," mocked Rular, whose raucous guttural sneer echoed in the blustery wind. "You have no idea how long I've waited for this day to come."

Tried as hard as he did, Nark couldn't make out the giant's face, which was hidden by the tempestuous climate. From his meager vantage point, all he could see was a tower rising up to the clouds. Although the vision terrified him, he wasn't as scared as he should be. He had a good luck charm clutched in his hand—the gold tooth Mister Dojo gave to him.

Every time, he entertained doubts about his ability to see

things through, he would grip the tiny molar harder. Although it wasn't exactly the hilt of *Gut Weed*, the sword forged of alchemy steel that he discarded in the woods, it was comforting enough to allay his fears and reinvigorate him with an energy to slog on.

"I figured that I should just step on you to end your miserable suffering," added Rular, shifting his weight forward a little, shaking the earth a bit. "But that would be too kind for your likes."

There were many reasons why Nark chose this course of action—confronting Rular alone, all by himself—moronic as it seemed. For starters, he wanted to teach his belligerent attack hound a lesson, and he was certain that he could—in spite of the great disparity between them in size and other things. He knew for a fact that, whatever happens, he wouldn't die. And he was certain of this because of Mister Dojo, his future self, still ticking fifty years from now. So if the old man says that he will be able to lay the Nanek Beast to rest, all by himself, that was good enough for him.

With the last ounce of his fleeting strength, Nark boosted his head up high to the monster, which turned out to be miles away removed from him horizontally, standing miles above the ground vertically. He squeezed the gold tooth in his hand as hard as he could, until he bled, before passing out. It was at that exact second that he shed blood that a champion appeared out of the blue.

"A spargolem? This is interesting! I didn't think you had another stone on you, boss. You sure are full of surprises!"

The champion forged itself out of the moisture in the icy air, sculpting the imposing form of a golden giant that could look Rular straight in the eye and not flinch.

Lean and brawny, it had the taut physique of a bantamweight boxer, only with the head of a balding old man with a handlebar moustache suspended under a large roundish nose. It looked like Mister Dojo, more or less, except for the eyes which were button-like and cartoonish.

Although its heft and size were immense, it was surprisingly nimble and light-footed, moving with the blazing quickness of a much, much smaller fighter. It had grace and elegance when it shuffled its polished feet across the snow swept plains. When it circled the Nanek Beast, throwing jab after jab into the air in a display of its boxing prowess, it also seemed to be dancing, gyrating its hips while it moved from side to side.

"How exciting!" applauded Rular, his tone and inflection thick with sarcasm. "I haven't engaged in fisticuffs in years! Not that it has anything to do, mind you, with the condition of my hands... or the lack of them."

Hunching forward and raising its bent arms over its metallic face, the spargolem took a pugilistic stance. It taunted the monster to attack, while orbiting it. Rular, however, didn't bite into the obtuse provocation. The Nanek Beast stood its ground and watched its foe carefully—very carefully—as it searched for weaknesses.

"Nark, where are you?"

The spargolem had completed one revolution around its unflinching adversary, when Sammy happened on the scene. He had diligently followed Nark's trail all the way up the sloping sides of the basin, to the stormy weathered plains where the two behemoths faced off in a distance. When he stumbled upon Nark's body, it was slumped face down on the snow, nearly completely crystallized in ice. It was Sammy's fear that his friend may already be dead.

"Come on, Nark. Let's get out of here."

Shortly after speaking these words, hostilities commenced between the pair of giants in the background. Although Rular was handicapped with only one working arm, he was no underdog in the ring. When the spargolem punched the monster with a right hook, he capably blocked it with the limp, lifeless body of the snake that doubled for his left arm. It absorbed the full impact of the blow, allowing Rular the luxury of launching a counter offensive right away.

"Thank you for the lovely sparring match," quipped Rular, blindsiding his adversary by coiling his last good serpent arm around the spargolem's neck. "But I have a previous engagement with my previous boss that I need to keep, so ciao!"

The monster tightened the noose, squeezing hard. And gold, being a soft metal, didn't hold out for long. It shattered in no time, effectively decapitating the spargolem, whose cumbersome body crumbled next, crashing down hard onto the snow.

****

By the time Sammy Tsunami set eyes on his dwarfish friend, Nark was face down in the snow, lifelessly still and frozen solid like meat cooling inside a freezer. He was cold to the touch as expected, but surprisingly hard as granite and, not to mention, heavy for someone of his unusually short stature. Latching his sleeved covered hands underneath the small boy's icicled armpits, Sammy gave it his all to lift his chum's waiflike body from the shallow grave of gathering snow it has been heftily resting on.

Heaved as hard as he did, however, it wouldn't budge—not a single tiny bit. It felt weighed down, which was odd, for he was pretty sure that Nark weighed less than seventy pounds roughly. His impish pal was definitely not a ton, although he did make a strong case for it. Regardless of how onerous it was to move his friend, Sammy was not one to just lightly surrender himself to the easy temptation of simply abandoning his pint-sized mate to the murderous cold. Much as he disliked Nark, Sammy was not about to let him perish.

"That's an awful lot of weight you put on there!" Sammy jested as he exerted his best efforts, resulting in a number of sores in the spent muscles of his arms. "Be nice and bend both your elbows and knees now! I need you to try to stand up on your own because I don't think that I will be able to carry you!"

ROARRR!!!

As if the difficult task at hand wasn't already arduous

enough, Sammy's stomach just had to throw its hat into the ring and get feisty. It reminded him of his urgent obligation to feed it—an obligation he thought he had fulfilled when he did nothing but stuff himself at the parking lot during lunch hour. Annie's sandwiches, apparently, had all been digested. In the end, they were insufficient to thoroughly satisfy the lingering hunger that has haunted him for days to no end. The truth was, Sammy had not eaten anything substantial for the longest time.

Prior to today, the last meal that he ate over two days ago hardly put any meat on his bone. It may have been a moderate serving of cabbages and potatoes, but it was just like consuming air, not enough at all to totally subdue the long term starvation that had him withering away into a human skeleton. Given his lethargic state, he plainly didn't have the power to boost up his keeled over friend, which probably explained why something so light seemed so strangely cumbersome to him for no reason.

"I know you can hear me!" Sammy kidded himself, fairly certain that Nark's been out for the count for quite some time now. "Three words: quit playing dead! You and I have to head on back so that we can get out of this wretched place! If you didn't wander away like you did, we would have been long gone by now!"

Normally soft spoken, Sammy wasn't one to raise his voice out loud to be heard. But this time around, he really needed that extra pitch to get his message across. It was just like what his mother often said. If a person needs to listen, speak your words; but if he refuses to listen, scream your words and he will hear them loud and clear.

"This is all your fault!" bawled Sammy, his throat pushed to its very limits and starting to hurt. He was not the slightest bit angry at his dwarfish friend as he was annoyed with his current taxing predicament. Undaunted though, he tried and tried again, while keeping an eye out for the two giants that were battling it out in the not-so-far distance. His efforts at lifting ultimately proved to be of no avail, so he finally decided to go with a different approach. Kneeling beside his fallen friend, he tried reviving him by tapping his frosted cheek, gently at first then vigorously later on.

SLAP! SLAP! SLAP!

"Aren't you going to get mad at me for pointing a finger at you, or slapping you around like this?" he demanded to know as he tried shaking Nark and flipping his statue-like carcass over. "Get furious, okay? Be anything—anything at all, but dead!"

It was then that a blustery wind blew out of nowhere, howling as it came barreling right into Sammy who almost fell back on his butt. Distracted for a second there, the boy failed to notice Nark's hand grip the dangling end of his red scarf. Suddenly, it was the incident on the school bus all over again.

"What's with the scarf and the sweater?" mumbled Nark through pursed lips, still half awake and half asleep. He jerked the cloth like he would a rope to ring a bell. One pull and the loop around Sammy's neck unknotted. As the looped cloth came undone, Sammy felt a sharp throb around his neck, almost like a knife was carving it.

"Let go, will you?" Sammy frantically insisted, fumbling to release his dwarfish friend's grasp from his scarf. It was a grip that practically bonded skin to fabric. No matter how hard he tried to uncurl Nark's fingers, they would not come off his precious fashion accessory. It was as if they were wedged deep into it, with the nails practically joined to the threads themselves.

"Quit it!" cried out Sammy, his neck screaming sick with pain as the ugly gash across it widened and stretched. His vision blurred, such that things all around him seemed to double in numbers, triple—and quadruple even! When he saw his shadow arrow stretched out flat on the snow, it had split into countless versions of itself that he got dizzy staring at them as they multiplied exponentially.

As he watched the world turn upside down, the pain on his neck became so intense and excruciating that Sammy himself blacked out completely. When he came to and finally regained consciousness long enough to see what was going on, a breath-taking, eye-popping, senses-shattering surprise greeted him. He was so floored by the enigma that he fell flat on his butt.

In front of him, laid out on the snow for miles, to his left and to his right, were thousands of arrows—shadow arrows— all pointed and aimed and ready to fly at a moment's notice at the hulking figure of the Nanek Beast.

"Now, where were we, boss?" scowled Rular, done with admiring his handiwork—the broken body of the spargolem he just trounced. Rearing his ugly head in the general direction of Nark, he spotted Sammy sitting next to the inert, face downed body of his former master. It would have been a pleasant reunion from his point of view, had he not seen the phalanx of shadow arrows in front of the two boys, all pointed right at him.

"Interesting trick, Sammy Tsunami," sarcastically raved the monster, stepping back and dragging the only living serpent arm that it had left, which hissed at the boy as it bobbed its scaly head in the air. "Where'd you learn to do this fascinating thing you do?"

Picking up the red scarf from where it fell on the snow with hands that trembled feverishly from the stabbing pain wracking his body, Sammy met with the fearful gaze of Rular as he desperately tried to hold on to consciousness for as long as he could. When it became too much for him to stay awake because of the unbearable throbbing, he resigned himself to another fainting spell, but not before uttering four more words—"*Weapons Free and Fire!*"

At his command, the swarms of shadow arrows launched into the sky, obscuring the sun with a billowing pitch black blanket as they soared with rapturous aplomb. They held together, like knitted fiber, for a few seconds before freakishly disintegrating into a fierce and relentless rain of sharp silhouetted steel. Hurtling down in the thousands, they ripped through the jinn-mera's scaly flesh, reducing it into an ugly bloody pulp. Its black robe was left none the better, itself shredded into threads as the pointed arrowheads slashed and sliced mercilessly through it, wave after wave after relentless wave. There was no time to speak, not even to breathe, as death came again and again and again for the listless giant, which struggled to keep its feetless bottom end from scraping the snow below. If it could have screamed, it already would have, but it was too busy dying.

Not that Sammy wasn't dying himself. The boy was writhing in pain as his frail body convulsed on the snow, the wound on his neck becoming more and more pronounced as it reddened and thickened, so much so that it seemed that his head was about to break off entirely from his neck.

He was right about ready to buy the farm and croak, when a miracle happened. From out of the blue, a Good Samaritan emerged, taking the red scarf away from Sammy's trembling hand and placing it around his neck where it should be. Once the wound was covered up neatly again, the shadow arrows instantly disappeared without a trace, leaving all but one at the edge of Sammy's feet.

"Leave now while you can," rang out a familiar voice to the near dead jinn-mera. Whatever was left of Rular's pulverized face then rose up and acknowledged the unexpected kindness by nodding once in the affirmative. Soon as the Nanek Beast had done this deed, it turned its back away to leave.

There wasn't much of the monster that remained when it

crawled across the snow back in the direction it came from. Its robe was nothing more than a tattered rag, no more than a quarter of what it was originally, while its head and arms resembled freshly grinded raw meat all strewn together.

"What just happened?" Sammy was slowly coming back. His eyelids gradually peeled upwards as the light streamed back into his eyes. It was a faint light though, whatever got through the tempest. Nonetheless, it was enough for Sammy to recognize the person of the hour who had rescued him from certain death.

"You trounced him, Sammy. You trounced him without lifting a single finger. Spectacular trouncing that was!"

Mister Dojo was looming over the boy, his sights lined far away towards the distance where a black raven was soaring through the storm, a piece of paper tied to one of its shadowy legs by a string. It was heading in the opposite direction, and not at the old man who had been the one who sent it on its way. When Sammy saw it before it vanished into the thick of the squall, he just had to ask.

"Where's that bird heading off to?"

"To someone who's worried about you," replied the old man in an affectionate grandfatherly tone. "Now, how does getting out of here sound to you? Are you tingling all over with excitement already?"

29

"Hopefully, he will have some manners now!"

Defeated and badly injured, the Nanek Beast cowered when it slinked back into the icy crater from where it sprung from, bearing in shame on its tattered body the countless shafts and fletchings of the shadow arrows that had pierced its scaly hide.

Proudly watching it slither away down into its underground retreat from a safe enough distance was Mister Dojo, who somehow managed to ascend the steep slope of the basin to be with Sammy and his unconscious younger self, Nark, who had passed out long before hostilities with Rular officially commenced.

"It's all yours now, Sammy," he told the boy, who was making doubley-sure—out of paranoia—to tighten the already tight red scarf around his pencil-thin neck. "Use it wisely."

The old man then took out from his pocket an egg-sized crystal, which seemed to look like a dozen tiny crystals pieced together with sticky glue. He had seen it before when Nark held it up for him to behold. It was still amethyst purple in color, still vibrant and gleaming. Mister Dojo gently placed it inside Sammy's hand and smiled.

"This is the Nanek Crystal," Sammy declared, sure of himself. "But I saw it fall into a crack in the basement! It should be lost!"

"It was lost, but I retrieved it before we got out," immediately confirmed Mister Dojo, turning away to pick up Nark's frozen and passed out body lying in the snow. "Even in pieces, it flies to its wielder when he calls for it, no matter how great the distance between them. Say, why don't you get us all home with it? Go ahead, and *will* it to open a doorway to our world. Go ahead now."

"But you said that it can only work once in one's lifetime— and no more," Sammy surly explained with cold certainty. "Those were your very words, sir."

"I did say those words, come to think of it," jokingly agreed the old man, having a bit of a chortle afterwards. "True enough, it can only open a doorway from here to our world once… for a wielder. And I certainly did use it for that purpose a while ago, didn't I? So that's it for me! But not for you, though… since you're the new owner of that busted piece of jewelry."

"How do you know that it's going to follow my orders from now on?" asked Sammy, feeling the crystal's smoothness and unevenness on the tips of his frosted fingers as he ran them over its glossy surface. "I don't know about this."

"Because I passed it on to you," responded Mister Dojo, slinging Nark's flaccid body over one of his broad shoulders as if it weighed no more than a plush toy won at a carnival. "Nobody can wield that shiny junk, unless it's been passed on to him or her."

Sammy examined the small jerry-rigged crystal more closely up closely, turning it around in his supple fingers. Although he wasn't knowledgeable on how exactly to make it work, he somehow managed to get a glowing purple rift to appear out of thin air around the string the old man carried. While this one wasn't as wide as the one in the basement, it was still adequate enough to fit one person through—if he squeezed right in, that is.

"I see that this one is standing up and not lying down on the floor," gratefully observed the old man, pleased with the portal's handsome appearance. "Passable. See you on the other side then."

Mister Dojo then bid the boy farewell after thrusting Nark's sleeping mass in first through the glimmering portal. "Don't be tardy, alright? It won't remain open for long as you already know."

As soon as they had gone, Sammy ruminated the events that had just transpired, breathing a little easier than he did when his scarf was stripped off from the skin of his neck. He combed the winter landscape after he was done with his contemplation, keeping an eye in particular on the Nanek Beast's descent into its craterous home in the bowels of hell.

"So small and so much trouble." Sammy spoke these words as he felt the tiny Nanek Crystal lying inertly in his grasp.

Its jagged jigsaw edges pricked his exposed skin, scratching it and even wounding it a bit. The gemstone weighed close to nothing. It felt fragile, breakable, easily crushed. He looked at it as if it was some unwanted insect resting calmly on the surface of his palm.

After growing tired of repeatedly viewing it, he let it slip through his clumsy fingers, letting it fall on to the snow. It struck the moist, frosted surface without a noise, then disappeared quietly into the layers of ice underneath—never to be seen again.

Uninterested in its final fate, Sammy didn't turn around anymore to check on how it had gone. He sauntered ahead in the direction of the shimmering but shrinking doorway, which waited a few paces away from him. It was calling to him to go home. Not one to turn down this attractive invitation, he readily accepted and entered through it, vanishing on the other side.

****

India, Sammy's mother was waiting for her son outside in the cold night air on their doorstep. She was thinly clad in her usual silky rose red dress, and was strumming a pleasant tune on her ukulele as crickets chirped in the background. The woods that surrounded her humble cabin were completely dark now, nothing more than the mere silhouettes of trees rising up from close nearby into the starry evening sky.

Torches burned brightly and dangerously around her home,

hot white and orange, forming a protective circle around it. They were planted high enough on tall wooden stakes to ward off the creeping darkness, as well as all dangers that it kept secret. Her tract of land may be small and pitiable, but it was secured and fortified as tightly as a castle fortress. The fires that marked her territory warned all manners of beasts lurking out there in the darkness not to cross into her little place—or else.

"Teach it a lesson."

She spoke these words out loud without lifting her head. A few feet across from her, a wolf emerged from the shadows with its fangs unsheathed. She was busy plucking the strings on her instrument, trying to scratch out some music when danger strolled into her midst on four legs.

Since she couldn't be bothered with her ukulele playing, her shadow rose up in her stead from the ends of her feet. Once upright and erect, it confronted the bothersome beast by charging right at it. One look at the approaching shade, and the wolf quickly made a three hundred and sixty degree turn back into the gloom from where it came, running off with its tails between its legs.

"Sorry, I'm late… mom."

Sammy Tsunami came in from the pitch blackness, his long awaited arrival heralded by the six glowing golden diamonds printed on the front of his black sweater. His eyes reflected how terribly exhausted he was, as well as the secret that he was trying to hide from his mother. It was so painfully obvious that she couldn't have missed it the second he stepped into the soft glow of the torch lights.

"It doesn't look like that's the only thing you're sorry for," she said contemptuously, rising to her bare feet to meet with her son's awkward gaze. "If it's about my shade, don't worry about it. It did its job. Here you are, alive, and with me. That's all that really matters. It did its job."

A tinge of melancholy strummed at Sammy's heartstrings as he struggled to suppress the hurtful memories of Shadow Ranger's tragic demise, all bubbling up again to the rim of the cauldron of his mind. The pain associated with those hurtful recollections quickly dissipated, however, when he saw another one of his mom's shades patrolling the fringes of their torch encircled border. It immediately reminded him of his fallen friend, from the refined appearance down to the peculiar mannerisms. They were all Shadow Ranger's, as if she had been resurrected from the dead.

"Those things are my eyes, my ears and my reach out there," India nonchalantly pointed out after noticing her boy's intense interest in her shadow familiar. "When the one I sent out to look after you was destroyed, I lost all contact with you. It's a good thing though that principal of yours over at your school sent me a message by shadow raven to inform me that you are alright. Otherwise, I would have been worried sick about you!"

After taking one last look at Shadow Ranger's silent twin from afar, Sammy diverted his full attention to his mother, who had then folded her arms across her flat chest as she fought off the shivers brought about by the cold and some vague fear.

"Mister Dojo, our principal, said that you're an alchemystic just like him. Is that true, Mom?"

"I've kept many secrets from you, Sammy, but the only thing that's no secret is how much I love and adore you."

"That sounds corny," teased Sammy, mortified by what he just heard his mother say. He was squinting his eyes and wrinkling his nose, and seeing him do all this made India laugh out loud hysterically.

"What's so funny, Mom?"

"You… us. Do you have any idea why we're poorer than a rat, Sammy? Poorer than a rat!"

"Bad luck, I guess."

"Partly, but did you know that I worked as a banker before I became a grocery clerk?"

"Now, that's a secret!" remarked Sammy, genuinely surprised with his mother's big reveal. "So what happened?"

"I hate money, so I quit!" she explained with a chuckle. "Imagine a banker who hates money!"

"So that's why we're poorer than a rat then!"

"That's why we're poorer than a rat!"

The boy nodded in agreement before turning towards the door of his home, dragging his tired, aching feet there. His mother followed, laughing so much that she was practically in tears. This went on for quite a while until, suddenly, her mood turned grave.

"I tried my very best to shield you from all these horrors that are cropping up left and right in your life," she said forlornly, keeping up a brave face that was tearing up, "but fate has other plans for you that I didn't know about."

She was being overly serious in Sammy's opinion, melodramatic to a fault. "They found you, just as you found them," she continued, choking back the sadness that was engorged in her throat. "You were meant to meet, but I had hoped secretly that you would be spared such an unfortunate introduction for the rest of your natural life. Now, things are moving so fast that I'm practically overwhelmed! It's like juggling too many balls—too many balls in the air—which to catch first, how to keep them from not falling, what to do?"

"We'll figure something out, Mom," Sammy cavalierly cut in, hugging his mom tightly with whatever feeble strength he had left ebbing in his weary muscles. "Don't worry too much about me. I'll be fine. We'll be fine."

Composing herself, India pulled away from the bony embrace of her son and smiled at him with little ease. A steely expression then washed over her face and she looked at Sammy with an affectionate fierceness, like that of a lioness to her cub.

"You're bushed," she said to him with much concern, tugging then at his arm to make him follow her into their tiny hovel of a house. "You must get some sleep because it's back to school again for you tomorrow. I'll tell you everything next time, alright?" Mother and son then slipped in through the door, and disappeared entirely. As soon as they were cozy inside, the torches around their home all burned out, gone in one violent snuffing, leaving only faint trails of ghostly smoke in their wake.

30

Class started the following day on time and on schedule. Mrs. Galactrix came extra early that windy Tuesday morning to welcome all her students back to room fifty-two. She was dressed as an airline stewardess, had braided her hair, and was all smiles. She bowed every time she greeted somebody coming in, even handing them out souvenir ballpoint pens with the school logo printed on them.

Her students were, of course, all shocked to see her back in the flesh. The memory of her vanishing in a cloud of purple smoke yesterday was still fresh in their minds. Even though she assured them that it was all a show she had put on, there was nothing she could say to extract the horror of that brief moment out of their heads. It was embedded there for the rest of their natural lives.

Reactions to her return were mixed. Some let out a bloodcurdling scream, like some people do when they come face to face with a ghost; while others expressed how glad and relieved they were that she had come back by hugging her affectionately. All those that did this were girls. The boys, for their part, preferred a polite handshake followed by a courteous 'thank you' upon receiving their presents. Secretly though, they were titillated by the fact that their teacher was cosplaying.

"My, you're wearing the same set of clothes you had on from yesterday," Mrs. Galactrix whispered in a hush tone to Sammy, as the boy awkwardly glided through the sliding doors draped in his usual diamond printed black sweater, black pants and red boots. Even his signature red scarf was flapping around his neck in the air-conditioner cooled breeze.

"You look good by the way, young man," the teacher then said with a friendly wink. "Now off to your seat now."

"Yes, ma'am."

When Sammy made it to his desk and chair, he was the only one in the back row to have arrived so far. Oleta was still out, and Timmy was probably going to miss school on a permanent basis, considering the turn of recent events.

Watching the classroom slowly fill up gave Sammy a sense of normalcy, which felt liberating. Things were settling back down to how they should be, quiet and uneventful. In fact, on his way to the bus stop earlier, Sammy was heartened to learn that there were no more wild spooks to chase him and give him a troublesome time. It was just like his mother told him, before he left home that day. The threat posed by the Shadows was gone.

"So did you read it already?"

Like a mouse, Ruby quietly snuck into Oleta's empty seat to be next to Sammy, who was completely caught off guard by her sudden appearance. She wore the same athletic apparel that she did the other day—the jersey and the knee long shorts—only that, this time around, the color scheme was golden yellow with purple trimmings instead of emerald green.

The other thing different that Sammy noticed about her, which he didn't quite catch on the bus ride earlier, were the tube socks and checkered keds that she sported. These were aside from the fact that she wore her flaming red hair down and straight.

"Come on," Ruby spurred, snatching the piece of paper Sammy had tucked away beforehand in one of his pockets. It was the letter Ruby handed over to him on the bus—the one that supposedly came from Nark who, according to the girl, wouldn't be attending school today for reasons explained in the letter. "Let's see what's written there. Share and share alike like a good classmate."

Sammy didn't protest when she mischievously snatched it away. His curious eyes were busy fixated on the new girl, who just came in—the one with the crutches and the hobbled gait. She had short curly brown hair, big circular glasses and a mild case of acne that were all too familiar.

She wasn't in class yesterday, so she attracted a lot of stares and attention, stirring up hushed whispers even from the remotest corners of the room. People talked about her, not really because she was the only handicapped person in their midst, but mainly because her fashion sense was downright atrocious.

She had a pink floral dress on over a pair of night black nylon pants, which was rounded up oddly by a couple of yellow leg warmers and moccasin flats. Before Sammy realized who she was, she was ambling over to him with a naughty smile on her face.

"Heya, I'm Mickayla," she affably introduced herself. "I'll be sitting on your left side from now on. Teacher's orders."

She was referring to Timmy's seat, which was unoccupied at the moment. Before the boy could put in a word on behalf of his absentee seatmate, however, she had already sat herself down and made herself as comfortable as she possibly could.

Seeing her settle in beside him, Sammy was seized with the urge to playfully scold her for not taking her seat over by Mick's desk. He had to stifle it though when she saw him looking at her weird.

"Pleasure to meet 'cha, Mickayla," Ruby addressed the new girl, shaking her hand across Sammy who reclined back on his chair to give them some room. "What happened to your leg?"

"Skiing accident," Mickayla tersely replied, maintaining a poker face. "Healing up nicely, so no worries there."

"Oh, I'm sorry to hear that. By the way, this fellow here is Sammy, and that lady over there is my sister, Annie."

Like Ruby, Annie showed up from out of the blue, this time in front of all of them. She was wearing a windbreaker over blue denim jeans and a stylish pair of winter boots. Her black hair was uncombed with a red headband across it. In her hand was a large transparent bag full of sandwiches.

"Glad to meet 'cha, Micks," she nodded at Mickalya before shoving the bag in her hand on to Sammy's chest. "Special delivery, Samms! Ruby made all of these just for you. I'm just the delivery girl, just to make it clear! I deliver, that's all!"

"Roast beef subs are my specialty!" boasted Ruby proudly, swooping into the conversation with a grin stretching from ear to ear. "I figured that you might not have anything to eat for lunch, you know? Just saying."

"Err, oh-kay," replied Sammy nervously, cringing and shrinking away, as he placed the bag under his desk. "Big, big thanks. I look forward to eating them all later."

"You're welcome," merrily retorted Ruby, to the chagrin of her sister, who quietly turned around and marched away towards her desk in the second row. "You're welcome too," she mumbled out of earshot. She was obviously feeling slighted by Ruby, who didn't bother to acknowledge her help in making the sandwiches.

SAMMY TSUNAMI, PLEASE REPORT TO THE PRINCIPAL'S OFFICE RIGHT AWAY. SAMMY TSUNAMI, PLEASE REPORT TO THE PRINCIPAL'S OFFICE RIGHT AWAY.

The intercom blared like a ten second fire alarm. Everybody seated or hanging around waiting for the bell was rattled to their bones by the principal's abrupt earsplitting announcement, which literally shook the room as if an earthquake was taking place. As soon as he heard it, Sammy Tsunami took off, but not before snatching back Nark's letter from Ruby's sweaty clutches.

"I'll tell you what Nark said later at lunch!" he told Ruby before darting past Mrs. Galactrix and out the door. He wasn't gone two seconds when his classmates started asking why.

Why was he called into the principal's office this early in the day? Why? Why? Why?

Fifteen minutes into the discussion, and there was already a consensus. Ninety-nine percent of the class agreed that Sammy was in trouble for cutting Mister Dojo's class yesterday. Although nobody remembers him sneaking out, he was definitely gone when… everybody woke up.

Strange as it was, nobody could manage to recall the lesson Mister Dojo taught. He came in shortly after Mrs. Galactrix poofed and vanished in a cloud of purple smoke. The next thing the students knew after that was that they were all sprawled on the floor with some of the desks and chairs in front either upturned or broken. The old teacher himself was in a daze, just like them, but he swiftly snapped out of it.

"How dare you sleep through my class!" he angrily reproached everyone as soon as he got back his bearings. After he made this furious declaration, he tossed a chair at the wall. Then, he continued his rampage by punching the large touch screen behind him. One hit on the glass, and he was shaking his hand in pain.

"Nobody—and I mean nobody—sleeps through my class, but me!" Following these head scratching final words, he stomped his feet on his way out of the class room, leaving everybody wondering:

What just happened?

31

Outside, the marble corridors were warm and toasty. It was also hectic and stressful, what with all the students there scuffing their feet to hustle over to their classrooms and wherever. By the time the tardy bell finished sounding off, they were all gone, leaving no trace of themselves to remember them by. Suddenly now empty and quiet like a cathedral, it was like strolling through a ghost town down there, which was exactly how Sammy felt when he moseyed along across.

Finally far away from prying eyes, Sammy took the opportunity that presented itself and immediately opened the letter that was allegedly addressed to him by Nark. It was still in his cold, sweaty hands where it weighed heavy. As he did so, he felt uneasy, tense and somewhat irritated. Although it pleased him that it wasn't written on a blood stained bandana this time around, he entertained serious misgivings about what it contained. For all he knew, this was going to be the beginning of another quest he would be forced to go on.

Could this be another one of those wild goose chases like

yesterday? he wondered, his heart beating fast and his legs weakening.

In the end, his own curiosity got the better of him. He had resisted throwing the letter away as soon as he got it, and now that it was ready for his eyes to scan, he quietly read it as he dragged his leaded feet over to the principal's office, one foot at a time.

SAMMY,

> *IF YOU'RE READING THIS, THEN I'M ALREADY FAR GONE. I JUST WANTED YOU TO KNOW THAT I WON'T BE RETURNING TO SIXTH GRADE ANYMORE THIS YEAR. I HOPE THAT THIS NEWS DOESN'T PUT A SMILE ON YOUR FACE, OR SENDS YOU JUMPING FOR JOY. IF IT DOES, THEN I WILL BE VERY MUCH DISAPPOINTED. REALLY DISAPPOINTED!*

The first paragraph had carved a loose smile on his face, long enough to let out a small, muffled laugh. Sammy didn't want to draw any attention to himself that he deliberately tried to stay as quiet as he could, Nark's unintended joke notwithstanding. Collecting himself after his muted outburst, he proceeded to read some more, his interest suddenly piqued.

> *JUST SO YOU KNOW, I'VE GONE OFF TO TRAVEL THE WORLD. HOPEFULLY, I'LL BE*

ABLE TO FIND MYSELF IN THE COURSE OF MY SOUL SEARCHING JOURNEYS.

FOR THE RECORD, YOU AND I KNOW THAT I'VE DONE A LOT OF BAD THINGS, AND I'M VERY SORRY FOR MOST OF THEM. I CAN'T STAY IN SCHOOL ANYMORE BECAUSE I CAN'T CONTINUE LIVING IN THE PAST. I HAVE TO MOVE FORWARD.

ANYWAY, YOU'RE PROBABLY WONDERING WHY I'M WRITING TO YOU NOW. I KNOW WE HAD OUR DIFFERENCES, AND I'M AWARE THAT YOU PROBABLY HATE ME FOR TRYING TO KILL YOU. JUST SO YOU KNOW, YOU'RE MY ONLY FRIEND IN THE WORLD RIGHT NOW, AND THAT'S THE TRUTH. I HOPE YOU COULD FORGIVE ME AND STILL BE MY FRIEND. I WOULD REALLY LIKE THAT. I HOPE THAT OUR PATHS AND OUR FATES CROSS AGAIN SOON.

UNTIL THEN,

YOUR BUDDY DUDE,

NARK

Sammy crumpled the letter as soon as he read it, then tossed it into a trash bin nearby. There was no need for him to keep it anyway since he has already committed all of its contents to memory. About how he felt about the message was an entirely different story though. To say the least, it was a mixed bag.

While he undoubtedly missed his scoundrel of a pal, he was actually quite mad at him for going off on an adventure without giving him a proper goodbye. Not that this was the only reason why he was angry. Truth be told, Sammy despised Nark for not inviting him to accompany him on his journeys. He would have certainly made the best travel companion if he had been given the chance to do so. In the end, after pondering these things deeply, he soon realized that there was no use crying over spilled milk. Besides, with Nark gone, he could now look forward to a quiet, uneventful academic year devoid of any thrills and excitement, which was just how he originally wanted it from the start.

Somehow though, the prospect of that didn't seem quite as appealing as he initially thought it would be.

****

"Why, hello there, Sammy Tsunami. Go right in. The principal's expecting you."

The receptionist at the front desk wore thick glasses and a mop wig. Even with the disguise, Sammy could readily tell that it was just Mister Dojo under there. The large overripe tomato nose, the handlebar moustache, and the moth eaten flannel suit with the chopped in half tie were all dead giveaways.

"Thanks," Sammy replied with a stoic face. "I'll go right in then." As soon as the boy went for the knob on the door to the principal's office, Mister Dojo quickly got rid of his costume and props, and dove in through an open door in the back. He made a loud thud as he hit the floor.

"Sammy!" greeted Mister Dojo, who was barely on his feet when he pulled the door open from his end. "Nice of you to drop by! I see that you've met my receptionist. His name is… Carl."

"Sir, are you suffering from multiple personality disorder by any chance?" Sammy ventured to ask as he took a seat in front of the principal's wooden desk. "I think that's treatable nowadays if I'm not mistaken."

"Whatever do you mean?" shot back Mister Dojo, slipping into his chair with the glasses still hanging on his collar. "I'm not crazy, if that's what you think. I'm just a hardworking man working many jobs that pay honest pay. I need the money to make alimony for my ex-wife every month. She's a bloodsucking parasite who lives to drain the very life out of me."

"You said that you're a time traveler, sir. Why not go back in time and… not marry this person?"

"That's a good suggestion, Sammy. Unfortunately, she's a time traveler too. And no matter what I do to avoid the mistake of making her my wife, I always end up marrying her in the end and then divorcing her later on! It's as if she's making sure that we get hitched! Sometimes, I can't help but think that she's out to get me! But enough of my personal and private problems, I'm here to offer you a job!"

His ears heard the old man right the first time, but they could hardly believe. If they could clap across his thinned face, they probably would have. Sammy couldn't have been more thrilled. With his mother out of work and sickly, and his family mired in deep poverty, the news broke like he had won the lottery itself. He was so excited at the prospect of having work that he could hardly breathe and find the words to properly thank the old man for the kind and generous gesture that he extended.

"I really don't know what to say," Sammy began nervously with his heart thumping hard on the inside of his chest, "except that you won't ever regret hiring me, sir!'

"Great to hear it!" exclaimed back Mister Dojo, thoroughly pleased with the boy's enthusiastic response. "You start immediately as my apprentice then!"

"Apprentice?"

"That means, you'll assist me in conducting the day-to-day affairs of the school. Sounds exciting, right? You will be the assistant to the assistant of the principal, the conductor on the school bus, the assistant chef and lunch person manning the lunch room, a substitute teacher's assistant, an apprentice janitor... hmm... let's see what else is there..."

"I'll do anything you ask of me!" Sammy passionately volunteered, interjecting himself as Mister Dojo was right about ready to add one more job title to his growing list. "I'll work hard, sir! I don't mind, even if you work me to the bone!"

A sly expression formed over Mister Dojo's puffy face, the kind that got people's heads scratching as to what exactly was he thinking. He smirked at the boy, then slouched back on his black leather recliner, fiddling with his handlebar moustache as he relaxed himself—a sure sign, Sammy was certain, that he was concocting something up in his bald, shiny cranium.

"Your mother might not approve of what I have planned for you, Sammy Tsunami," he began grimly, crossing his legs before leaning forward for dramatic effect. "But I think that it's time I taught you a little about the art and science of alchemysticism… for your own good and *protection*, of course."

"What do you mean, sir?" Sammy asked a with confounded look, his tone turning serious and concerned as he recalled back his mother's words from last night regarding a similar matter. "Am I in danger or something? Why would I be needing protection?"

An awkward silence doused their conversation, which was suddenly heating up. Mister Dojo had to pause for a while to collect his wits in order to say what he needed to say next to the boy. It was as if something was stuck deep inside his throat, and he was trying to expel it from, difficult as it was.

"They already know where you are, kiddo," he told Sammy with a heavy heart and in a grieving tone. "And they will not rest until they find you… and take you back with them."

"Who, sir?"

"The ones who made this world," the old man replied sullenly. "They're coming back to unmake it."

ABOUT THE AUTHOR

Luke Gatchalian was a semi-finalist in a local PBS Kids Go! Writing Contest before embarking upon penning this novel. He plays acoustic guitar and the violin, and is also an avid martial arts enthusiast. He lives in Las Vegas, Nevada with his parents, Cathy and Elmer.